KRIS LONGKNIFE'S SUCCESSOR

GRAND ADMIRAL SANTIAGO ON ALWA STATION

MIKE SHEPHERD

KL & MM BOOKS

Published by KL & MM Books
February 2018
Copyright © 2018 by Mike Moscoe

I would like to thank my wonderful cover artist, Scott Grimando, who did all my Ace covers and will continue doing my own book covers. I also am grateful for the editing skill of Lisa Müller, Edee Lemonier, and, as ever, Ellen Moscoe.

Ver 2.0

eBook ISBN-13: 978-16422110203
Print ISBN-13: 978-1642110210

ALSO BY MIKE SHEPHERD

Published by KL & MM Books

Kris Longknife: Admiral

Kris Longknife: Emissary

Kris Longknife's Successor

Kris Longknife's Replacement

Kris Longknife's Relief

Rita Longknife: Enemy Unknown

Rita Longknife: Enemy in Sight

Short Stories from KL & MM Books

Kris Longknife's Maid Goes On Strike and Other Short Stories:
Vignettes from Kris Longknife's World

Kris Longknife's Maid Goes On Strike

Kris Longknife's Bad Day

Ruth Longknife's First Christmas

Kris Longknife: Among the Kicking Birds

Ace Books by Mike Shepherd

Kris Longknife: Mutineer

Kris Longknife: Deserter

Kris Longknife: Defiant

Kris Longknife: Resolute

Kris Longknife: Audacious

Kris Longknife: Intrepid

Kris Longknife: Undaunted

Kris Longknife: Redoubtable

Kris Longknife: Daring

Kris Longknife: Furious

Kris Longknife: Defender

Kris Longknife: Tenacious

Kris Longknife: Unrelenting

Kris Longknife: Bold

Vicky Peterwald: Target

Vicky Peterwald: Survivor

Vicky Peterwald: Rebel

**Mike Shepherd writing as Mike Moscoe in the Jump Point
Universe**

First Casualty

The Price of Peace

They Also Serve

Rita Longknife: To Do or Die

Short Specials

Kris Longknife: Training Daze

Kris Longknife : Welcome Home, Go Away

Kris Longknife's Bloodhound

Kris Longknife's Assassin

The Lost Millennium Trilogy Published by KL & MM Books

Lost Dawns: Prequel

First Dawn

Second Fire

Lost Days

1

G rand Admiral Sandy Santiago scowled at the two staff members as they sat down. They had requested this meeting first thing to explain what had been going on in the Alwa System while Sandy was away. She'd been busy fighting crazy alien monsters and peeling back the ancient wreckage of their home planet to better understand the bug-eyed monsters (BEMs for short) that looked too damn similar to humans.

She had to admit, she might be a bit behind on the local news.

Certainly, what she'd heard on the voyage from the jump point to Canopus Station had not sounded good.

Still, what Sandy really wanted was a briefing from her key science staff on the studies done on findings from the alien raiders' home planet. She'd put off that pleasant conversation to talk to these two.

Across from Sandy, on the opposite side of her desk, sat two women. One was in uniform, the second was a primly dressed civilian, though her tummy might be just starting to show that she wasn't all that conservative around her boyfriend.

Admiral Amber Kitano's four stars were well and quickly earned by the young woman. A tall, willowy blond, the admiral wore her uniform like a second skin, the same way she wore command of a battle fleet. Amber was Sandy's second-in-command and made the first report.

"All is well, Admiral Santiago," she said before she sat down. "The aliens picked off just one of our automated outposts. They were long gone by the time we got out there to replace it. As per standing orders, we added an additional layer of outposts and came back. As far as the Navy's concerned, things are shipshape and Bristol fashion. I wish the same could be said for the civilian side."

With that cryptic remark the four-star had turned the meeting over to the civilian who'd followed her in. The olive-skinned woman sat in her place like a powerful spring at rest but on a hair trigger. Abby Nightingale had been Kris Longknife's maid, spy, assassin and general dog robber. Any of those jobs could have been a killer, yet the woman had survived five years of it and now was well into her fourth year as the chief expediter for Nuu Enterprises in the Alwa System.

Oh, and she'd also organized the workers into a union and led them out on a system-wide strike. All in five days.

Sandy's respect for the woman was exceeded only by her caution around her.

"Say again," Sandy said, trying to restart the conversation that she had missed while reflecting on the messenger.

"Alexander Longknife has sent a new management staff out here to retake control of the Nuu Enterprises portion of our industrial base," Abby repeated.

"I thought it was supposed to take him more time to find

out that Kris Longknife shipped his last bunch off to Chance?" Sandy asked.

"Yes, ma'am," Abby answered. "Kris sent the last batch packing and we figured dropping them penniless on Chance would keep them too busy earning their bread to afford an interstellar phone call."

Here the former maid shrugged. "I guess they were more creative in their financing than we thought they were. However they managed it, just after you left, a convoy arrived with an entire boatload of Alex's best. Managers, thugs, lawyers, and his very own judge."

"Lawyers? Judge?" Sandy said slowly. She did not like the sound of this. Lawyers and judges never meant any good as far as she was concerned.

"Yes, Admiral," Abby said. "It seems that as a dependent colony of Wardhaven, Alwa does not have the standing to organize its own court system. Least of all a court to hear claims involving trans-stellar cases. It turns out that anything involving Nuu Enterprises is a trans-stellar matter."

"So, they already knew about Granny Rita nationalizing their industry, huh?" Sandy asked.

"Actually, no," Abby answered. "They thought they'd just be handling a matter of who had the right to run Nuu Enterprises: them or the team Kris Longknife put in place. They'd hardly stepped off their ship before they were telling me Kris didn't have the right to decide how the Nuu Enterprise business was run. She was just a shareholder. Alex was the CEO. He decided such matters."

"So said the lawyers," Sandy said, dryly.

"So said the judge," Abby appended.

"He's sounding as if he's been bought lock, stock, and barrel."

"A conclusion most of us here arrived at quickly," Abby admitted.

"And the lawyers' and judge's reaction to discovering that everything in the Alwa System had been nationalized?"

"It was merely a speed bump in their plan to blitz us. They took a night to rewrite their briefs and presented their complaint to the judge the next day. Meanwhile, the thugs, I mean security guards that had come out with them, were strutting around Canopus Station trying to start fights. It seemed that the pet judge had established that his writ held sway on the station for all things. It was pretty clear that if someone threw a fist at them, they were looking forward to suing them for everything they owned."

Sandy did not like the tone of this. Not at all. "Did my Marines have a thing or two to say about this?"

This got Amber's attention. "I had my best JAG officer look into that. It seems we never bothered to declare martial law. While the USMJ holds sway in the shipyards, private quarters and private businesses are another matter."

"So, the bullies bullied."

"Sad to say, Admiral, but yes."

"How much trouble are we in?"

"We let the word out quickly and, so far, everyone has walked away from a fight," Amber said. "However, that's not going to last forever. Yesterday they started harassing women on the A Deck promenade."

"Admiral, do we have some young female Marines that need some practice at hand-to-hand combat?" Sandy asked.

"Yes, ma'am," Admiral Kitano said through a shit-eating grin.

"Get them into civvies and turn them loose on A Deck. Tell the Marines that I'll pay any fines levied against them."

"Aye, aye, Admiral," Amber said and made a quick call.

"Implement Plan A. The admiral and I will be picking up the tab for any fines."

Amber's grin was even bigger as she rung off. "The gals will be out in ten minutes."

"You reading my mind, Admiral?" Sandy asked with a jaundiced eye.

"No, ma'am. I think you read mine."

"Meanwhile," Abby said, "things are not going as well as the new kids on the managerial block expected. They figured they had the only lawyers in the system and they could hold their court hearing and get a snap decision from the bench. They forgot how many JAG officers the fleet has with it."

"But they're my JAG officers," Sandy said. "Not that I wouldn't mind loaning them to you, but defending Nuu Enterprises from Nuu Enterprises hardly passes as 'other duties as assigned'."

"Yes, ma'am," Abby agreed. "But your officers on shore leave do have the right to take odd jobs."

Sandy turned to Amber. "Do we have any lawyers skilled in fighting hostile takeovers? Do we have any that even know where to look for the statutes covering corporate law?"

"Ma'am, we have lawyers trained in just about every aspect of the law, including divorce law, which is starting to come in handy. You'd be surprised at the number of lawyers we have who studied every aspect of corporate law and then volunteered for duty in the Alwa System. We even have one senior former corporate lawyer who volunteered for the Navy and Alwa just to get away from something or other. She's leading the team we put together."

"How's the fight going to keep control of the nationalized property?" Sandy asked.

"Not as well as we'd like," Abby admitted. "They countersued for compensation. It seems they brought some cash with them, and since we lack much cash in the system, they're bragging that they'll force us to auction off the fabs and they will buy them up for chicken feed."

"We have plenty of chicken feed," Amber said. "Or at least bird feed."

"Unfortunately, they want cold, hard Wardhaven dollars," Abby said.

"So, we're in a mess," Sandy concluded.

"Not even close," Abby said, grinning like she'd just dined on several fat canaries.

"I'm listening," Sandy said. "Make it quick. If you've got a solution to this, I want to hear it."

"Actually, Granny Rita pulled one of those Longknife grizzly bears out of her hat."

"Oh lord, not Granny Rita again! Is everyone about to go out on strike again?" Sandy asked. The last time she went off on an independent mission and came back, Granny Rita had nationalized everything and Abby had organized a system-wide strike to oppose the old girl. Strangely enough, the former Rita Nuu-Longknife-Ponsa, and whatever other names she'd worn in her many marriages in the Alwa system, had submitted to the unanimous decision of just about everyone that they did not want her running things.

She'd been fired from her job as viceroy for all things Alwan.

Still, the nationalization of all means of production in the Alwan System had been too tasty for the locals. Everything had stayed nationalized and was working out pretty well.

"Nope, no one's on strike," Abby said. "We've been thinking of doing that, but to date we haven't had to."

"Okay, I know I don't want to know," Sandy said, slowly,

"but what's this grizzly bear that Granny Rita has managed to get to do her bidding?"

"When you're really mad at the old harridan," Amber said, "you want to call her Rita Nuu-Longknife, right?"

"Yes," Sandy admitted.

"Say those words again. Only slowly, and think about where they come from."

"Rita," Sandy said. "Nuu. Longknife."

"Mata," Abby said to her computer, "Would you fill us in on the history of Granny Rita's early life, please?"

"Granny Rita," Abby's computer, one of Nelly's kids, began in lecture mode, "was born Rita Nuu. The only child of Earnest Nuu and Clara Stirling. She married Major Raymond Longknife and they had two children together, and a third born after her ship became lost in space . . ."

"That's all we need to know," Sandy said. "Nuu Enterprises is . . ."

"The same corporate empire," Abby's computer continued, "that Earnie Nuu created and passed to his daughter on his death. Upon her apparent death, control of all stocks in that corporation passed to her surviving husband, Raymond Longknife. He lacked interest in running the business end, so it passed through various CEOs before their son, Alexander Longknife gleefully took over the job. He has run it for the past twenty years."

Sandy eyed her two visitors. "You can't be telling me that it's Rita Nuu-Longknife who really owns all the stock in Nuu Enterprises?"

"That is exactly what Granny Rita is claiming in court," Abby said. "She's also threatening to go back to Wardhaven and have it out with 'little Alex.' Our JAG officers had a nearly impossible time keeping a straight face as they presented this case with her sitting, plain as day, at their table. She even had a modiste put together a business suit that was the height of fashion when the last convoy left Wardhaven."

Amber paused in her chuckling just long enough to add, "The old commodore hasn't forgotten any of what she learned at her old man's knee. She's not dead, and everything that was done assuming she was is now piffle."

"You never want to pick a fight with that old gal," Sandy said, shaking her head, "if you can avoid it. So, where do we stand?"

"The court's in recess. I don't think even a bought judge is willing to rule against Rita Nuu-Longknife. There has been a motion for her to provide a DNA sample for comparison to the sample from other Longknifes in the official records database. It seems to be taking more time than they planned."

"Did it get lost?" Sandy asked, drolly.

"Maybe. Don't know because the judge ordered it sealed and then adjourned. It won't be opened until the next time he holds court."

"So, they're running."

"Yep. Also, with you back, Viceroy, would you mind extending the USMJ to all of Canopus station?"

That reminded Sandy of one of the many hats she now wore. She was King Raymond I's Viceroy in the Alwa System, as well as Commander of the Alwa Defense Sector. Kris Longknife had worn both those hats as well as CEO of all Nuu Enterprise property in the Alwa System.

As far as the means of production in the Alwan System at the moment, no one was quite sure who effectively owned the nationalized property. The native birds to the system had no idea what property was. The human colonials squabbled among themselves a lot, although they had agreed that the nationalized property would stay nationalized. The immigrants from human space and the assigned Navy personnel had not organized themselves in any civic manner. However, Sandy would not put it past them to form a city, country, or other political unit if Abby so much as dropped her hat.

"Is it time for us to try and organize a planetary government?" Sandy asked.

Abby shook her head. "We've been talking about that, both with the colonial government and the honchos running things up here and we don't think that's a good idea. At least not yet. All the humans in the system could, however we're just a minority out here. The birds own this planet. It's their home and no one wants to take it away from them. We humans have had enough experience with aboriginal and native peoples getting the short end of the stick when immigrants with high tech show up."

Sandy nodded. "Kris Longknife was insistent that this bird civilization be protected, unlike the historical mistreatment of her native American ancestors."

"That's our problem," Abby said. "Most of the birds are still at the tribal stage. Even the Roosters only have their Assembly of Assemblies, and that was more a debating society than a decision-making body. Whether dealing with the Roosters, Ostriches, or other birds that were just now being contacted, their concept of private property and ownership, as well as cash money, was limited to only those individual birds that had accepted jobs with the humans. And even there, most of the first-generation workers just wanted to work long enough to earn something they could take back to their tribe. Say, a rifle, solar-powered TV, commlink, or bike. Barter, yes. Cash, no."

"So, what we have is what we have?" Sandy said.

"It sure sounds like that."

Sandy considered all that had been dumped on her in the last half hour. "The colonials weren't all that excited about having Granny Rita running the stuff she nationalized. How will they take to her owning everything?"

Abby got a strange look on her face. "Well, if she is the one that owned it before it was nationalized, then she'd be the one demanding payment for everything. There's talk that she's willing to accept twenty-four dollars' worth of glass trinkets. I can't actually say that, but that's the story on the street."

"Glass trinkets, huh?" Sandy said through a grin.

"Twenty-four dollars of glass trinkets," Abby corrected the admiral.

"Yes," Sandy said.

"Can you imagine how this will play out back on Wardhaven?" Amber said. "What will happen when Alex Longknife realizes that his greedy grasping ways have brought his mom back, and she's pissed?"

The three of them took a minute to enjoy a good laugh at that thought.

When Sandy was ready to get serious again, she said, "Is Granny Rita ready to go back to Wardhaven and take on the full role of Rita Nuu-Longknife?"

Abby shook her head. "She's spent most of her life here. She'd much rather be called Granny Rita by her great-grandkids than get into a fight with a bunch of corporate lawyers and her son. I'm told that she's willing to settle for a quit claim on all the Nuu Enterprise property in the Alwa System and her proper share of the corporate profits next year. I don't know how everyone will work that out, and no doubt, it will take time with travel between here and there so infrequent. Still, no one, except for maybe some high power corporate lawyers, are losing any sleep. Nice to see those vultures get turned into a roasted turkey dinner."

"So, I can relax and do my job," Sandy said, leaning back in her chair.

"Actually, not so much, Admiral," Amber said.

"Oh?" Sandy answered, giving her subordinate the eye.

"It seems that the last couple of ships from the cats have showed up with no additional cats on board. None of those here have gone back, except the spies we sent packing, but there haven't been any more workers Those cats make really good workers."

"Is there a reason for this absence? A reason we know of?"

Amber nodded. "Admiral Drago reports that the cats want to renegotiate their contract with us."

Sandy leaned forward in her chair. "What do these cats want?"

"More battlecruisers to defend them from the aliens and some of our wonderful industry to work out there, in their system. They've got letters back from our workers telling about the fabs as well as lunar and asteroid mines. They want in on the pot of gold."

"Lord love a duck," Sandy scowled. "Back to the bargaining table with those damn kitties. This time, I'm keeping a tight hold on my pants."

2

———

Sandy's commlink buzzed. "Your next meeting is set up in the wardroom," her chief yeoman informed her.

The other two stood as Sandy got to her feet. "Abby, please have Pipra see what sort of fabrication and mining facilities we could ship to the cat system. No need debating what they want if we can't provide anything. I doubt if after Alex's folks get back to Wardhaven that we'll get any more factories flown out here."

Sandy turned to her admiral. "Amber, I want two threat assessments from your team. What would it take to protect the Sasquan System at a decent level? Also, how much of a threat are those damn cats and their atomics to the rest of us? I have no doubt that they're as sneaky as we humans are. I'm not sure that I'd let us into space back in the bloody twentieth century."

Amber nodded. "Still, ma'am, their people are a damn sight better at working our fabs and fighting our ships than the birds are. If we can afford them, they're a good addition to our forces."

"Yes, but that may be the problem. They're too damn close to being as nasty as we are. Do you trust all the humans under your command?"

Amber said nothing, but gave a neutral shrug.

"Now, if you'll excuse me, I have a meeting with a bunch of boffins who have promised to tell me a lot of things that I don't know about our main problem, the alien raiders."

"Have fun with the science types," Abby said. "Both Pipra and I would love to get copies of their reports."

"You get me a nice report, and I'll see what I can do about getting you some in return," Sandy said. If she had to work with tradesmen, she'd learn how to trade.

They left, and Sandy followed them out.

"Hold all my calls," she told her yeoman as she headed for the wardroom.

It was only a few paces down the passageway to Sandy's flag wardroom. What she saw inside was a complete change from the room where she occasionally dined. Penny and Jacques were in charge here, and both had one of Nelly's kids. The dining room tables had vanished into the floor and one large table had been extruded in their place in the form of a hollow rectangle. The walls, usually a familiar beige required by a tradition that must date back to sailing ships, were now converted to glowing huge monitors that covered them from deck to overhead, wrapping all around the room.

Sandy wound her way through a crowd of boffins and intelligence types to the head of the table, where a chair had been reserved for her between Penny and Jacques. Amanda sat at Jacques' other elbow. Around the table, women and men in shipsuits with shoulder boards or ship-suits with lab coats fiddled with their commlinks, readers, or computers. Behind them, the bulkheads danced and flashed as data of one type or another was brought up and displayed.

Sandy sat down and waited for the room to subside to a dull roar.

Penny stood and gaveled the meeting to order by rapping a spoon on a glass of water. That was enough to end most conversations. "We are here today to give Admiral Santiago a briefing on what we've discovered so far about the alien raiders. Jacques, would you begin the overview?"

"By the way," Sandy said, "have we finally gotten a high level of confidence that this is, indeed, actually the aliens' home planet?"

Jacques glanced around the table before answering her question. "We think we have at least one piece of solid evidence that connects the alien raiders we've found wandering the galaxy with the two bodies that we recovered from the rebel base on what we're now calling 'Bug-Eyed Monster Home.' As strange as it may sound, it's a question of blood."

"Blood?" Sandy asked.

"Yes, Admiral. Blood is one of the simplest cells in the human body. The red blood cells carry oxygen and nutrients to the tissues and remove waste on the flip side. It's a very simple and very important basic building block of a complex organism. While the additional DNA proteins are used in much of the modern alien bodies, their red blood cells are identical to the red blood cells in the two bodies we recovered from that deep fissure. The bone marrow that produces the red blood cells in the modern alien may have more DNA protein than what was in those two soldiers' bodies, but only the four original proteins are used to produce their red blood cells."

Sandy stared pensively at the scientist. Two questions immediately came to her mind.

"Okay, answer me this. If the blood cells are produced from only four proteins, why does every other cell in their bodies have six? Also, has anybody given any thought to how the alien occupation force managed to replace everybody's DNA on that BEM's home world?"

Jacques nodded towards a young scientist. The fellow was a tall string bean with an unruly shock of red hair. He grinned with delight at being pointed out and quickly came to his feet.

"I'm so glad you asked, Admiral. The extra proteins in the DNA are there to assure that the basic code of life does not get muddled. It's there to prevent mutations from taking place in the general population."

Sandy was shaking her head even as he spoke. "Excuse me, but I was led to understand that our early analysis of the first raider bodies to fall into our hands showed their genetic drift to be reasonably close to the rate that our genes drift."

The young scientist grinned. "Yes, Admiral, we applied our genetic drift theories and we were comfortable with the results. We still are. However, we do not spend our entire life in space. The space-raiding aliens do. They've been absorbing a whale of a lot more radiation than you and I. If it were not for the extra checking done by their DNA, each of those ships would probably be filled with a crazy mob of mutants eating each other's brains."

Sandy eyed the young fellow. "Can you prove that?"

"Ma'am, the entire population of the second continent, the one without the pyramid, has a population with practically no genetic drift from the northern-most point to the very southern-most point. We'll get to the reason why that doesn't apply to the first continent in a minute, but for the space-based raiders, those extra DNA proteins are the difference between surviving with minimal drift and being a total cock-up, ma'am."

"So, whoever did this wanted to create a race that could survive wandering the stars?" Sandy asked.

Jacques shook his head. "As best we can tell, the only intent of the occupiers was just to create a slave labor force that would be obedient, docile, and not at all subject to the wandering variables that flesh is often subjected to. They wanted no troublesome surprises."

"So, what was that surprise that freed these docile, subservient slaves to overthrow and destroy their masters?" Sandy asked.

Jacques pointed to a different boffin. The young man who had the floor sat down with only a slightly contained scowl.

A petite young woman with a mane of brown hair stood immediately.

"Admiral, connecting specific DNA to specific physical expressions such as a hereditary disease or hair color is not easy. Connecting specific DNA to behavioral traits is even more slippery. Especially when you're dealing with dead bodies," she said dryly.

"However, we do have a growing database of interesting subjects that one might venture to consider statistically significant. For example, we have the three dead males from the most recently captured alien cruiser whose bodies were found in the command center. Comparing their DNA to other bodies we have from the other shipwrecks we recovered allows us to identify some specific genetic markers."

Sandy shook her head. "Yes, but they were scattering

their seed rather widely. How many of the young women aboard were carrying their children?"

"Thirty-four," the young scientist said. "That would appear to be a significant flaw in the ruling class's plan to keep the underclass both docile and subservient. However, they may have already arrived at a solution to that potential problem.

She paused for a moment while she tapped the computer that lay on the table in front of her. On the screen behind her, photos of two cadavers appeared. One showed an attractive woman. The other a tiny infant.

"We still have the body of the young mother and infant that Kris Longknife tried to bring back here the first time she visited the alien home world. We also have a wide range of DNA samples that we collected this trip from a large number of the small nomadic hunter-gatherers who were roaming in the immediate vicinity of the raiders' trophy pyramid."

The young woman hurried on. For a scientist who was nonplussed by data analysis, she looked quite excited by her report. "If we assume that these castoffs from the alien base ships were people the powers that be wanted to get rid of, we have an interesting subpopulation of people who no longer fit into the subservient class. Surprise of surprises, Admiral, over half of them share the same genetic markers that we found in the three men from the cruiser's command deck. They are also held by the children they had engendered on those young female crew members."

Sandy turned to Penny. "So, they've been dumping their troublemakers on the home planet with damn near no ground survival skills. No doubt, they expected them to die and be done with."

"Yes, Admiral," Penny said, "but with the genetic disposition to be stubborn sons of bitches, an amazing number of them have succeeded in making a go of it. Before you ask, Admiral, we also ran a DNA work up on that hunter-gatherer tribe who succeeded in bushwhacking our scientific research team and its Marine escort at the end of Kris Longknife's visit to this planet. I don't think you'll be surprised to learn that most members of that tribe carried the SOB marker."

"Do most of the tribesmen on that continent carry what you're calling the SOB marker?" Sandy asked.

Attention turned back to the young woman scientist. "Yes, ma'am. The marker is very prevalent on the continent with the pyramid and almost nonexistent on the other. Several hundred times more prevalent."

Sandy frowned at that, immediately seeing both good and bad aspects to that bit of information. "We'll need to examine this from a fighting perspective. Looked at from one side, those who command, the Enlightened Ones, were mean enough to not only throw off their conquerors, but also wipe them out and obliterate all life on their world of origin."

Penny, the superb intelligence officer that she was, nodded agreement.

"On the other hand," Sandy said, going on, "What are the chances that the social tension within the raider wolf packs might end up tearing them apart and bringing revolution to the underclass? We all saw the way the command structure broke down in that battle I fought at the home world. How often does that happen?"

"There's also the matter of the cruiser we captured," Jacques pointed out. "They were out to pull our whiskers and race back to the base ship with their trophy. They were involved in a kind of rebellion, it would seem. How much social distress is their repeated defeats at our hands causing their ruling class? They hold their position at the top based on the need to roam the galaxy, destroying all vermin. How many times can you lose to vermin before your subordinates begin to wonder if you're as enlightened as you say you are?"

Sandy nodded. "We are certainly throwing shade on their claims to superiority. Few ruling classes can survive that very long."

"May I point out," Amanda put in, "that we're throwing shade on some of the Enlightened Ones, yes, but most of the Enlightened Ones that crossed swords with Kris Longknife are blown to hell and gone. It's only since Admiral Santiago arrived that we've had meeting engagements where the high command of the wolf packs kept their base ships well back and safe."

Sandy again nodded. The O Club on Canopus Station had eight banners hanging from its overhead. Eight banners representing the eight alien mother ships that the Alwa Defense Force blew away under Kris Longknife's command. Sandy had yet to add a banner since taking command. She'd destroyed a lot of alien battleships and cruisers. Of mother ships, however, she'd not seen a one.

The Enlightened Ones had learned at least one new trick. Keep their own noses out of the human meat grinder that they were only too willing to send their young men and warships out to test.

Sandy had her own thought to toss into this stew pot. "There's also the minor matter that we estimate that there are thirty or so more mother ships that we haven't heard from. If the raiders have sent out the bat signal to gather the clans, they'll be bringing in a whole new batch of troublemakers."

"So basically," Jacques said, "we have no idea if this

social tension is working on their society, or how it will express itself. I hope the admiral will forgive me if I say that this potential for revolt is just something that we must wait and see how it develops."

Sandy frowned in thought as she leaned back in her chair and stared at the overhead. Part of her was not surprised that the boffins had found a genetic strain for rebellion in the aliens. After all, they looked far too much like us human beings. We humans were a pretty cantankerous bunch. Occupiers had a very bad track record on Earth of keeping the downtrodden down and trodden. Of course, no human conqueror had ever been able to genetically modify an entire population into a beaten-down population that was satisfied with being oppressed.

This brought Sandy back to one of her first two questions. She leaned forward in her seat and eyed the first boffin who had spoken.

"I take it you have not finished your brief, so, I'll ask you this question. How did the occupation force manage to change the DNA of every living person on that planet? The best I have heard about gene modification involved snipping out a little here and there to get rid of an inherited genetic defect. Even then, it's best done in the embryo stage. It's been attempted in adults, but certainly not for a population of billions of adults."

The young boffin was nodding even as Sandy posed her question. He took a deep breath as soon as she finished and immediately gave her an answer.

"Ma'am, we don't think they changed the DNA of a massive population of adults. They had control, apparently total control of that planet. What I'm going to describe is appalling. Appalling to me and my associates who have formulated this hypothesis, as it must be to you. However, it's not like we humans haven't done a few things like this to our fellow man during our long and bloody history."

The boffin tapped his reader several times, and the screen behind him changed to show examples of the speed with which disease could spread through the Earth's global population. The Black Death. The Spanish Flu. The Great Bird Virus of 2045. "If you modify the male population of a planet so that they can't engender children on the females of the species, you find yourself with a blank canvas to paint on."

"Every male on the planet!" Sandy exclaimed.

"Ma'am, we had sea raiders in our history who captured men and women and hauled them off to be slaves on their farms back home. Based on genetic evidence, every one of those male slaves was castrated. They made no contribution to the gene pool of the area of their captivity. We have evidence that the women did, but not the men. As I said, ma'am, this is not something I want to talk about too close to lunch. All of us who've come up with this model find it appalling, but it's the only model that explains the evidence."

"Excuse me," Sandy said. "Go ahead with your briefing. I'll try not to interrupt again."

"Once the male population was taken out of the genetic competition by either physical or chemical castration or another form of contraception, the occupiers gained complete control over the female breeding population. There was no chance for any conceptions that they themselves did not control. It does not take a high level of technology to create your own zygotes and insert them into any and all available wombs."

The room froze. If someone took a breath, it would have thundered like an avalanche.

Sandy was a mother. Yes, her daughter had been conceived and grown in a uterine replicator. Still, she had loved her husband. Together, they had expressed his sperm donation in bed one loving night. The very thought that she might be forced to carry a pregnancy that was not one she shared with Alan was repugnant.

Sandy found part of her breakfast back in her mouth. She swallowed the bile, and reached for a glass of water to clear the taste from her mouth.

She was not alone in needing water.

"I wonder how many of the women committed suicide rather than carry such a forced pregnancy to term?" Amanda said softly. "The despair must have been over-whelming."

"We can only imagine the hopelessness of the situation," the young scientist said. "But even if we were to assume that half the population committed suicide, the occupiers would still have billions of slaves. Within two or three generations, the entire population of the planet would have been replaced with subservient slaves formed from the DNA they modified toward their own ends. A slave force that could not even conceive of being anything but submissive. After that, the overlords could go back to letting the slaves reproduce in the old fashioned way, knowing that the resulting children would be just as obedient as the parent."

"Good God!" Sandy muttered. "After ten thousand years of that, no wonder those that broke their chains would want not only their overlords dead, but their entire planet ripped out down to the bedrock, unable to maintain life even at the virus level."

That level of hatred sent a deadly chill through Sandy. That level of hatred was now aimed at the human race. How much had it cooled in the last hundred thousand years? To date, there was no evidence that it was any less intense now than it had been then.

"It kind of makes you want to get a good look at the next planet over," Sandy said. "If that planet isn't the actual home planet of the overlords, then I sure would like to find the other one. Did they demolish it as well? Or is it out there somewhere still? Is that one of the reasons the raiders are so intent on destroying populated planets?"

"Several of us have talked about the need for a thorough survey of the next planet over from the raider home world," Penny said. "Our problem is one of security. What type of a survey do we conduct and how do we make sure that whatever teams we send to conduct it don't get caught and massacred by raiders?"

Sandy glanced at Penny with raised eyebrows. She'd just led a force out to explore the aliens' home world, and space raiders had done their best to cut her off and cut her to pieces. She'd lost ships fighting her way out of that trap. Was the study of a barren wreck of a planet worth a ship or one human life?

At the moment, the exploration of this end of the galaxy was on hold. Yes, they had visited the planetary systems around the planets that humans were defending: Alwa, and the cat world. Beyond that, knowledge was limited to the systems that convoys dropped into on the way from human space to here and back again. It would be nice to conduct a broad-reaching mapping and exploration program, but few people were willing to volunteer to go jaunting about space in a small exploration vehicle that might very well run into an alien raider cruiser.

There were so many questions Sandy wanted answered, but there were even fewer that she was willing to send people out to die for.

"There is one thing that you might want to look into personally," Jacques said. "You haven't yet visited the alien raider children that we've got in school down on Alwa. About twenty of them are from the aliens we destroyed in the cat system. None of them have the alien rebel marker in their DNA. Their teachers tell us they are model students. They do their work diligently and can memorize entire stories, as well as data. When it comes to creative problem-solving, however, they tend to work best in groups with human children who provide the ideas that they then make real. Two kids from the hunter-gatherers have the rebel marker. They are giving their colonial playmates a run for their money when it comes to ideas and surprises."

"That doesn't bode well for us fighting them," Sandy grumbled.

"I don't know," Jacques said, with a chuckle. "It could be argued that our rambunctious kids are being a bad influence on those two from the home world."

"Don't be so sure," Penny said, "I was there when we rescued a shame-faced Marine gunny. They walked right into the middle of that tribe. It takes a pretty savvy bunch with stone-tipped spears to ambush a Marine patrol."

The room fell silent as Sandy mulled this picture. There was not a lot to like. "So let me see if I've got this straight. We are extremely confident that this planet we studied was indeed the home planet of that huge force of alien raiders that do not want to say one word to us, but only wipe us out and all the other intelligent life in the galaxy."

Sandy paused to look around the table. Everyone met her eyes. Many nodded. None objected.

Sandy went on. "There is a strong likelihood that the population of that planet was subjugated in a very brutal way, most likely by the inhabitants of the system that can be reached by one jump. During this subjugation, the entire population of the planet was replaced by genetically modified beings that were specifically bred to be subservient slaves."

Again, Sandy looked around the room. There were fewer scientists nodding. Still, no one objected to her conclusion.

Sandy went on. "The enslaved population rose up and destroyed those who enslaved them. They took off on a mission to sanitize the galaxy of all intelligent life. At the moment, they appear to be divided into two groups. The much larger group are very much like the subservient slaves from the occupation. They do what they're told to do. A smaller group, however, have mutated somehow. They are more like us cantankerous humans. They may even be subject to things like ambition and the urge to have a long line of beautiful women waiting to jump into their beds."

That grew a chuckle from both the men and women around the table.

"Not that it is necessarily a totally reprehensible objective, from a human standpoint," Sandy said, and got a full-fledged laugh from most. That seemed to clear some of the poison from the atmosphere.

Sandy shook her head, ruefully. "If only we could take a few of the Enlightened Ones out for a drink and let them know we aren't that much different. You know, bond while we get drunk," the admiral said with a sarcastic snort.

"We'd likely need to add ourselves a strip club on the station," Penny said, "if we really wanted to try for that kind of diplomacy, Admiral."

That drew frowns and scowls from most of those there. Penny was only a captain. She didn't have the rank to get dutiful laughs, and she knew it.

"Getting back to the serious matter at hand," Sandy said, "there is the question of how we can exploit this weakness to somehow destroy their command and control. Any suggestions?"

"That's something we'll have to work on," Penny said. "Psychological warfare against your fellow human has been part of human warfare for thousands of years. Still, those are human-on-human interactions. Trying to figure out the psychology of aliens who command fleets of obedient slaves is something else entirely."

"No question about that," Sandy said. "Have you got anything else for me?"

"We've got lots of information for you Admiral," Jacques said. "There's a lot of people sitting at this table who would really love to bend your ear. Problem is, I'm not sure that you really need to know what's down in the weeds underneath what we've been talking about."

"Have I got written reports from all of you with good executive summaries?" Sandy asked those around the table.

There are quite a few nods. Put that way, no one wanted to admit that they had not prepared a good and full report.

"Let me peruse those for a couple of days, Jacques," Sandy said. "Maybe we could have a dinner or cocktail party once I know what you have, and those of you who really feel a need to bend my ear can do it while I have a nice drink in my hand."

That grew a chuckle from everyone present.

Everything done for the moment, Sandy stood. So did everyone else in the room.

"Admiral, if you don't mind us tying up your wardroom for a bit longer," Jacques said, "I'd like to hear more about what some of my folks have to say. I think Penny would find it informative as well."

"That's fine, Jacques, I've got several small fires I need to put out before they become larger ones. You continue this meeting, then drop in to tell me if anything new has come up."

That said, Sandy headed back to her desk to see what the gremlins had done while she was busy elsewhere.

3

Santiago returned to her day quarters; her desk had a stack of readers on it. She settled herself down in a comfortable chair her computer generated and got ready to 'enjoy' the rest of the morning. She quickly skimmed the executive summary of several of the reports. None of them raised any questions in her mind that hadn't been answered during the meeting.

Sandy dove down into a couple of reports that looked intelligible. None of them added anything more than she'd gotten from the summaries. Apparently, scientists would be pleased with the granularity at that level; Sandy was just bored.

The entire time she read, her mind was only half paying attention to what she had in front of her. The short conversation she'd had with Amber about the Alwa Defense sector had not satisfied her.

"Computer, raise Admiral Kitano."

"Yes, Admiral."

"I've been sitting on my butt in meetings all morning. Would you care to accompany me on a walk?"

"Of course, Admiral."

"I'll be at your flag in a few minutes," Sandy said and punched off. She passed quickly from her quarters to the *Victory's* quarterdeck, to the pier, then up to A Deck of the station.

An electric station truck silently rolled past her, towing three trailers full of frozen food. Whether it was bound for a ship or a restaurant, there was no way to tell. Around her, people strode purposefully in singles, pairs, or groups. Similar groups ambled along, taking time to window shop at many of the stores and eateries along the A Deck Promenade.

A couple; one Navy, one civilian, studied the window of a jewelry store, then hugged and hurried inside.

The smell of food, lubricants, and ozone tickled her nose, with a hint of trash and garbage underlying the more pleasant scents.

It looked like any other day in a busy downtown, except here some of the people were humans, some Ostriches, some Roosters, and there were a few cats. All that was missing were a few Iteeche to make for a complete mix of humanity's interstellar relationships.

Amber must have posted a lookout at the top of the *Princess Royal's* pier; the admiral was standing there as Sandy approached. The two exchanged salutes and the four-star admiral fell in step with the five-star as they proceeded briskly down A Deck.

"Did I really have all of the SOBs nipping at my jump gates at the alien home planet? Did you really have a quiet time here?" Sandy asked.

"I said the BEMs didn't cause us much trouble. I didn't say we had a quiet time."

"I thought there might be more lurking behind your brief this morning. You've got my undivided attention."

"The bug-eyed monsters only popped one of our jump warning buoys. As per our practice, we replaced it and added another layer," the commander of Sandy's Battle Force said. "My problem was more with our allies than our enemies."

Sandy allowed herself a groan. "I was kind of expecting that. What's happening besides the fight between Rita Nuu-Longknife and her son, Alex?"

Amber paused and the two admirals faced each other. "The two fortresses guarding the jump points are turning out to be a bitch to crew," Amber said.

"I assigned a task fleet of thirty-two battlecruisers to each of the two fortresses. That would be a quick reaction force to any surprises we might get along the edge of our perimeter outposts. The single time we dispatched them, the little nuisance was long gone and it turned out to be just a 'march up the hill and then march down again,' drill. The wear and tear on the ships was minor. The wear and tear on the crews was another matter."

"Our crews?" Sandy echoed.

"All the ships tied up at Canopus and Portsmouth Stations have just under half their crews aboard. The rest are dirtside on their week off. One week on ship. One week dirtside on their farm, ranch, hunting lodge, golf course, whatever. Then switch. We do the same for the yard workers."

"I know. You're slipping colonials, birds, and cats into the workforce to cover for the folks on leave below. Is there a problem with that?"

"Between these ships and down below, no problem. Between those on the two jump point fortresses and the ships assigned to them, not so much. Two, four, maybe six hours at the most, and anyone here can be down there. It's a two- or three-day passage to the jump fortress."

"Volunteers?" Sandy asked.

"We initially tried filling the ships with couples that volunteered for say, two months out there, then seven weeks dirtside with one week of travel. I know people have pulled worse duty before, but we're putting a whole lot of people out there and the facilities on the fortresses haven't developed as well as we would have liked. Recreation is still what you make of it. Maybe in time it will get better, but it's still pretty primitive for both the fortress troops and the fleet personnel.

"We might have been able to work all this out, but a lot of the birds and some of the cats proved to have serious problems being cooped up for two months that far from dirt. We had to ship quite a few of the first watch back home under sedation. Even the cats that stayed out there are grumbling that they aren't learning a whole heck of a lot staring out of the fortress waiting for something that may or may not happen. Right now, we're having to cover the forts mostly with Navy and colonials. That straps the rest of us."

"Do you think the cats back home found out about this and its part of the reason they're playing hard to recruit?"

Amber shrugged. "We are sending mail back and forth between here and Sasquan. No way to tell if this is coordinated or they're just cats being cats and being overly picky. You ever have a cat, Admiral?"

Sandy shook her head.

"Feed them their favorite food today, and they eat it. Tomorrow, they turn up their nose at it. I never could understand the cat my sister adopted. Or who adopted her. The more I see of these cats, the more they remind me of Goddess."

"Can we do anything to help the cats learn what they want to?"

"Most of the cats are here on a one year worker training program. They spend one week working in the shipyards or the lunar fabrication plants and the next week standing watch on one of the ships we've got here on the pier. They love a day of exercise and, so long as we give them light duty for a weekend, they're ready to go back to work on the moon."

"But that only works if we've got a yard or fab within a few hours sailing time," Sandy said.

"Yes, ma'am. We considered putting the ships at the station on a heavy training cycle and let the cats spend two months getting thoroughly drilled up Navy, but that means driving the Navy and colonials just as hard, and that's hard to do for two months at a Spartan base."

"What can we do about that Spartan base matter?" Sandy asked.

"I've talked to most of the best cooks on the station restaurants. I've even gone dirtside and talked to several places around Haven. No joy. No one wants to be a long cruise from dirtside."

"So, the fortress is a great idea for defending our jumps, but not so good when no one is under the threat of total annihilation, right?"

"Right. I've cut the number of ships at each fortress in half. There are only sixteen now. We've discussed among the sailors the idea of switching out the ships' crews every two months, but no one wants to be rotated through a ship that's not their own. Besides, who takes care of their ships while they're out there?"

"Have you looked at rotating ships and crews every two months?"

"That's about all that's left," Amber said. "Still, no matter how we cut the cards, that's going to be a hardship post. We may be only crewing the ships at 75% of wartime levels, but it's still a major drain on morale to have everyone knowing they'll be spending two months out there at least once a year."

"Are the cats still the most able seamen among the aliens?" Sandy asked.

"Yes, ma'am. They grasp the concepts of what we're doing. I think a lot of them have at least some idea of how lasers work. You don't have to field strip a 24-incher too often to figure out the working parts. Of course, there's no way they can manufacture what gives the laser it's kick, but they have the concept down, now."

"In six months or so, we'll be releasing the first bunch of cats back to their home world knowing there's something there and we are hell-bent on discovering it," Sandy said, shaking her head.

"Yeah. I can't throw any stones. I've gotten too much good work out of these cats to complain about what we did, but I think there may be some really wicked unintended consequences in what we're doing."

"I've got to look into this," Sandy decided.

"Talk to Penny. Have Mimzy research the West's intervention in Japan during the last half of the nineteenth century. I've been reading up on that."

"What happened?"

"Japan had locked itself away and refused all but the most minimum of foreign contact. Then the West decided they wanted to sell stuff to the Japanese and they opened the country up to trade and other contact. The Japanese got a good look at what the Western powers were doing to the next country over, China, I think. The Japanese took off to modernize themselves as fast as they could."

"How'd that work out for them?"

"They ended up with a lopsided economy with the Army driving the entire country. The West had colonized much of the world. Japan not only tried to modernize, but also become a colonial power. Unfortunately for them, they got into the colonial thing as most of world was discovering that it didn't work all that well, for both the imperialists and the colonials. Japan ended up being the first and only country to get atomics used on them."

"Ouch," Sandy said. "What I'm hearing from your cautionary tale is that we need to keep the technological, sociological, and political capabilities close to even."

"I think so. Still, neither I or anyone else know how to do it. Strange, I had my ship's computer search the historical archives, and there weren't a lot of good examples of how you introduce high tech into a lower tech world and didn't get a mess."

"So, I foresee another trip to see the cats and a whole lot of bargaining in my future."

"Yes, ma'am. By the way, while you were gone, we completed another squadron of battlecruisers. They're sitting at the pier. We can't find more than a skeleton crew for them."

"We need cats?"

"We need cats."

"Okay, you get me that threat assessment and see what you can do about working out a rotation schedule to swap task forces between the forts and here. The crews get to keep their ships, no swapping crews between ships. At least we won't get into that mess. Me, I'll look into the cats."

"Thanks, Admiral. Ain't it wonderful to be the head high muckety-muck?" Amber said with a dry-humored grin.

"Oh, I thank Kris Longknife every night for going home and leaving this mess in my lap."

"You think she's really enjoying her desk job?" Amber asked.

"I had a desk job once," Sandy said. "I never thanked it properly for driving me to drink."

On that laugh, they parted ways.

4

I t was a good thing that Sandy ate most of her meals in the *Victory's* main wardroom. When she left her office after wading through more information that added little, but provided a stronger back up to what she'd already been told, the wardroom in Admiral's Country was still loaded with boffins carrying forth on their pet part of the issue.

Sandy was halfway through her meal when Jacques and Amanda joined her.

"Any surprises?" Sandy asked as the couple settled down to their meal.

"No, but the xenobiologists are going apeshit over the collection of species samples we recovered from under the pyramid. They want you to send out scouts to see if we can locate some of those worlds. One sample of a species is hardly enough to study. They want a good look at the entire ecology."

Penny shook her head as she joined them. "They left nothing to study on the planet we assume conquered and occupied them."

"Yes, but that first planet Kris Longknife discovered? There was still a lot of evidence left behind about the world and its ecologies," Jacques pointed out.

"That was a fairly recent destruction," Penny countered. "There won't be a lot left of the planets that got massacred ten thousand years ago or more."

"It doesn't matter," Sandy said, putting her foot down, even if it was just under the table. "I am not sending out exploration ships. First, I don't want to lose them. Second, if there are motherships that haven't gotten the word about us, I don't want one of them getting brought into this war because they intercepted a strange little vehicle with strange vermin that look too much like the properly enlightened ones. Okay?"

"Oh, we've got something to add to your pipe," Jacques said. "After we captured the alien cruiser, the one we caught before we all headed off to the home world?"

"I remember the ship," Sandy said.

"We sent off a request to Wardhaven asking for the genetic work-up on the people that Kris first ran into. They were a family or something. They were running a small mining operation."

"Yes, I asked about that before we left. The word was that they'd been lost."

"Just about everything from that circumnavigation of the galaxy disappeared down a vanishing hole," Penny said. "They were none too happy that we'd let the others in the circumnavigation corps know that we could find fuzzy jumps when they couldn't. Anyway, it was all classified somewhere up there above God almighty."

"And?" Sandy asked.

"We got them to give us at least the genetic work-ups for them, the couple of raider females we found murdered on the first raped planet, as well as the gene report on the two babies we rescued when we blew up that alien scout in Iteeche space."

"Where are those kids?" Amanda asked, patting her own stomach. While Sandy was gone, Amber had signed a general permission order for everyone who wanted to have kids. Apparently, many wanted to start a family, Amanda and Jacques included.

"They gave us their genetic picture," Penny said, dryly, "not their address."

"What's interesting about the work-up," Jacques said, ignoring the side tracks, "is that most of the members of that independent family all had the rebellion markers. The aliens must have more than one way to get their independently-minded types off their base ships."

"And the others?" Sandy asked.

"Two of the three women who were murdered and their bodies hidden among the slaughtered local bodies also had the rebel makers," Penny said. "I guess they weren't as docile as some guys wanted them. The two kids also bore the marks. I wondered how it was that their parents had attempted to escape the general death that the aliens accepted with defeat. I'm sorry we didn't get to meet them."

"Me too," Sandy said.

"Have you met the kids we do have here on Alwa?" Jacques asked.

"No, not yet."

"Admiral, I really think you'd benefit from spending some time with them. They may not be our enemy, themselves, but they're the closest we have."

"How would I arrange some time with them?"

"Cara, Abby's niece, is working a lot with them. Call Abby for an introduction."

After a couple of calls, Sandy had an invitation to the children's school for the next morning. "Please don't wear your uniform, Admiral," the young Cara told Sandy. "Some of the alien kids get anxious when they see someone in uniform."

Sandy wasn't sure what that meant, but the next day she was in a mufti as she stepped from the longboat to the shuttle landing dock at Haven. A taxi was waiting and quickly drove her to the school. She arrived about ten a.m. local time.

The school didn't look all that different from the middle school she'd visited when her own offspring was growing up. Built of adobe brick with red clay roof tiles, it fit in nicely with other colonial buildings. Sandy reported to the office where the principal offered her coffee, then took her to a play area in the open space surrounded by classrooms.

Twenty kids in their early teens were getting set up under the care of Abby's niece, whom Sandy recognized from her file picture. All of them were dressed in the same clothes; khaki shorts and green t-shirts. Whether it was a uniform or just what they wore, Sandy didn't know. The kids had the lankiness of early teens who were shooting up so fast they could hardly find their feet, much less keep their feet on the ground.

The principal offered Sandy a seat in one corner and handed her a tablet. On that screen, she could monitor all the kids.

The students were about to play one of their favorite games. It was a multi-player game. They were divided up into five groups of four. Two of the groups, Sandy learned from a glance at the information displayed on the tablet for her, were made up of colonial kids. Two other groups were made up of kids that General Montoya had succeeded in sleepy darting before the female alien managed to incite them all to suicide.

Like most people in human space, Sandy was familiar with the grandmotherly woman who spewed invectives and threats at any human who would listen. A lot of battle-cruisers were being paid for and built by people who'd made her short acquaintance.

The kids, however, were bright-eyed and eager to play. Spending a morning playing a game was great sport for them.

The last team was a mix. Two of the kids had been brought out from human space when their parents immigrated to teach at Haven University. The other two kids were aliens, members of the hunter-gatherer tribe that had ambushed a Marine patrol protecting a science team. Sandy spotted a scar on the boy's leg. It was an infected wound that had almost turned lethal which had driven his parents to risk taking on the sky gods in search of a miracle.

Beside him was a slightly younger girl who seemed inseparable from him.

A dive into the student file of the aliens showed that the two tribal kids had the full rebel genetic fingerprint. The eight ship-borne aliens were untouched by any of the markers.

Sandy leaned back to watch and learn.

The kids hurriedly went through the opening moves. Some aspects of the game became clear quickly. The objective was to exploit resources to build and expand your small village. Each child in the teams needed to cooperate with their teammates. One of the colonial kids tried a sleight of hand, committing to a trade, then reneging after he got his half. That didn't work out for him; the other three ganged up on him the next turn.

The four kids needed to cooperate, although fighting and conquest was an option. However, with only four players in each group, there was no way to settle on a course of action, except unanimously or with a vote of three against one.

The untrustworthy player apparently tried his trick every game. The kids had learned to land on him heavy when he did it the first time. By the third time, he'd fallen into line.

The five teams, however, did allow the overall game to fall into two-on-three if one student could get the other eleven to join in a game of conquest.

Today, one of the colonials, Nancy the Hun, as she was known, tried to turn the game into a war, but the other players would have none of it. Quickly it became clear to Sandy that the kids were out to maximize their growth, while seeing if they could edge out the other teams for the lead.

It was there that the internal dynamics of the four-player teams began to show itself.

The two colonial teams settled for a good strategy that balanced resource exploitation and population growth with care for the land. They might suffer natural disasters or have a good year with abundant crops. They'd roll with the punches, help where they could, but keep working towards the goal they'd set for themselves.

The two teams that had children from the alien ship teams had a problem. They understood the basics of the game; they enjoyed playing it, and did so often. However, they couldn't seem to agree on an overall strategy. Each year, they would have to make their decisions all over again. Each time, a different kid seemed to get into the driver's seat and they'd go off where he or she wanted to go.

Sandy noted that her monitor kept track of who was the leader of each group. Leadership was collegial for all the teams, but some of the ship aliens would talk more one time, less another. Depending on who was talking, the team went one way or the other.

The strongest argument among the eight aliens always centered around risk. All of them were very risk averse.

The fifth team was anything but risk averse. The two immigrant kids and the two tribal ones weren't reckless, but they weren't averse to a gamble. Most of the time, they won. When they lost, they'd laugh and set about recovering.

Sandy went deep into the teacher's materials. The mixed team had won ten of the last twenty games. The other ten were split between the two colonial teams, often by little more than a nose.

The ship aliens always came in last, frequently by a lot.

Sandy waved down Cara when she stood back to watch her students play their game. The admiral pointed at the results. "How does the trailing team feel about that?"

"They're fine with it," Cara said. "They just love building. When we finish this game, we'll mix up the teams and I'll show you something."

Sandy leaned back, keeping one eye on the kids and the other eye on the readouts, and watched the game develop.

One of the colonial teams was almost wiped out by a volcanic explosion. All four of the other groups accepted refugees, fed them, and allowed them to pass through their lands on their way to an area that had no burning mountains.

One of the ship-borne groups suffered a major flood. They had to retreat into the hills and survive as hunters again before they came back down to the flood plain and rebuilt. This time, they split their population between seven hills with only those that needed the river for fishing or transport.

The mixed group got carried away. They tried to expand their population fast and split out to form their next town. Unfortunately, mother nature didn't cooperate. They suffered a year of bad crops. Those that stayed behind had food stored in their granaries. The new town had no such reserves. Survivors fled back to the mother town, and there was civil strife and famine.

They recovered in a few years and tried again. This time, crops were abundant.

This was the cycle of the game for two hours.

With lunch only minutes away, the students made their final moves. Cara totaled the score. Again, the hunters and the immigrants came in first by a significant margin. The two colonial teams were neck-and-neck for second place and the ship-borne were well back. While the eight colonials ribbed each other for their mistakes, the eight raider kids showed no reaction to last place but took it all very placidly. They were more verbal about how fun the game had been, not who won or lost.

Sandy found it interesting, yet also disturbing. This was how slaves would react; quiet, servile, well-behaved.

There was a break for lunch which Sandy spent in the teacher's lounge listening to the usual good-natured pleading of cases for more farm implements, electric cars, and other goods as well as more teaching tools. Sandy listened, but made no commitments. They knew as well as she that defense had a strong demand on them.

After lunch, the game continued. Only this time, Cara divided up the kids differently. The two colonial teams swapped two kids each. It was the other three teams where reorganization got the most interesting.

The mixed team was distributed between the ship-borne aliens. Each of the hunter kids was assigned to one of the other teams. Each of those teams contributed one person to the mixed team, leaving two immigrants with two ship-borne raiders.

The internal dynamics of those three teams was totally different in the afternoon game.

The two hunter kids dominated the ship-borne. They quickly arrived at a strategy and began to implement it within the group. The other three kids became more cheerful and enthusiastic as they went about fulfilling the orders they had been given.

The mixed group, however, was the most verbose. The two immigrant kids drew ideas out from the two quiet aliens. Some of their ideas were quite good and they were the basis for the final strategy. The assessment of Sandy's tablet was that they were implementing a plan that was the closest to optimum.

Meanwhile, the two other mixed groups ran into a few problems. With three following the leader, the boss didn't have anyone to question some of their worst ideas which led to a catastrophe or two. They met adversity with good humor, but still, you could see that the two hunter kids had a pretty good idea where they'd screwed up and went back to the game with a strong intent to get back in the lead.

Sandy nodded to herself as she watched the game play out in a small space all the strengths and weakness of government by the strong man. When the leaders were right, things went very well, but when the policy was wrong, there was no one there to spot it before it went south, or offer alternatives when it did.

That left Sandy wondering about the command structure she faced among the alien raiders. The Enlightened

One called the shots; that was clear. What wasn't clear was what the internal processes were. Was there a committee of Enlightened Ones that chose how the wolf pack did things or was it a top-down dictatorship? From what Sandy knew from Earth's history with dictators, they were far more worried about keeping their jobs than the average elected official, usually because losing an election was bad. Being dethroned usually involved losing a head.

The one data point that Sandy had of an Enlightened One's job performance related to her recent battle. The boss guy had failed to prepare for the attack she launched, and when it hit, he ran like a chicken, screaming for his subordinates to sacrifice themselves to save him.

In the end, one of his subordinates had blown him out of space.

"I wonder how well the aliens with rebel markers play with each other?" she asked herself. Sadly, she had no answer, but she was getting ideas.

Her commlink buzzed.

"Yes," she answered.

"Admiral, we have a problem," came in Admiral Kitano's smooth voice. "A convoy just arrived from human space and it got into a fight. You might want to get up here so we can debrief the convoy commander."

Sandy stood. The kids ignored her, so intent were they in the final few moves of their game. Cara, however, quickly came to her side.

"I take it that you have to go," the young woman said.

"Something is always boiling over."

"I learned that with my Aunt Abby," she said with a sad smile. "Thank you for coming."

"Can I see the final results?" Sandy asked.

"If you want to," Cara said, more sparkle in her smile this time.

"I'd like to study how it all comes down, if you don't mind."

"Take the tablet. It will stay connected over the net and I'll see that the final readouts are sent to you."

"Thank you."

With that, Sandy was soon racing to the shuttle port to catch a ride back up to face this new crisis.

5

No sooner had the longboat landed in the *Victory's* docking bay than Sandy found she had an ensign at her elbow. The youngster was cute as a puppy and just as eager.

"Admiral, ma'am," he stuttered. "Admiral Kitano is waiting for you in your flag plot with all of your available key staff."

"How many of my key staff?" Sandy asked. The answer to that would warn her as to how big of an issue she faced.

"All of them, I think, Admiral," the ensign choked out.

"All?"

"All the admirals of the fleet, ma'am, and a whole lot of captains, too, Admiral."

No wonder the kid was on senior officer overload. "Thank you, Ensign. I can take it from here."

"Yes, ma'am, Admiral," and the nervous fellow fell in behind her. Did she hear a gulp of relief?

Ensigns were just so cute. Too bad they grew up to be intense admirals, but, no doubt that kid would have lots of fun memories by the time he had to make life or death decisions.

Two Marine guards were waiting for Sandy outside the door of her occasional wardroom. A corporal opened the door for her and announced, "Attention on deck."

Sandy's "As you were," saved wear and tear on a lot of knees which they doubtlessly would be thankful for when her staff got to be her age.

There was a vacant chair at the end of the table closest to the hatch. Admiral Kitano sat on one side; Captain Paisley held down the other. Along both sides of the table were all the admirals that commanded her fleets, including Admiral Benson who commanded Base Force and her ship-yards. Arrayed along the wall were more key staff that didn't rate a seat at the table but might be needed to inform or execute the orders Sandy would soon be issuing, as well as the admirals' chiefs of staff.

"What's the excitement about?"

Admiral Kitano had continued to rise. Now she turned to face Sandy. "The every-other-month convoy from human space jumped into the next system out," she reported in clipped tones. "It's decelerating now, but they sent ahead a combat report. One of the systems they passed through had alien raiders in it. They fought a brief fight and jumped out. Unfortunately, they both entered and exited the system using fuzzy jumps."

Uh, oh!

"Did any of the aliens survive the encounter?" Sandy snapped.

"With your permission, Admiral, I'd like to turn the briefing over to Captain Paisley to bring you up to date on what we know and don't know."

"Carry on, Captain," Sandy said, as she took her seat and Amber settled into hers.

Penny stood, and both the long walls of the wardroom suddenly became huge monitors showing identical tables of ships, star maps and the other types of information that would show up on a battle board.

"For the last year, we've been getting resupply convoys every even month from human space. They usually consist of sixteen battlecruisers and eight fast transports. They've been bringing out approximately sixteen thousand new sailors and immigrants, in addition to mail, entertainment, news, journals, technical data, and Smart Metal. It seems crazy to ship machinery and stuff when we can fabricate what we need out of Smart Metal, so we don't. They also bring livestock and some of the food choices that we don't yet grow here."

"All the comforts of home," Sandy said. "They go back on every odd month. What happened this time?"

"Nelly, Kris Longknife's computer, calculated a thousand different courses between here and human space. We have yet to use fifty of them. Still, we hit the jackpot this voyage."

A holographic star map appeared above their conference table. Alwa pulsed green. Planets in human space were gold. The Iteeche were brown. Closer to the green than the gold, a system pulsed red.

"The convoy was making its last fast passage across a star system. This jump would take it to the system next out from here and they'd decelerate in that system before coming through our jump at a decent speed. I point out the velocity of the convoy so you can understand that slowing down to fight the alien, or going back to finish them off, was not an option."

Sandy scowled. This way of racing around the galaxy was the only way you could get from human space to Alwa on the other side of the galaxy before every one on aboard died of boredom. Still, it involved risks. Two ships might collide in, or right next to, a jump point. Humans did their best to route their ships well away from each other. However, there were thirty to forty alien raider wolf packs out there. Also, if luck really abandoned a convoy, one of their ships might run into some other race's first go at interstellar travel.

This problem, however, was more basic. This convoy had stumbled on the alien raiders doing whatever alien raiders did when they weren't doing their best to slaughter other sentient beings.

Sandy brought her mind back to the problem as it developed.

"The convoy jumped into this unvisited system and immediately found noise. Sensors detected reactors of an as yet unidentified type. They were close enough to Wolf Pack George but different enough to tell us this was part of an extended family but not George."

"Did a lot of George's pack escape when we fought them?" Sandy asked.

"A handful of door knockers, but nothing else," Penny answered. The door knockers were huge alien battleships that had grown from 500,000 tons to around a million tons. All the extra weight came from blocks of granite or basalt cladding the hull. They might now be adding ice armor as well. All that extra weight made the door knockers slow but hard to kill as they led the way through a jump point. The aliens hoped that with a bit of luck, we'd still be trying to kill these heavy warships when the smaller ones zoomed through the jump. Thus, they'd force the jump and earn their name, door knockers.

Sandy had commanded the force that chased down and destroyed about half of the door knockers that survived the massive Battle at System X. Still, the alien ships split up and she had to let some get away.

"Did our convoy face door knockers?" Sandy asked.

"No, ma'am. The hostile force was thirty battleships and a dozen cruisers."

Battleships were what the humans were calling the original alien warships. They were half a million tons of brute force, too many short-range lasers to count, all with a strong overdose of viciousness and hatred. The cruisers were smaller ships, smaller than the human battlecruisers. They were a lot faster than the battleships, but still not as fast as the human warships.

To date, the quality control measures the aliens applied to their construction worked fine if the ship was used only moderately hard. If they really pushed their reactors, they might end up blowing themselves up.

Still, the alien base ships, (the size of a small moon with fifty billion souls aboard,) could park itself in a planetary orbit and start a production line that could turn out ships at a terrifying pace. While the crew of a battleship was approximately a million, when you had a pool of 50 billion people to draft crews from, you could crew a lot of battleships.

An alien grandmother had screamed that they would drown us in their blood just before she'd ordered the very same kids Sandy had spent the day with, to suicide with her.

These aliens were crazy.

And now at least some of them knew there were jump points they did not know about.

"Tell me about the encounter," Sandy ordered.

"The aliens were orbiting a large ice giant," Penny said. "It was not on the direct path between our two jumps, and they didn't appear to be expecting us. It took them a good twelve hours before they got underway and broke orbit. We're not sure, but we think they had one of those lattices the aliens are using to swing their ships around and get something like gravity."

"So, we found an outpost," Sandy concluded.

"It does appear so, ma'am. Our convoy accelerated from 800,000 kilometers per hour to several million. They did their best to dodge out of the way of the alien attackers. Still, they were in range of the aliens' gun batteries for approximately one hundred and five seconds. The aliens followed their standard policy and concentrated on two of our battlecruisers. Their crystal armor held, but they suffered major damage to the crystals and overheating to the underlying hull. They will need some serious yard time," Penny said to Admiral Benson.

"We're already made ready to receive them. I've asked for some extra crystal as well."

"Very well," Sandy said.

"One of the fast transports suffered some damage. We might want to suggest that these ships get crystal armor, too. At least those on the Alwa run."

"Examine the option," Sandy said to Benson. "Also, could you get enough crystal to armor these eight before we return them to human space?"

"We can, but it's going to cost in consumer goods, boss."

Sandy rolled her eyes at the overhead. Everything the Navy needed had to be paid for from the consumer goods that the civil economy needed. Still, there was no choice.

"Penny, send this briefing along to Abby. Tell her I'm open to any suggestions as to how we do it with the least displacement to our world."

"Yes, ma'am. Mimzy and Mata are exchanging data.

Abby is in a meeting at the moment and will get back to us later."

"Very well. Okay, how many of the aliens got away?"

"Two battleships were left drifting dead in space," Penny reported. "They might or might not make it anywhere, but the real problem was that one of the cruisers was sent racing off to a far jump just as soon as the rest of the fleet got underway to intercept. They watched the entire battle. There was no way the convoy could chase them down and nail them."

Sandy shook her head. "Don't you hate it when the evil galactic overlord starts getting smart?" she said with a sigh. "I guess after losing as many ships to us as they have, they decided they need a few survivors to report back some lessons learned."

"They got a very important lesson this time," Amber observed. "There are bits of space we can disappear into that they can't see. I guess we better add some explosives around our Mark XII fire control systems. Can't have them finding it in the wreckage of one of our ships."

Admiral Benson nodded. "I'll have the design teams get on that immediately."

"There is one more thing I need to share, Admiral," Penny said, "before I sit down and hear I've totally ruined your day."

"Hit me," Sandy said drolly.

The star map added a second flashing green system. "That is our cat planet, ma'am. While those skunks are a long way from Alwa, they're just outside the picket line for the Sasquan System."

The room took on the silence of a tomb.

Sandy leaned back in her chair and stared at the overhead. The cats were a pain in the butt. When they weren't causing her trouble, they were squabbling among themselves. The last time she'd paid them a visit, one of the factions among the bickering felines had kidnapped her, though for what purpose, Sandy was still not sure. Likely the ones that kidnapped her had no idea of what they intended.

Now, those blasted cats were on strike, refusing to send her more workers, and the bloody fur balls were the best workers she had, where aliens were concerned.

"So, we withdraw Admiral Drago and his Fourth Fleet, or do we dig in and defend the cat system? Opinions anyone?"

Admiral Betsy Bethea, Commander, Third Fleet, spoke up first. "Kris Longknife swore that we weren't going to let the sons of bitches get another intelligent species, ma'am. I think we all would like to keep that promise."

"As I would also," Sandy said, "but can we?"

"Despite the problems getting crews for the fortresses," Amber said, "we have been drilling the crews. We've found that we can operate a gun with a quarter of the normal gun crew for one aboard a battlecruiser. That's not to say that we can keep that up forever, or that if a laser goes down we can fix it, but even with the gun crews spread thin, only two thirds of the lasers have gun crews. If one of the guns goes down, they've got another they can bring up."

"Can they do that?"

"Ma'am," Admiral Benson said, "it's not like we're talking about a long siege. A hundred and sixty operational 24-inch lasers backed up by three beam guns can pick off a lot of ships coming through the jump. Unless they've got three or four wolf packs all in line to charge the jump point, sooner much more than later, they're going to run out of targets for us."

"I take it that you'd still rather have a full gun crew?" Sandy asked.

"Spreading one gun crew over six guns for preventive maintenance is a bitch, ma'am, but to date, if we order them to unlimber those guns, they come up ready to fire on the tick."

Sandy nodded. There was some risk involved, but it looked like an acceptable one.

"There's also the matter of an alert," Admiral Kitano said. "We've got pickets out twelve or thirteen star systems deep. Penny tells me that even if the aliens stumbled onto a fuzzy jump, they couldn't jump all the way into the Alwan system. For one thing, we don't have any of those jumps in this system. I guess we're on a spur for the galactic highway system." Amber's dry humor drew a chuckle from around the table.

"If we know that an alien attack is on the way, we can deploy a fleet of battlecruisers, maybe two if nothing is coming up behind the other jump. We can also reinforce the gun crews to make the fortress even more deadly."

"I like that idea," Sandy said. "I want a plan to do just that on my desk by 0800 three days from now. Ben?"

Admiral Benson stiffened in his place.

"I want you to jack up battlecruiser production. Work with Abby and Pipra to figure out how we can avoid disrupting the production lines as little as we can, but I want your yards back to laying down sixteen battlecruisers a month."

"Can you hold to twelve?" Benson asked. "We've got a plan to increase the production tempo to that level which doesn't harm the rest too much."

"Work it out with all the interested parties. If you need to bring me in, do it before the convoy arrives. As soon as it gets here, I'm hijacking the fast transports, their cargo, and a lot of their passengers."

"I suspect I know why, Admiral," Amber said, "but I don't want to guess wrong."

"I propose to take half of the ships we have now, three fleets' worth, and go visit our feline friends. I will take all the Smart Metal the convoy brought here and ship it over to Sasquan, as well as any yard workers. I also want to include any fab operators and lunar miners that came out this convoy. I propose to expand Kiel station to support three fleets and use what's left over to start some heavy fabs on the cats' moon. I figure we can use the lunar resources, along with what the cats ship up to us, to get heavy fab production up to speed. We won't start building ships for a while, but we'll be getting everything set up for it."

"Pipra's not going to like that," Penny said. "I had supper two days back with Abby and she told me they were already making plans to use this shipment to expand the heavy fabs here."

"Tell her that momma's got to love all her kids, no matter how much of a pain they are."

"Well, if this doesn't get Abby out of that meeting, she really doesn't want to be disturbed," Penny said.

"Now, I think we have everything well in hand. Amber, I want to reorganize our fleet here into six fleets of forty-eight battlecruisers. I intend to take three with me when we sail. Admirals Bethea and Miyoshi will bring their fleet. Also, let's give Admiral Nottingham one. We need an Earth officer commanding a fleet. Amber?"

"I've got Shoalter and L'Estock. I'd propose to give Admiral Kaeyat her third star and a fleet."

"I approve," Sandy said, eyeing the young woman who'd come out as a division officer on the first eight ships given to

Kris. She looked too young to be trusted with the family car keys, but she'd proven to be a fighting admiral. "You'll have Admiral Benson doing his best to knock out some ships for his yard workers to fight. Be sure to steal them regularly for the other fleets. That should keep production humming?"

"Admiral, you wrong me," Admiral Benson said, his hand placed mockingly over his 'wounded' heart. "We'll always keep the yards humming. It's just so mean of you to rob the grain from the kin that grind the corn."

"Keep robbing," Sandy said.

"No doubt, I will," Amber agreed.

"Now, ladies and gentlemen, I have some plans I want to see, and see quickly. Dismissed."

Amber called the room to attention and Sandy withdrew. As the door closed behind her, the hum of happy voices were balanced against dismay and disappointment. No doubt, those sailing for the sound of the guns were the happy voices. Those left behind were the disappointed.

Of course, they both could end up in a battle if this was just an alien ploy to pull her and half of her fleet off to guard the vulnerable cats while the real attack was aimed at the birds.

You pay your money and you take your chances.

6

No surprise, Sandy wasn't even halfway through her supper that evening before Abby and Pipra came storming into the *Victory's* wardroom.

Sandy spotted them when they paused at the door and stood glaring at all the officers as they searched the room for her. She knew she shouldn't have, but Sandy gave in to the devil and waved cheerfully at the two of them.

While they stomped toward her, Sandy flagged down two ensigns who were leaving and sent them over to the steam tables to select two dinners for her guests.

As the two plopped down in the chairs across from Sandy she said, "Today is roast beef night, at least I think they're cutting on a real cow. You never can tell, but it tastes good. How do you like yours served?"

"Rare," both snapped.

Sandy waved at the two ensigns. "Rare," she said in a soft voice that carried across the room.

"So, I suspect I know to what I owe this visit, but tell me anyway."

"You are not only a juvenile delinquent," Pipra growled,

though she did keep her voice low, "but you are also a thief. Stealing what is not yours to take."

"Hold that thought while I check on it. Let's see, I'm Viceroy of the Alwa System. I'm responsible for defending this system and negotiating treaties with any other aliens we come across. I have negotiated a mutual defense treaty with the cats. Ergo, I'm responsible for their defense as well."

"Yes," Pipra hissed. "But the cats don't need any help with their economy and I need bird workers and that means I have to pay them. I was hardly caught up on the delivery of consumer goods from that crush you created with your last sudden maximum effort. Now you want to make a mess of everything again. Christ, woman, what do you expect from me, a miracle every day?"

Sandy carved a small bite of roast beef and eyed the two women of business and industry. "No, I just expect a miracle every month or so." So saying, she delivered the meat to her mouth and began to chew.

"Well, why didn't you say so? Just one miracle a month is manageable," Pipra growled. Her voice showed none of the acceptance of her words. "If it doesn't upset the entire damn production line."

Sandy took the time to chew the meat carefully. No doubt this meeting would deliver a lot of excess acid to her stomach, but it was better to chew her food very well. With luck, it might not come back up on her.

"Pipra, if you reviewed the meeting notes I sent you, I'm asking you to up the priority for defense. We've got a threat to the cats and we need to add a hundred and fifty ships to the thirty-two Admiral Drago has there right now. That means we need to add some fifty ships to our own fleet as fast as we can. Admiral Benson figures it will take three or four months, assuming we produce twelve ships a month.

How much disruption will an extra four to eight more ships a month cause you?"

Pipra scowled, but turned to Abby.

Their meals arrived, so conversation died, as Sandy hoped it would, while baked potatoes were prepared to taste. It continued as the first few bites were enjoyed. Roast beef, potato, and mixed fresh vegetables, some of Earth, some Alwan, were best enjoyed while warm.

Abby, born and raised in the slums of New Eden, was willing, at times, to talk with her mouth full.

"We can absorb the jump from eight ships to twelve without too much dislocation. We'll likely have to slow industrial growth a bit, but the product for the birds, Colonial, and immigrant consumption should be only slightly impaired. Say five percent. People will see deliveries slide by two, maybe three days. You should warn the Colonial Prime Mister that this will be coming her way over the next month."

"Me? Not you?" Sandy asked around her next bite.

"You're the Viceroy," Pipra snarled. "You're making a mess of my plans. You tell the birds and Colonials we're back to robbing Peter to defend Purr."

"I will, as soon as Abby can give me a comparison of deliverables that I can pass along to her."

"Mata already has the tables drawn up, Admiral," Abby said. "It should be in your mail queue right now."

Sandy glanced at her wrist commlink. She had mail. A check showed it was from Abby and it was a huge document.

"Thank you, Abby. I appreciate your promptness."

"Glad to be of service, Admiral, but you ain't out of the woods. We'd already told Prime Minister Ada that we were expecting some four hundred thousand tons of Smart Metal on the next convoy. We planned to spin up a couple of fabs, both heavy and light. I told her she could expect some serious deliveries in two, maybe three months. You're stealing her future largess. She ain't gonna be a happy woman when you tell her that you're taking all those nice goodies and hauling them off to that furry red-headed stepchild of yours."

No doubt, to the birds and Colonials, the felines were illegitimate barkers and biters. However, they were now Sandy's barkers and biters whose parents had only been to church to nip at the parson's heels. Sandy had to protect them, and somehow, she would.

"I'm sorry about the dislocation," Sandy said, "but Kris Longknife swore that no more intelligent species would get wiped out, with one body in glass and a pile of heads displayed in the aliens' trophy room under their pyramid. I'm so glad to say that we cleaned that place out and sanitized it. If they get mad at Alwa, we've got the jump point fortresses to defend you. The cats are in a totally different situation."

"Yeah, we got the fortresses," Pipra snapped. "But in the last attack the aliens made on Alwa, Kris chose to defend forward, to fight them at every jump we could. You're taking all our reserves and forcing us to defend at the last ditch. That's a lousy strategy, Grand Admiral."

"Suddenly, every businesswoman is a general," Sandy quipped.

"Admiral," Pipra interjected.

"Okay, Admiral," Sandy said, only a small amount of sarcasm in the rank she gave the woman. "Yes, I'm taking all our reserves. We'll have plenty of warning that the aliens are headed here. Admiral Kitano can defend forward with what she has, and the sooner she has more, the better."

"The general who is strong everywhere is strong nowhere," the putative admiral pointed out.

"Yes, but we have good communications between here and there. If we need to reinforce one part of the defense, we should have enough warning."

"So you're going to trade me one military platitude for another, huh?" Pipra said, after a brief pause for reflection.

"If you want, I can give them to you in the original Greek," Sandy said, dryly.

"Okay, I had to try. Will I get any of the new immigrants arriving with this convoy?"

That was a good question. Those people had signed up for a dangerous assignment, but Alwa was one level of danger. Sasquan was another one entirely. Kris Longknife had shanghaied people when Alwa was just getting started. Could Sandy dare to do it again?

Sandy ran a worried hand through her hair, supper forgotten.

"What do you think the chances are that they'd volunteer to fill in where we need them?"

Pipra shrugged. "Your guess is as good as mine. However, I will point out that we have a few folks that aren't happy in their present jobs. They don't get along with the boss. They just had a messy break-up. Why don't you let me get out the word and look at what we get? I know you Navy types are more used to 'I want three volunteers: you, you, and you,' but the rest of us like a chance to at least think we're in control of our lives. The new arrivals. Hell, girl, they volunteered to come here. Is the cat system all that different from the birds'? They haven't been plugged into jobs out here yet. The odds are that, given a choice, they're actually quite likely to volunteer. After all, vacuum is vacuum."

"So, you're suggesting I treat civilians like civilians and trust."

"Yeah, I know that's a mighty strange thought, but you know, you really could be a grand admiral to these folks if you just gave them a chance. And hell, if you don't get enough volunteers, you can send out the press gangs."

"But I like press gangs," Sandy said. For the first time since the two stormed in here, there were smiles between them.

"I'll even loan you Abby to run your press gang."

"Hell no, boss gal," Abby said. "Remember, I'm the union's chief steward. I can't do nothin' like that."

7

W ith Abby's estimate of deliverables in hand, there was no reason for Sandy to delay her meeting with Ada. Thus, she found herself again in a longboat headed for Haven. By not calling ahead, Sandy figured this late in the day, she might find the Colonial Chief of Ministries alone in her office.

That proved not to be so.

Apparently, either Ada or Granny Rita had good spies on the station. There was a government car waiting for the admiral as soon as she departed the longboat. It whisked her straight to Government House where a Rooster and a Colonial were waiting for her.

Officially, they smiled and showed her the way to Ada's office. In fact, they seemed ready to grab Sandy's elbows and steer her there if she deviated so much as an inch from that flight plan.

Sandy walked into Ada's office to find a full cabinet meeting waiting for her.

"So nice of you to finally get around to letting us poor

benighted souls in on your high and mighty plans," Ada said, her words dripped in both sarcasm and vitriol.

"I came right down here as soon as I had a plan," Sandy pointed out as she settled into a chair at the foot of the long table. Ada had the head. Various Colonials and Roosters sat along each side. There was even an Ostrich. Apparently, they'd been added to the Colonial council.

Granny Rita sat at Sandy's right elbow. The two of them exchanged nods, but neither blinked.

"You could have included us in the development of this damn straight jacket you're strapping us into," Ada demanded.

"There was no development," Sandy said, evenly. "The situation calls for increasing monthly battlecruiser production from eight to twelve or sixteen. Mata Hari had already done a plan for Abby that increased production to twelve ships a month. It should only reduce the consumer production by five percent. Maybe less, depending on what you order. I accepted the smaller number."

"Why does the Navy get to eat our lunch again?" a Rooster seated half-way up the table demanded.

"Isn't this problem just something for the cats?" Ada asked. "The cats that are not pulling their weight? I hear they're on strike."

"The cats here are working hard," Sandy said. "I'm headed out to speak to the cats and resolve this labor problem. I expect to settle it quickly."

"And give them our Smart Metal." This time it was a Colonial at mid-table that jumped in.

"Yes," Sandy said.

"Why, for the love of God, are we stripping our defenses? Defenses we've worked hard to build ourselves," Ada pointed out.

"Because you have the jump point fortresses to defend your system and the bug-eyed aliens are sniffing around the cat system."

The room fell silent at that.

"We didn't hear that part of the story," Ada said.

"The latest convoy from human space," Sandy said, "stumbled upon a couple of dozen alien warships and cruisers. They were just outside the picket line we've set up around the cat world. I need to reinforce our fleet there. I intend to get the cats set up to mine their own moon. Get them producing their own battlecruisers on Kiel station. That's what the Smart Metal is for, as well as the draft of workers. It will not be easy to get a fabrication base started with only four hundred thousand tons of Smart Metal, but that's what we'll start with."

The room stayed silent as those around the table absorbed the rest of the story that somehow had not made it down to the planet's surface.

"Must we protect the cats?" asked the Rooster who had spoken before.

Sandy eyed Ada, then Granny Rita, then turned back to the first minister.

With a sigh, Ada spoke. "Yes, we must come to their aid, just as others came to ours. I have been up to the O Club on Canopus Station. I've seen the eight banners hanging there. Eight flags for wolf packs that Kris Longknife blew away before they could get to our doorstep. We have to give them the same help that we were given."

"Are you going to want us to make jump point forts for the cats?" the old commodore asked from Sandy's elbow.

"That is not in the initial plan. At least not for Alwa to make it. Those huge stations are a bitch to sail. I have no idea how long it would take us to get something even half that size from here to there. There is also the matter of the beam guns. We can't make them here. If we want something like that, we'll need to have human space send them out."

"So, what do you intend to do?" Granny Rita asked.

"Tell the cats that they've got a problem," Sandy said. "After they recover from that, I expect that we'll see what we can do to survive it. I'm willing to put four hundred thousand tons of Smart Metal into the pot, along with several thousand workers to help them jump start a whole new level of tech. Still, a whole lot will depend on them. I expect there will be a lot of yowling and maybe some scratching."

"Better you than me," Rita said.

"I can provide everyone with a copy of the plan we intend to implement," Sandy said, tapping her commlink to send the entire plan to everyone in the room. "Within the confines of the resources available, I'm willing to entertain suggestions. I intend to depart with one hundred and forty-four battlecruisers in three days. I hope you can provision us for a month. I expect the cats will need some time to develop a logistical support network."

"I think we can do that," Ada said.

"Now, if it's okay, I'd like to meet with Ada and Granny Rita for a bit," Sandy said.

With much scraping of chairs and low rumblings of conversation, the others left. Ada came down from the head of the table to sit at Sandy's elbow, across from Rita.

When the door finally closed, the admiral turned to the old commodore. "Rita Nuu-Longknife, can't I ever go away and not come back to find you in the middle of a hornets' nest?"

"Not my hornets," the old gal drawled.

"But it is our nest," Ada added. "Sandy, this isn't just

Rita's fight. It's all of ours. We've got to cut the apron strings from human space."

"But if human space doesn't keep shipping us people and extra Smart Metal," Sandy pointed out, "we're going to be in a world of hurt. We are not yet ready to stand up our own defense. Yes, we're adding Roosters, Ostriches, and Colonials to our ships and fabrication work force, but without the immigrants, there just isn't enough highly trained people to support those training up."

Both of the other women were nodding long before Sandy finished.

"But now you're talking about dividing what we get from the United Society and the other associations," Ada said. "We hardly have enough, and now we need to survive on half of it."

"Yeah," Rita said, "but I think we've got a leg up on the cats, Ada. We've got land here we can offer the immigrants. I doubt that the cats have much empty space if they're fighting as much as I hear tell."

Ada eyed Sandy.

The admiral shrugged. "I have no idea what their land use policies are. I know they don't much care to have humans walking their planet, and we can't get the right to protect our people with extraterritorial status. Their legal system is not at all like ours. They seem to settle a lot of things with screams, claws, and capital punishment. For now, our folks are staying on the station."

"So, we can offer land and the cats can't," Rita said.

"I think that's the way of it," Sandy agreed.

"Now," Sandy said, "not to radically change the subject, but what's this I hear about you being alive and wanting your stocks back?"

"Not to change the topic," Rita said, " but it seems reasonable, don't you think?"

"Reasonable is one thing. The law can often be something else," Sandy pointed out.

"Yeah, I seem to have heard that a time or fifty from my dad. I may have to go back to fight little Al for the company, but I think I still have some pull with my former husband. If a king can't keep the judiciary honest, who can?"

"You want the entire company, lock, stock, and barrel?"

"Oh, God no, honey. This is my home. Once I get the brat to give me a quit claim on all the Nuu property in our system and my appropriate chunk of the annual dividends, I'm coming home. This is where my kids and babies are. Of course, they may have to add two or four more frigates to the Alwa run to bring out all the additional Smart Metal I buy with my money."

"Are you going back on the next convoy?" Sandy asked.

"Likely so. I may be taking a few of your Navy lawyers with me. I hope you won't mind. They've also named a few lawyers I might want to retain once I get back there. I don't think Alex will know what hit him."

"Good God," Sandy breathed, "being around Longknifes fighting their enemies is bad enough. Longknifes fighting Longknifes? I'm very glad I'm on the other side of the galaxy."

"A smart move on your part," Rita agreed.

"Anything else left on our plate?" Sandy asked.

Both shook their heads. Sandy found her way back to the entrance to Government House through cool halls, now dusky and empty. Only her footsteps sounded on the wooden floors. The government car was waiting for her.

Back at the landing dock, her longboat was tied up and waiting for her.

"Admiral, we just missed a launch window. We'll have another one in seventy minutes."

"No problem, Bos'n," Sandy said. She pulled out her reader and began pacing up and down the dock. The evening was the kind of cool you get after a long day. The air smelled of fresh water and healthy dirt. Birds flew by, flapping their wings and honking. Other small birds were flitting about, catching insects.

It was a wonderful evening to be alive.

The reader showed that, true to her promise, Cara had sent the game results. The afternoon game went long; the kids were still playing an hour after the final bell rang. Cara finally had to break up the game and send them home.

The results of this game were much different from the first. It was a neck and neck race among all five teams. The two teams led by kids with alien rebel genes and three ship-borne kids in support positions had their ups and downs, but they finished right up there with the other three teams.

All were within one percent of each other.

Inwardly, Sandy groaned. This did not bode well for her fight with the alien raiders. If their "Enlightened Ones" could get their act together, they could give the humans a run for their money. The question was, could they get their act in order?

For a hundred thousand years, they hadn't been in a real fight. You had to wonder if the laser design they'd hit the humans with five years ago had changed any in all that time. So far, the humans had changed a whole lot faster than the aliens.

Were the kids raised as hunters with the rebel gene more flexible than the ship-borne "Enlightened Ones?" Were the ship lords willing to learn? Were they able to learn?

The bos'n announced it was time to motor away from

the pier. Sandy boarded the longboat and quickly strapped in. She mulled her problem over as she did so.

In the end, she found there was no real answer. The aliens were out there and they'd likely make her fight them again and again.

The human race would have to keep adapting faster than they did. It was either that, or die.

8

Grand Admiral Sandy Santiago, Viceroy to Alwa and Minister with Full Portfolio to Aliens didn't relax until her fleet jumped into the cats' star system.

Since the trip out had been made at high speeds, it was not possible to tiptoe up to a jump and put the periscope through to get a look at what was waiting on the other side. Instead, the battlecruiser *Steadfast* stayed a good ten minutes ahead of the main fleet. It would go through the jump and send back a near instantaneous messenger rocket with a report on what was within a million klicks of the jump.

Fortunately, all the reports were negative. The aliens did not show their face this voyage.

For that, Sandy was grateful.

Now, she looked down on a system she was getting to know all too well. She had Comm send off a query to Admiral Drago for a status report on the cat situation. Her last report had been a month ago and had not mentioned that the cats were refusing to send more workers to Alwa.

The first message from Admiral Drago arrived several hours later.

The main screen lit up with his smiling face. "I'm glad to see you, Admiral Santiago, but to what do I owe the honor of such a huge battle fleet? It can't be good."

A few minutes later, a reply came in to her first query.

This one showed him shaking his head, ruefully. "If I didn't know better, I'd think these bloody felines were related to the common house cat. They never seem happy with anything. Well, most things. They're always happy when we sell them some new tech. It's just that they keep complaining that we're charging too much. They whine that we're taking money out of their economy that they need to grow. I hope you brought Amanda Kutter back with you. I need some advice on what monetary policy helps an economy grow. At the moment, we are taking in a lot more money than we can spend on the fleet."

The admiral who had to ride herd on the cats paused for a moment before going on. "As for their refusal to let us tap their labor force, I think it's a try at renegotiating our royalty system. I've tried to explain that I don't have the authority to revise a treaty you signed, but I've gotten nowhere. I'm glad you're here. I hope you'll have Jacques La Duke at your elbow. I swear, the social practices of this cat house is driving me crazy. Sorry to be such a wet blanket."

Drago's gaze then took on a hard glint. "You still haven't told me why you brought such a huge fleet. It's not that I won't be able to feed you all. The cats will be glad to sell you damn near anything to get their money back, but I can't believe you brought a couple of fleets out here just to negotiate a labor agreement."

Sandy's reply advised Drago that she did, indeed, have Jacques and Amanda at her elbow for negotiations, but the fleet was there for a more sanguine purpose. "We have a report of alien raiders sniffing around your perimeter." That said, she went on to brief him on what she knew. She also sent him a full report on the battles she'd fought around the Alien home system.

"You have been busy," was Drago's later reply. "I'll try to stretch Kiel Station out to handle a few more battlecruisers, but we won't be able to dock your entire fleet here."

Sandy let him know she had four hundred thousand tons of Smart Metal™, some of which he could use to enlarge his station.

A lot of planning and preparation was done on the voyage in from the jump point. While the *Victory* and her squadron mates docked immediately, four of the fast transports docked right next to them. While Sandy prepared to meet with Admiral Drago and his staff, Smart Metal™ streamed from three of the frigates into the station. It was quickly spun out into an extra couple of kilometers of A Deck with piers attached.

Cameras on A Deck showed Sandy the weird process of the aft of the space station distancing itself farther and farther from the camera as stairs, elevators, and escalators sprouted to take people up and down to the docked ships.

"Ain't Smart Metal wonderful?" Admiral Drago drawled as he reported to Sandy's day cabin. He brought several of his staff, along with four civilians. They greeted Jacques and Amanda as if they'd just found water in the desert.

"Is it that bad?" Jacques asked the two that seemed intent on wrapping him in a bear hug.

"Those cats are crazy like foxes," a young woman said, stepping back under the glower from Amanda. "I think they all need ten years in therapy before we come back here."

"And the economy?" Amanda asked the two that had been only a bit more reticent in their greetings to her.

"It's tearing itself apart," a young woman answered before an older male could organize his thoughts.

"I think we should settle in for a formal briefing," Sandy suggested, and under her watchful gaze they gathered around a conference table that had suddenly appeared in her day quarters as the right bulkhead, the one between her day and night quarters retreated, squishing down her bed and furnishings to make more room for her guests.

It was a reality of how much Smart Metal™ was becoming normal that no one batted an eye at the magic.

Sandy sat at one end, Amanda and Jacques at her elbow, Penny next to Amanda. Admiral Drago took the foot of the table with his intel officer at his elbow. The economic team settled on the side of the table across from Amanda. The sociologists took the other side.

"Would anyone care for tea?" Sandy asked. When no one objected, she had Penny order up service.

"Now," she said, eyeing four-star admiral Bret Drago, "What's going on below our feet?"

"The planet is in turmoil," Bret said, and eyed the economists.

"Actually, it's hard to say whether the cause of the uproar is the economy, or the sociology and psychology of the cats," the young woman economist said. The other three civilians leaned back in their chairs, apparently ready to let her run with it. She glanced at them, then launched into her report.

"All of the feline governments have to walk a careful balance between a lot of competing demands. They have the usual forms of government. There are strong woman dictators ruling over a few countries. To maintain a grip on things, there is the usual amount of graft being passed around and a lot of full prisons. The other two options, oligarchies and democracies, try to harness the factions and bring them into the government in one fashion or another. Still with me?"

Sandy nodded.

"Then we arrived and change hit them like a run-away space ship. Just the sight of us was enough to get all sorts of things going. You saw a few of those splinter factions last time you were here, Admiral. One of them kidnapped you."

Sandy scowled. She still had nightmares of standing sans pants in front of her command team.

"Amanda, Jacques, you were still here as the governments fell and reformed around the approval or disapproval of letting their bright youngsters come work for us. It got easier to swallow that deal when we started sharing our technology that was ancient to us, but cutting edge to them. We thought that would keep them happy for a while."

"I gather that it didn't," Sandy said.

The young woman nodded. "Not for much more than a week after you shipped out. Our technology was a lot more disruptive than we thought. Maybe some of us were a bit too helpful, but it seemed like they needed some assistance figuring out how to make the new electronic gizmos, and set up the infrastructure for cell phones, computers, and nets."

"Some of our people were way too helpful," Admiral Drago growled.

"How so, Bret?"

"They're crafty, these cats. The more they played dumb, the more some folks wanted to help the poor little pussies."

"They suckered us, Admiral," the economist admitted. The other three civilians nodded guiltily.

"At least we got payment contracts signed for the extra tech we delivered," the guy economist said.

"Which caused the money drain," the gal said.

"Well, yes," he admitted.

"Okay, let me interrupt this tale of folly to check on a few things close to my heart," Sandy said. "Are the cats involved in a world war?"

"No, Admiral," Bret shot back. "Actually, they've closed down several of their long-running wars. We embargoed tech to both sides that had a war going on. If they'd held out, they might have managed to steal some of it, but all of them caved real fast when they saw the way the tech was helping the countries we gave it to. It didn't take the little buggers long to figure out how to use computers and better comm-links in their military. No one dared being left behind. Also, I offered to set up tribunals to hear the claims that were at the root of most of the wars. I think we managed to settle most of them in a fair and even-handed manner."

"Even-handed?" Sandy said. "No one got taken advantage of? No one was occupied by us?" Sandy well remembered how the British Empire 'accidentally' ended up owning most of the Indian sub-continent back in Earth's history.

"Ma'am, none of us want to spend too much time dirtside," Bret said. "It's way too easy to piss off one of those cats, and we don't have the claws for one of their little cat fights."

"Okay," Sandy said, going on, "So they got more technology fed into their economies faster than we intended, and they got stuck paying a lot more money to us than they felt like they were making? How'd that go?"

"We ended up with lots of paper money and not a lot we wanted to spend it on. Hell, beyond food, clothes, and minor personal items, we were pretty much banking the money."

"Hold it," Sandy said, puzzled. "If they're using fiat money, and we're taking a lot of it out of circulation, why don't they just print up some more to replace what we're hoarding?"

"Nothing is stopping them, ma'am, and they did," one of the sociologists, the older fellow, said. "However, the howl went up that we were wrecking the economy, which was just a smoke screen to cover the disruptions tech was causing. Every new technology has some winners and some losers. You start selling cars and suddenly blacksmiths aren't shoeing horses and buggy whip manufacturers and workers are out on the street. What we're seeing below is a major economic reorganization being done at breakneck speeds. It's been a lot more than their culture or society can handle."

"And we space aliens are right here to take the fall for all the problems," Sandy growled.

"Yes, ma'am," Bret said. "I've been tempted to pack up, leave, and let them stew in their juices for a few years. Now I understand that is not an option."

"Oh, it's an option, just not one I want to take," Sandy said. She turned to Jacques and Amanda. "How much trouble would I cause if I asked the cats to launch into a major military buildup? We may have the cash on hand to start buying stuff, but what would we need to keep it going without making things worse?"

"What's their labor market?" Amanda asked two resident economists.

"The larger, industrialized nations are suffering a bit of a recession, what with all the new stuff coming on-line and the old jobs evaporating. They are at something like six or seven percent unemployment."

"Resources?" Amanda asked.

"Some of the shifts in the economy are causing shortages. Steel is in short supply as they build new factories. The whole idea of pure silicon wafer chips has them starting up an entirely new technology and industry that has never been thought of. Their quality control is poor, but getting better. They had just stumbled on a large supply of rare earths before we got here and weren't quite sure what to do with it. They're digging like mad right now. It all depends on what you want."

"Doesn't it always," Amanda said to herself.

"Okay, you can continue your briefing in a moment, but first I need to organize a dinner in the honor of a whole lot of boss cats. Bret, can you send Penny a list of who leads the top thirty or forty countries and invite them up here for a black-tie affair?"

"Yes," and the admiral tapped his commlink.

"I got it, Admiral," Penny said.

"Call them and put them on screen."

The wall to Sandy's left turned into one huge screen, divided into some forty windows. Most showed minor functionaries, very panicked and busy making apologies for their leader being unavailable at this moment.

"Penny, get me a direct line."

Admiral Drago's intel guy shot Penny a different list of commlinks. A moment later, the windows began to fill in. Some showed cat leaders sitting at their desks or around tables. One was just getting out of the shower. At least four were sitting up in bed. Behind two, male cats were fleeing the frame.

"I apologize for barging in on you so indecorously. However, I have just arrived at our space station."

"We notice that you have a very large fleet," the President of Columm Almar interrupted.

"We will likely discuss that at our dinner that we are holding in your honor," Sandy said.

"Is this an honor we will be able to walk away from?" the Prime Minister of the Bizalt Kingdom asked, dryly.

"I assure you, all of you will be sleeping in your own beds tonight. That is, assuming you are able to sleep after our post-dinner discussion."

"So, you're here to discuss the labor treaty?" the President asked.

"I bring assurance that the failure to meet your obligations to send some of your subjects and citizens to work with our technologies is a minor matter to me right now."

"Then what is the major issue?" the Prime Minister asked.

"For that, you will have to come and see. Will you please advise Admiral Drago's staff of where you wish to be picked up? We will have a longboat at those coordinates in eight hours. Again, I apologize for disturbing you, and I wish you a pleasant day."

Sandy paused for a moment. The screen went blank. "Penny, is the commlink broken?"

"Yes, ma'am. I've transferred it to Admiral Drago's Operations Officer."

"Good," Sandy said.

Now Bret about split a gut as he laughed. "Wishing them a pleasant day. After you dropped that bomb on them, and dropped it after showing them that you can get through to their very personal commlink . . ." The old admiral had to pause to guffaw and then catch his breath.

"No doubt," Sandy agreed, dryly. "Okay, folks, we've got a formal dinner to plan, a major revision to the cats' economy and culture to sketch out, and only eight hours to do it in. Bret, can your people arrange for the necessary cat food as well as human food?"

"How do you want your steak, Admiral?"

"Bloody rare," Sandy snapped back.

"We will have dinner arranged for fifty, eighty, or five hundred, ma'am."

"Good. The guest list did grow last time," Sandy admitted.

The easiest thing settled, Sandy sat back to listen to a whole lot of talk. Some of it was actually helpful.

andy gave herself just enough time to shower and dress carefully in her formal dinner jacket. Tonight, she settled for a skirt. After all, among the cats, it was the women who made the rules and it was better that she distinguish herself from her male subordinates. She sent word to all the women attending the dinner to do the same.

After some thought, she switched to a skirt that was as short as the regs allowed. These cats wore nothing but coats, jackets, or harnesses. It would be better to show some leg, just not as much as she'd ended up showing upon her last visit while needing rescue.

The *Victory* had no Forward Lounge like Kris Longknife's ships had, and it was still dry. Still, Sandy was able, through the magic of Smart Metal™, to create a large ballroom just off the landing bay. The cat leaders would walk straight from their barge or longboat directly into the banquet hall.

Sandy did not want to parade the cats past a lot of high-level human technology. Just knowing that a room like the ballroom could be created in eight hours was enough shock and awe for one night.

Clearly, the night would hold enough shock for them.

A quarterdeck had been established at the doors from the docking bay to the ballroom. As usual, it was marked off by ancient artillery shells and a fine, complex macramé. There, Admirals Santiago and Drago awaited their guests.

The bosons on the barges and longboats worked with the landing control team on the *Victory* to do a fine job of landing the guests. No lander missed a hook and had to go around. Thus, Sandy was presented with a long and continuous line of dignitaries and their associates.

Admiral Drago's intel officer sifted through the national leaders and those accompanying them to separate out those who were the most important; they, their deputies, and leaders of their opposition parties were introduced to Sandy and Bret.

Lesser officials were shifted to a receiving line made up of Sandy's three fleet commanders. Those lower down were sent directly into the Banquet Hall through two doors on either side of the quarterdeck that magically appeared when it became clear that, once again, the cats had brought quite an entourage.

Once inside, those junior members of the party were treated to three of the four walls retreating to make room for them, and more tables and chairs oozing up from the deck. Their comments were preserved for later review by Mimzy. Most of them were getting used to the aliens doing strange things, but they still found it a shock to actually see it done.

Junior officers directed them to round tables, or groups of tables, depending on their delegation. A dozen of the most important would be seated with the five admirals at the long head table. That way, Sandy or one of her fleet commanders would have a cat at either elbow. It should make for a fun meal.

With the last longboat unloaded and the last honoree's paw shaken, Sandy headed in and quickly went to her seat on the dais. Immediately, Marines in dress blue and reds began delivering plates to each place. There was no salad course; however, a meaty barley soup won praise from Sandy's seatmates.

Madame Gerrot, the Prime Minister of the Bizalt Kingdom, sniffed at a spoonful of the broth, dampened her tongue, and found it worth the risk of eating one spoonful. "Not bad," she said. "Surprisingly good. You humans are full of all sorts of surprises."

"As are you cats," Sandy said, obliquely.

For a few moments, Sandy, Madame Gerrot, and President Almar enjoyed their soup.

"What is the source of the meat?" President Almar asked.

"I could have someone check on it."

"Not if it would take too long."

"Penny?"

Instantly her chief alien intel officer was up from the table right in front of the dais and standing before them.

"Yes, Admiral?"

"Can you ask the cook the source of the meat in our soup?"

"Of course, ma'am," the captain said and tapped her commlink. A moment later she was talking to the senior cook. A moment more, and she was answering.

"A hoofed critter from one of your southern continents. We call it a wildebeest. Did that translate correctly?"

"Yes, thank you. Is there any chance that we might get the recipe for the soup?" the Prime Minister asked.

Penny asked and quickly had an answer. "Yes, we can send it to your commlink, or just distribute it to your media outlets. However, the barley and several of the seasonings are not grown on your planet."

"Would you like us to bring you seeds for barley and the rest?" Sandy asked.

"How much will you charge us?" The Prime Minister wanted to know.

"The price for seed corn is minimal. I think my pay can support you getting a ton of seed barley and whatever grows the seasonings. They could be here next month, assuming they all grow on Alwa. If we have to bring in the seasoning from human space, it could take six months for it to get here. You also have to understand. If it grows on trees, they often take several years to mature and begin yielding fruit."

"Everything with you humans takes time," the President put in.

"We have a saying. Rome, a world capitol, was not built in a day. Don't you have one like it?"

"Several," the two cats said as one.

The fish was the next course. The chef had prepared filets of a white fish in a light wine sauce. The plate included a small cup of Hollandaise sauce as well as a wedge of lemon. The cats addressed it enthusiastically with forks, a device they'd learn to use when eating human cooking.

"Very good," President Almar said.

The Prime Minister dribbled a small amount of the sauce on one flake of her fish and ate it slowly. "This is also very good. Could your officer also get us the recipe for this?"

A minute later, she was adding a request for lemons as well.

"I can get you some lemons, maybe even small lemon sprouts," Sandy said, "but they take time to grow."

The two cats nodded. "Time," President Almar scoffed.

The main course was meat. Plates of raw as well as cooked meat were available. Fortunately, the cook had prepared enough to feed all the cats from either menu. Few chose the raw. The roasted small red and golden potatoes and the long string beans took some getting used to for the cats. Most tried some, and many found them to their liking.

"I don't know what spices went into these," Sandy said.

"I have eaten of your roasted potatoes and these long beans," the Prime Minister said. "I think we already know how to prepare them."

Admiral Drago had suggested that they do without desert. While the cats liked warm chocolate that was thin and had no sugar, they tended to get the trots if they ate too much sugary foods.

Sandy took a deep breath, and stood. Penny rapped on her water glass and the humans immediately fell silent and looked to the head table. It didn't take the cats long to recognize the signal and focus their attention on Sandy.

"I wish to thank you for coming to this dinner on such short notice. I would not have called it if there was not something of great import to share. I noticed, as I listened to the conversations here at the head table and snatches of talk I heard from out there, that the issue of some of your young cats working for us was studiously avoided by you. I had, of course, ordered my officers not to bring it up and to avoid comments if it was."

Sandy turned to glance at President Almar first, then Prime Minister Gerrot. Could a cat be shame-faced?

She turned back to the room and took a deep breath. "I did so because I believe that we will all find what I'm about to say far more important than the minor differences we've been having lately."

The room fell deadly quiet. Few of the officers from Admiral Drago's fleet yet knew The Word. Sandy had passed The Word down the line to officers on the fleets she brought out to keep it on the down low until she let it out.

Apparently, they had kept their mouths zipped.

"Penny, could you project a star map for us?" Sandy asked.

"Yes, ma'am."

The lights in the vast room dimmed so that the picture of the Milky Way galaxy glowed bright in the air above their heads.

"This is the star cluster we live in. We call it a galaxy. The Milky Way galaxy. We started on a single planet and expanded over the last five hundred years or so to occupy hundreds of stars. Penny, can we see human space at this scale?"

"Ma'am, I just colored it all red and ordered it to flash, but I don't think anyone can see it."

Sandy eyed the 3D holograph of the galaxy. "I don't think I can either. Try slowly zooming in until we can see it."

It took a lot of zoom to bring the human sphere into a tiny globe, hardly bigger than a golf ball. There were whispers among the room. A cat rushed out and was heard retching in the hall before the door closed.

"Yes," Sandy said. "It makes you feel kind of small when you look at it from a galactic scale. Now, your system and Alwa are on the other side of the galaxy."

Penny planted a flag pole in human space and began to zoom out. The flag had to be rescaled several times in the process. Then another flag appeared on the other side of the galaxy.

"That's us," Sandy said. "Penny?"

And the view shifted over to the other side as it shrunk

and shrunk and shrunk until the cat system was on one side of the room and the Alwa system was on the other. They glowed bright red. The rest were white.

"As you can see, we're a long way from home, and you and Alwa are a long way from each other. We have ways to cross the stars from human space to here. It takes about a month and we do it each month. A convoy goes from Alwa to Wardhaven one month, and another convoy sails from Wardhaven to Alwa the next month, and so on."

Sandy paused and took another deep breath. She found herself trembling at the words she was about to speak, so she took a second breath and calmed herself.

"Penny, concentrate on the Sasquan System. Let's show the pickets we've got up around the planet to give us warning."

Now the star map concentrated on the cat home. One bright green dot moved over to the center of the overhead. Several yellow dots appeared, with white ones farther out.

"As you can see, we've put warning buoys out in all the systems within four jumps of you. The aliens can only come by the jumps, so we've got a pretty good warning system in place."

Sandy wasn't about to mention that the pickets around Alwa went twelve, thirteen or even fourteen jumps out. That would come later.

"Penny, light up the system we're concerned about."

A bright red light began to flash.

"You will notice that that system is exactly one jump out from the picket line around you. It is also one of the systems that we just happened to have one of our convoys drop into as it was slowing down so that it could arrive at Alwa at a reasonable speed to dock on Canopus Station."

Sandy paused and focused on the flashing red star.

It seemed as if everyone in the room held their breath.

"Our convoy ran into a small fleet of the alien raiders that attacked your planet and which Kris Longknife defeated. The convoy's escort engaged the aliens, destroying most, but the aliens have a new policy. As soon as they see us, they detach a single ship to run for the nearest exit. While that ship was running, the battleships and other cruisers engaged our ships.

"The convoy had too much energy on their ships. There was no way they could slow down and engage the aliens. The battle lasted a little more than one of our minutes. We left only two damaged ships behind.

"As you can see, we have met the enemy and destroyed them as an effective force."

Sandy paused to look at the President and the Prime Minister.

"As you can also see, the aliens were stalking you. Getting as close as they could without being noticed by you.

"After my last visit with you, as I left you, my eight ships ran into thirty-six blood thirsty alien raiders' ships. They fled and I gave chase. I chased them until they had me exactly where they wanted me, at a high velocity, approaching a dead planet. Huge banks of lasers were hidden in a crater just out of my line of sight.

"I chose to assume that they were there. Fortunately, you had provided me with several thousand of your huge atomic devices. I put a dozen of them on rockets of our design and we walked them into the crater and across it. With your help, we turned the alien trap into a trap for them. Not one alien survived that failed ambush. As for the thirty-six cruisers, the aliens turned against us and threw their lives away trying to kill even one of us."

Sandy paused.

"They harmed not so much as a hair on any human's head."

Unfortunately, they'd gotten a few human ships when they sent three fleets up against her around the alien home world, but there was no reason to mention that.

"This is the reason I have brought three fleets here to join the one that has guarded you. To do this, I have had to strip Alwa down to three fleets. Our shipyards there are busy adding a fourth and will likely try to build a fifth and sixth fleet. We have the facilities to build them. Unfortunately, we don't have the skilled people to crew them."

Another pause.

"Do you understand the problem *we* face?" Sandy said, starting with the President on one side, glancing up to the rest of the major cat players seated to her left, then turning to sweep the ballroom. She finished with the cats to her right and the Prime Minister.

"I think we can see your problem," Prime Minister Gerrot said. "It is clear that we were short-sighted when we reduced our contribution to your labor force. I know I can talk for the Kingdom of Bizalt when I say we are ready to send ten thousand cats to join you in the Alwa system to build ships and crew them."

"So will Columm Almar," President Almar said.

"I thank you for that," Sandy said, "but we need more than a willing work force at our own fabs and shipyards. We need more shipyards building ships."

"Are you saying what I think you are saying?" President Almar asked.

"Yes, I am," Sandy said. "We need to begin construction here of the most high-tech warships and weapons in the human arsenal. We need to build industry on your moon that can ship material to the space station so we can extend the yards on Kiel Station. I hope this won't shock you, but those paying taxes back on the other side of the galaxy are starting to wonder if we out here are just a huge hole in the ground that they are throwing their good money into."

Sandy moved her hands to her hips. "We need to do as much for ourselves as we can."

Both of the politicians nodded at her words. The room was soon full of nodding furry heads.

"I see," said the old Prime Minister from the Bizalt Kingdom, rising from her seat beside the admiral. "I cannot make any promises today, but I can assure you that I will lay before the parliament tomorrow a proposal that half of our defense expenditures be assigned to this planetary defense effort. It may take a bit more time to figure out what other funds can be tapped, or if a wartime excise tax is in order."

"I will do the same," President Almar said, also standing.

One at a time, all the national leaders at the head table stood and made the same commitment. Then the wave of solidarity swept out from the dais. There were some who took their time standing. Some leaders who had to speak with one, two, or even six opposing leaders before they could stand, but in the end, all fifty-two world leaders who had risked riding the tower of fire up into the sky to share a meal with the alien humans were standing.

The room broke out in spontaneous applause.

When the happy noise began to quiet, the President of Almar, still standing, reached for a fork and tapped it on her untouched water glass. It rang out and the room calmed as most took their seats. Only the two cats and Sandy remained standing.

"There is something that we must address," President Almar said. "We are committed to halving our defense. I expect that putting up a space defense will be more of a defense than I have ever dreamed of. However, not everyone on our world is sitting here tonight."

That drew concerned nods from both the head table and those at the round tables.

"You know that I have always been one for a strong defense. A defense using my own strong arm. Using my own troops, ships, and aircraft. So, I expect that you will be astonished at what I am about to say. We need to stand together. We need to stop our squabbling and face out to the common enemy."

She paused to survey the room. "I propose that we, the leaders here tonight, not leave here until we have knocked together a treaty that commits all of us to defend one another. A treaty that says that an attack on one of us is an attack on all of us."

There was a lot of shocked looking around by the leaders in the room. The silence grew long and began to bend into a pretzel. Finally, one cat on the floor stood again.

"President Almar, I am amazed at what you now say. I assure you that I would very much like to see such a treaty go into force. I would be happy to sign it. My problem is that my country has boundaries that some of our neighbors do not accept. They believe that some of what is now my country should be part of their country. You understand?"

"I certainly do," President Almar said, frowning. Finally, she turned to Sandy. "Do you have any advice that might be helpful to us?"

"Penny, what arcane history can Mimzy dredge up for us?"

The Navy captain stood and spoke, no doubt, the words her computer was feeding to her.

"When our home planet was the only place we humans walked on, we were divided, and our many nations, some one hundred and sixty or more, did not trust each other. They did form a mutual defense pact, or organization. However, before any country could apply for membership, it had to solemnly announce that it had no claim on anyone's territory. That was not easy to do, because many of the boundaries had changed quite a bit in the last fifty years. Still, they did, and countries that had been at war with each other only a few years before swore that they would accept the lines as they were drawn. I should mention that fifty years later, the lines on the map were of little importance. Trade and populations moved smoothly across those boundaries without so much as slowing down. But first, they had to agree that those boundary lines were valid. They were not open to change by force of arms. We did allow for the citizens of small areas to call for a vote to change allegiances, however I don't think there were any."

"Is there anyone in the room that finds that an impossible commitment?" the Prime Minister asked.

"You're one big island," someone from the floor shouted. "It's easy for you to say your boundaries won't change. Those people have land that my grandmother and her grandmother fought for."

"And if you keep this up," the President of Columm Almar said, "your granddaughters and their granddaughters will be fighting and dying over that bit of land. That assumes that the murderous alien raiders don't pounce in here and kill us all. Then you'll have no daughter to remember your name at all."

The room fell deadly silent. Sandy considered the matter, crossed her fingers for luck, and opened her mouth. "If you wish, we humans could become co-signatories to this treaty. We could commit ourselves to fight on the side of the nation that is attacked."

The two cats beside her looked at her, their faces hard and unreadable. Then they looked past her to each other.

Prime Minister Gerrot spoke first. "We have all seen what your Kris Longknife did to President for Life Solzen. No one has found so much as a hank of hair to bury. I appreciate that you have made this as an offer to us, rather than an ultimatum. We need to talk. We have much to talk about. Can we have this room?"

"Navy, the cats have this room," Sandy announced. "Would you like the tables rearranged?"

"What would you suggest?" the President asked.

"Penny, there are fifty-two chiefs of state or chief executives here. Could you arrange something that would be comfortable for them?"

"Would everyone please stand up?" Penny called. They did, and their tables disappeared into the deck, along with the dais. Then, fifty-two rectangular tables rose out of the deck. They formed a rectangle themselves, but none of them touched. There was a second and third row of tables behind the first, all with comfortable chairs for cats.

"If the delegations would decide where and with whom they'd like to sit, I can try to adjust the first row of tables. As it turned out, Columm Almar, Kingdom Bizalt, and one other nation occupied one entire short leg of the rectangle. Penny assured that everyone got a table in the first row, although several were small. A fourth row had to be added behind some delegations, but before ten minutes had gone by, everyone was seated.

Then Penny was asked for several hundred pads of paper, pencils, and a dozen containers. Fortunately, Admiral Drago's intel officer had stayed and he was able to quickly lay his hands on such obsolete technology.

"We have this in a store on the station. Some of the

locals trust it more than their commlink," he said, with a shrug.

Penny couldn't help but smile as the containers were passed around the room and filled with commlinks and all other electronic devices. She had Marines march them out into the docking bay. Mimzy pulled up tables and the Marines scattered them around so they'd be easy for the participants to find when this meeting ended.

Done, Penny and her intel associate headed for the exit Admiral Santiago and the rest of the Navy had left through and walked right into a room with much of Sandy's key staff.

There were tables set up, chairs, a screen showing the meeting room from several angles, and, depending where you stood, you could overhear several different conversations. Penny learned this quickly, when Jacques called her over to listen in on four cats debating the military problems of aligning themselves in such an unequal treaty.

"Face it," one cat said, "not even one of us on this planet could have stood against the fleet that they had up here in our sky. Now they've got four. It's going to be a long cold night before we get anything."

"But they are offering to share their most violent technology with us?"

"Are they? Will they really share it? From what I hear from the cats that have come home, they're just junior workers on their ships."

"Of course they are. They're staring at magic and trying to learn how it really works. Would you trust a cub to fly your fastest hunter plane?"

The conversation petered out after that, with the four going their separate way in pairs that agreed with each other and disagreed with the other two.

Penny spotted Sandy and quick marched for her. She

stood while Sandy finished talking with the four fleet admirals. When Sandy paused for a break, Penny said, "May I have a word with you, Admiral?"

"Are you going to tell me anything I don't already know?" Sandy said with a happy smile.

"Probably not. I guess I shouldn't have worried when the cats walked their high tech out of the room."

"While you had Mimzy busy, Jacques's computer was able to set up this room. We may not be involved in the bargaining, but at least we'll know who hates us and who doesn't. He's tickled to death to get a good chance to watch the cats in conflict resolution mode."

"Yes, ma'am, and if the cats figure out what you're doing here?"

"They shouldn't."

"Yes, ma'am, but their room is just one open doorway away from here. What if some cat needs a trip to the litter box?"

Sandy got very serious. "Good point," she said. "Penny, correct it."

The room got a lot deeper, and the wall on the far side of the door moved over until it was on the far side of it. "I've set up bathrooms for cats right past the door. May I suggest that you station Marines in the hall just past the bathrooms to keep any cat from getting lost, accidently or on purpose. Mimzy, is there another door out of the banquet hall?"

"Besides the one to the landing bay, there is one on the opposite wall facing this door."

"Create a hall and bathroom off that wall," Penny ordered.

"Bret, you might want to get Marines in that hall as well," Sandy ordered. "Add some to the launch bay, and a couple at this door. I don't want anyone with fur in here."

"Aye, aye, Admiral," the four-star said, and began talking into his commlink while Mimzy created another set of bathrooms.

"Penny," her computer said, "is it okay to put bathroom signage over the doors? We didn't mention facilities when we were talking to the cats."

"We were expecting a shorter meeting," Penny said. "Yes, go ahead and put a sign over each door so they'll know there's someplace to pause within."

With the preliminaries over, Sandy and her key staff settled in to see how long the night would go.

10

T he initial debate in the ballroom involved whether they should negotiate one treaty or two, and which one would come first. This grew from a desire by some to resolve the conditions for the cats to work with the humans in the new technology transfer and military build-up and then tackle the thornier issue of a united defense pact.

That left Sandy shaking her head. The tech transfer and military build-up struck Sandy as the more difficult. She had a hard time figuring out how a mutual defense pact could be a bigger problem. However, it seemed a major concern for about half of the cats.

The other half wanted to resolve the labor pact first.

Since President Almar was on one side and Prime Minister Gerrot was on the other, it was not an easy matter to resolve.

After a bit more than an hour, they agreed to work on both simultaneously.

During the debate, coats and jackets had come off, and most of the cats were down to just fur. Since the tables were arranged with a lot of space between countries, none of them had come to blows, although with the Columm Almar and the Bizalt Kingdom right next to each other, at times, it had been a close thing.

As the cats got down to work, junior members of both those delegations were dispatched to the bathroom. Rather than use the facilities, they went to talk to the Marines. They wanted to see Penny. One of the Marine guards was dispatched to Sandy's command center, but Penny was already on her way to meet her.

"We have come to ask you to assist us in rearranging the room," one of the cats told Penny.

"Of course, I will be happy to assist," Penny said, and followed them back to talk with President Almar and Prime Minister Gerrot.

"We would like to have some more private rooms where small parties may talk alone," President Almar said. "Can you make us some?"

"No problem," Penny said. "Anything else?"

"Could we have some cots to nap on?" The Prime Minister asked. "Some of us are not as young as we once were and these all-night sessions are not so easy on old bones."

"Crafty old bones," President Almar said, not quite under her breath.

"Certainly," Penny said.

YOU HAVE ALL OF THIS, MIMZY?

GOT IT. ASK THEM TO STAND A DOZEN PACES FROM ANY OF THE WALLS.

"You might want to have your folks move ten or twelve paces away from any walls," Penny said.

That set a lot of cats scurrying toward the center of the room.

Walls began to edge up slowly from the deck. Any cats that hadn't scampered far enough, either stepped over the rising wall or went around to where each room would have a door. In some rooms, tables and chairs began to grow, in others, beds flowed from the deck in singles, pairs, or bunk beds.

Beside Penny, the feline heads of state were shaking their heads, but they said nothing, until President Almar could not keep her question in, "You will be giving us the secret of this kind of, ah, well, it just looks like magic."

"It is likely that we will need for you to build foundries to produce Smart Metal. How much control you will have over the metal will depend on what kind of skills your programmers acquire and the level of their computers."

"You used a computer to do this?" the Prime Minister said, not quite concealing the awe in her voice.

"Yes." Penny said, very much aware that Nelly and her children were still something the cats knew nothing about.

"Will we get such a computer?" the President asked.

"No. My computer is special, given to me by Kris Longknife. There are only two computers with this capacity present in your solar system. You will likely get commlinks and computers as capable as the ones Grand Admiral Santiago has."

"Strange for an underling to have a better machine than her superior," the President said.

"Actually, no. Admiral Santiago did not want something this complicated. When she needs something done, she tells me what she wants, and I make it appear."

YOU MAKE IT APPEAR? Mimzy said in Penny's head, clearly feeling left out.

WE'RE NOT SUPPOSED TO TALK ABOUT YOU AROUND THESE CATS, REMEMBER?

OH, RIGHT. SORRY.

NO PROBLEM.

The bulkheads were reaching the overhead. "There are breakout rooms of different sizes along the back and left wall. Most of the sleeping rooms are on the right. You can decide who gets a single or double room or who has to bunk down in the big rooms."

"Thank you. Did I see beds with mattresses and sheets?"

"Yes, ma'am, I assumed some of you might need a few hours of good sleep."

"In our own room," the Prime Minister said, slowly. "By all the ancestors, we must have this technology."

"We use it for many things, beside warships. However, the ability to duplicate just about anything just by programming a block of Smart Metal can be very disruptive. You might want to take this slow. On Alwa, just about everything is manufactured by conventional means from natural materials."

The two world leaders nodded, but were exchanging glances as Penny turned to leave. Then she paused. "If you need me again, just send a messenger to the Marines. I'll likely be in bed, but they'll get me up."

"I think you have done much, and given us even more to think about," the President said.

Penny quickly made her way back to the admiral's command center. There, one screen still showed the entire room, however, other walls had smaller windows focused down on a small group or even two cats talking, often animatedly. As Penny watched, two angry cats finished their conversation and stomped away. The window closed and Admiral Drago came away, smiling to himself.

"Trouble?" Penny asked.

"Yes, but I was more interested in whether they'd come

to blows. I'm going to need one of our sociologists or psychologists to study how it was that those two deescalated their verbal battle so they could both walk away. Hey, Jacques, come look at this," and the window opened again.

Penny made her way to Admiral Santiago.

"They seem to be happy for the moment," Sandy said.

"At least they like their new amenities."

"You better make some sleeping arrangements for our team. No need for anyone to get a full bedroom. Just create some beds in their own small cubbyhole with a door and a light they can turn off. Oh, and an alarm clock."

"I'll have the lights come up slowly at first, then maybe feed in music to wake us," Penny said.

"You do that. Then get yourself some sleep. Have that guy of yours take the first watch, then you two switch back and forth. I expect this to stretch into tomorrow. Maybe the next day. At least we have most of the decision makers right here, locked up in our room. Oh, check with the cat restaurants on the station. See if they can ship over some snacks and beverages. These cats are going to need to keep their energy up."

"Aye, aye, ma'am," Penny said. The wall farthest from the shared wall was sprouting a honeycomb of sleeping spaces, a meter high and wide at their main point, with mattresses. No one made a beeline for them. Penny checked in with her fiancé, Commander Iizuka, gave him their orders, then crawled into a bed cell, had Mimzy close the door, and dim the lights. With some relaxing music playing in the background, she was surprised at how quickly she fell asleep.

11

Admiral Santiago split her attention. Half the time she watched the cats as they debated what to do next and how to do it. The other half she spent watching her own staff.

The sociologists and psychologists were in hog heaven. They viewed the events taking place in the next room with delight. They spotted dozens of cases that they'd study over and over again before writing a paper on the interrelationships taking place.

"Admiral," Jacques said, calling her over to watch something he and several other specialists had watched several times.

"Yes, Jacques."

"We think we've got something here. Watch the heads on both of these guys. They've been shouting at each other for the last five minutes. Notice how others have been giving them a wide berth. It sure looks like they're about to go at each other. See, the claws are edging out now."

Sandy nodded. She'd seen the shouting and the claws come out in meetings she'd had with the cats. The wooden tables in their conference room had a lot of claw marks cut deep into their surfaces.

"Here it comes," Jacques said. "There, see what they just did?"

"I didn't see anything,"

"Computer, run it back ten seconds. Now, watch what the both of them do with their heads."

"They seemed to lean back."

"Both did, almost at the same time."

"What's it mean?" Sandy asked.

"I think that's an instinctive signal that one of them wants to break off the argument before they come to blows."

Sandy nodded. That would be good to know, assuming she could spot it fast enough and respond to it quickly enough. It might be instinctive for cats, but not so much for humans.

"What happens if one leans back and the other doesn't?" the admiral asked.

"That's harder to say. We have samples where one side of an argument leaned back and followed it up by stepping back. It was a clear sign of surrender. We're still hunting for a situation where one leaned back and the other didn't and the argument went on further. None of the cats have come to blows, but the morning is yet young."

"Thanks for bringing this to my attention," she told Jacques. "Next time I talk to a cat, I'll be careful not to lean back unless I want to send that signal."

"I'll let you know if we get any other juicy tidbits."

Sandy went back to the middle of the screen, took a few paces away from it so she could keep it all in view, then had her computer pull up a comfortable chair. She settled down for a long night.

It had been a long day, and Sandy found herself yawning. She became more comfortable, and soon drifted off to sleep despite all the noise around her.

She awoke several hours later with a start. A huge racket was coming from the main screen. Two cats were caterwauling. Their claws were out and they were leaning well forward.

"Jacques. What's happening?"

"I think we're about to get our first fight. The black cat with the light belly is from Columm Almar. The tawny one is from the Bizalt Kingdom. They are senior officials from both delegations and they've been the most vocal in the argument over separating the mutual defense pact from the tech transfer negotiations. I think we're about to see how far they'll go. Now, where are the President and Prime Minister?"

Sandy studied the scene before her. Quite a few cats had formed a large circle. The president of Columm Almar and the Prime Minister of the Bizalt Kingdom were on opposite sides of the circle.

Suddenly, the black cat leapt at the tawny one. The attack was swift, just one pass and the two swapped sides. Both showed scratches that were deep enough to drip blood on the deck.

Now the two cats hunched low and continued their caterwauling. Those in the circle were absolutely silent.

Again, both leapt at each other, slashing and biting, but only in a quick pass. Both were bleeding more freely now. The black cat had a bad cut over her eye, but the other cat was bleeding from deep cuts in her belly.

"Admiral, alert sick bay. We'll need a surgeon versed in cats real soon."

"Aye, aye, ma'am," Drago said and quickly was talking

into his commlink. "I'll have the med team waiting out of sight from the Marines standing guard by the restrooms."

"Good. We don't want the cats to think we're watching them."

"No," Bret said. "That would be most undiplomatic of us."

The two enjoyed a chuckle.

Another pass had been made while they talked. The black cat was bleeding more profusely from a head wound, but the tawny cat was slowing down. The belly wound was starting to look like a seriously deep cut into her most vulnerable organs.

They charged again, this time both biting toward the others' neck. They locked together, both with jaws clenched on the other's shoulder or neck. They both now clawed at the other's belly.

They broke apart, not so much walking away as rolling. Both struggled to get up, even on all fours. The black cat managed to work her way up to her elbows.

Prime Minister Gerrot stepped forward. "Enough. We accede to your position. We will have two different negotiations and treaties. Now, ask the humans for a doctor."

"Bret, get a Marine to the door. He can ask what all the noise was about."

Admiral Drago spoke for a moment to his wrist unit, and a Marine sergeant quickly show up at the door into the ballroom.

"Is something wrong? We heard a lot of noise," she got out as if she'd been practicing the line. Of course, she also got a good look at the two bleeding heaps of fur on the deck.

"We require medical assistance."

"Corpsman, Corpsman! Cat down," she shouted into her commlink. She signaled to a Marine guard who raced into the room, a buddy rescue pack in his hand. He slid to the deck beside the cats and began basic first aid.

"Good God, this guy's guts are falling out," one Marine said.

Jacques had joined the two admirals.

"I guess that tells us how far they'll go to settle their differences. You noticed, neither of the two fighters would call it quits. It had to be in the instigating feline's DNA to throw in the towel and end the fight."

"I wonder how it would have gone if they hadn't been fighting as surrogates for a political issue?" Sandy asked.

"Your guess is as good as mine," Jacques admitted. "I wonder if the black one would have slit the other's throat. He could have."

"You may get an answer to your question later," Sandy said. "This settles only the first issue. I see a lot of fights in their future."

The med team arrived and began stabilizing the bleeding pair. They were quickly loaded on gurneys and rushed out of the room. One med tech stayed behind.

"If you're going to be doing stuff like this a lot tonight, could we set up a battalion aid station either in here or just outside?"

The two world leaders from Columm Almar and Kingdom Bizalt eyed each other for a moment, then nodded.

"Yes," Prime Minister Gerrot said. "Please establish a medical facility just outside that door. If you hear shouting again, you may want to send in a medical team."

"For two?" the chief petty officer asked.

"Yes, for two."

"Aye, aye, sir," the chief said, saluted and marched out of the cats' space.

"That was interesting," Admiral Drago said. "Note how they didn't call for a feline doctor, but accepted we could take care of their wounded."

"Surely by now we know what makes them tick, Bret."

"Yes, we've had accidents on the station. We've even taken to running blood drives for the cats to build up a blood bank." He chuckled. "I'm not sure we've got enough if many more fights go this far."

"Can you issue a call for an emergency cat blood drive?"

Drago was back on his comm link before Sandy finished the suggestion.

Now that it was settled that they'd have two treaties, the cats got down to some serious bargaining over the Mutual Defense Pact. It was not easy for Sandy to watch politicians do their thing, and she rested. Before she knew it, she was being awakened by Admiral Drago.

"Did you catch some shut-eye?" she asked him.

"A bit. I woke up a few minutes ago and Jacques says you might want to see what's about to happen next."

"Jacques?"

The sociologist was at her elbow in a second. "The cats managed to hammer out a pact that looks amazingly close to those humans had when we still engaged in wars back on Old Earth. The problem is that there are several countries that don't want to come into the pact. The biggest five are in agreement. So are the smaller. It's some of the middle-sized powers that don't like the deal. I don't think some of them trust any cat, much less humans, to settle their boundaries."

"Are we going to?" Sandy asked.

"That's what the big five agreed upon. None of them share a border. They don't expect to put any cases before us."

"So, we'll have to figure out what's fair," Sandy said.

"More likely, we'll have to figure out some way to split the baby. Although, just a few minutes ago there was a modification to the pact that if both sides agreed, we would be bound to use only one line or the other."

"That won't make friends." Sandy muttered.

"How many do you think will want to go all or nothing?" Jacques asked.

Sandy eyed the screen. Once again, a circle was being formed. President Almar stood on one end, a cat in a bright red and blue coat was on the other side of the circle. One huge grey cat stepped past the President to enter the ring. Another large cat with calico coloring entered from the opposite side. The two went into the pre-fight cater-wauling. The translator failed to make out words; the two were just making loud noises, showing how loud they could be.

Suddenly, the calico charged the grey. They raced at each other. At the last moment, the grey threw itself to the side and rolled out of the way. Still, it managed to rake the flank of the other. One cat was bleeding. The other cat wasn't.

The noise began again. About the time it reached a crescendo, they charged again. This time the grey stood almost upright, on its back paws, towering over the calico. That cat stood high as well.

At the last moment, the grey ducked low and got herself under the calico cat. While her flanks got raked, the grey sank her claws deep into the lower abdomen of the other cat, then rose and tossed the calico over her shoulder.

Her claws did brutal damage to the other cat's underbelly as the cat's body flew over the grey and her claws came free.

The calico did not get up.

At the door, the Marine sergeant was waving in a medical team.

The leader in the red and blue jacket bowed, and called the duel finished. Her country would join the pact.

There were two more fights, one with the prime minister's champion, again, another giant of a cat, and then the other world leader that had sided with them. All ended the same, with the emergency medical team racing in to help keep one alive while they put some bandages on the other.

When the great powers presented a fifth champion, the other countries decided to cut their losses and unanimously approved the Mutual Defense Pact.

Then they began to discuss their starting position in negotiations with the humans for tech transfer.

Sandy turned to Jacques. "Did you notice how big the cats were that fought to get the reluctant lions into the pact? Compare them with the two that fought over dividing the two treaties. You know, if I didn't know better, I'd think Columm Almar and Kingdom Bizalt gamed the system."

"It does appear that they sent in a middleweight there, but they were both well-matched, and they fought themselves to a bloody mess," Jacques said.

"What's your guess?" Sandy asked.

"I suspect, from what I saw going on around the room, that some of the middle players really felt strong about one treaty verses two. If I was a betting man, I'd give you three to one odds that it didn't matter all that much to the President or the Prime Minister. Still they had their middleweight champions fight it out and let the fur fly as it would. It just so happened that the black won and we ended up with two treaties."

"That's what I was thinking. Bargaining with these kitties is not going to be an easy task," Sandy thought, and she didn't have a lot of people with negotiation training, much less experience.

Of course, she had none equipped to settle an issue with claw and fang.

"Computer, ask the fleet commanders to query their personnel. Do any of them have people with negotiations experience? We may need them."

The call went out. While it would, no doubt, cause a flurry of activity after breakfast, Sandy expected a report before things closed down.

The admiral went back to watching the cats. They were now debating the tech transfer treaty. Watching kids turned loose in a candy store would not have been more fun. They might not know exactly how this would work, but they wanted it. All of it. Right now!

Sandy would need to get some civilian manufacturing experts for her negotiating team. She was about to tell her computer to expand the search for negotiations when the computer gave voice to something Sandy did not want or expect.

"Admiral, the duty officer reports that aliens have been sighted four jumps out from here."

12

"**A**dmirals, with me," Sandy snapped as she stood and quick walked from her observation station. Quickly, fleet commanders Vice Admiral Drago, Bethea, Miyoshi, and Nottingham followed Sandy out. Together, they silently headed for Sandy's flag bridge.

There, officers, chiefs, and ratings moved purposefully. Around Sandy's flag plot, the walls came to life with star charts. Beside the images of a single star system, a table showed two counters: one for alien battleships, one for their cruisers.

So far, the third category, alien mother ships, was blank.

"Messages are coming in every fifteen minutes. This is the latest report. We estimate it's five days old.

Sandy eyed the screen. Five days ago, four jumps away, one hundred and sixty-two battleships and fifty-nine cruisers had jumped into a system where they had a picket.

As Sandy studied the reports with narrowing eyes, a fourth category appeared in the count. Labeled UNKNOWN, it showed ninety-three.

"Where'd that come from?" Sandy demanded of Captain

Velder, her chief of staff.

He quickly took a few steps that left him looking over a chief's shoulder at his board.

"That's the latest report, Admiral. For the last fifteen minutes, no battleships or cruisers came through the jump. Instead, the report is that ninety-three don't fit our parameters for the others."

"Can you tell me anything about those unknown?" Sandy asked softly. This situation was hard enough without her adding more stress to her good crew.

Captain Van Velder sidestepped to another station. "That jump had a basic search buoy. The one on the inner side of the jump is one of the advanced design. As luck would have it, the basic version was out there when the new bogie jumped in. In fifteen minutes, we'll get a full work-up on the new warship."

"Very good," Sandy said, then turned to her fleet admirals. "How soon can you get underway?"

Drago spoke for the others. "The cats have been delivering fresh meat to all the ships. We even have some of them growing fruit and vegetables as well as grains for us. We've got shipments coming up here, but not enough for a fleet the size you've got here. If you give us twenty-four hours, we should be ready to sail with as much fresh food as we can give you."

"And if I sail sooner?" Sandy asked.

"There will be a lot of fresh meat and fish on the menu, but it's kind of low on berries and melons, as well as vegetables."

"We'll see how things develop, folks," Sandy said, "but we'd better have the midwatch begin the process of getting us squared away."

"Aye, aye," came from four admirals, and they turned

away to speak into their own commlinks. A boring watch was about to get exciting.

Sandy pulled a chair from the deck, settled in it, and prepared to wait out the clock. She eyed the system that now was harboring a wolf pack of murderous alien raiders. It had two jumps besides the one that had been outposted. The aliens had come in through the jump farthest from the one that led to the cat system.

"Computer, assuming a one point five gee acceleration and deceleration, how long will it take this attack force to reach our picketed jump?"

"Four point seven days, Admiral."

"Thank you," Sandy found herself saying automatically.

"You're welcome, Admiral. Ask any time."

Sandy snapped her head around. It was bad enough she'd slipped up and started treating her computer like an associate. Who had programmed it to be civil to her? Neither Penny nor Jacques were here. Her intel captain was sleeping and Jacques had stayed behind with his wife who, as an economist, was living a life of bliss as she watched the cat economy being laid out before her.

When she got them back together, she'd have to ask them who was messing with her computer.

Of course, it would help if she kept her distance from the dang machine.

"The report is coming in," Van announced, bringing Sandy out of a quick nap she'd fallen into.

"What have you got?"

"The unknown has six reactors, Admiral. They are much smaller than the three reactors we use for our battlecruisers. They're packing nine lasers. Until we can get a mass count on the ship, I think they're about the size of our larger frigates."

"Do we know which wolf pack these are from?" Sandy asked.

Now her chief of staff rested a hand lightly on the shoulder of the chief. She quickly answered, "Admiral, it is not a match for any of the wolf packs we've ran into to date. However, the battleship reactors are closest to the reactors in the first wolf pack to make it into the Alwa system.

"And we haven't seen anything close to it since?" Sandy asked.

"These are rather distinct. The reactors are larger and have a particularly noisy electromagnetic containment system for their plasma."

Sandy mulled this over. So, another clown was putting their nose in her business. She really didn't need another challenge at the moment, the cats were proving problems enough.

Still, this looked like a problem she could put to her use.

"Keep an eye on developments," she told her chief of staff, then turned to the admirals who had pulled up chairs behind her and were waiting on her word.

"Ladies and gentlemen, what do you say that we go visit our cat friends? Computer, rouse Penny from her slumber and tell her to meet me at the door into the ballroom with the cats."

"Aye, aye, Admiral," her computer answered.

Sandy bit her lip to avoid adding a thank you as she would have for a human. Then she decided she was being small.

"Thank you," she said.

"Penny is awake. She asks for a moment to freshen up."

"Good," Sandy said, as she marched for her next meeting with the troublesome cats.

13

S andy found Penny waiting for her beside the
Marines who blocked the passageway just past the
cats' restroom. She looked chipper, and her uniform
hardly looked slept in.

"You get some rest?" Sandy asked.

"Yes, ma'am," the young woman answered.

"Well, let's take you and Mimzy in and see what the cats
are up to. Did your computer brief you on the alien raider
situation?"

"Yes, ma'am. Four jumps out. Different wolf pack. New
frigate-like ships."

"Yep. No need to tell the cats we're facing a new ship."

"Aye, aye, ma'am."

"Penny, would you step inside and let the cats know I
need to talk to them?"

"Will do, Admiral," Penny said, and slipped through
the door.

A few minutes later, the captain was back. "They'll see
you now. They had to rearrange the tables."

Sandy found herself walking into row upon row of

tables now formed into a u-shape. There was a table at the apex of it, but Sandy ignored it and walked out into the middle of the felines.

"I have an emergency development and I will need to move you to Kiel Station to continue your negotiation."

"Can we ask what the emergency is?" President Almar asked.

"As I think you know, we have put warning buoys out as many as four jumps from your star system. One of those has reported the approach of an alien battle fleet. I have ordered my fleet to prepare to sortie as soon as it is possible and we know what the situation is."

"The aliens are coming here?" came from a lot of cats. The room broke into a roar as cats talked among themselves.

Sandy waited patiently for the chatter to subside. She did not want to shout at these world leaders.

President Almar tapped a fork on her water glass and the noise came down to something Sandy felt she could talk over.

"While the message moves with the speed of light, alien warships are much slower. We think this information reflects a situation five or six days ago. For all we know, the aliens may have turned around and headed back out. We are waiting for matters to develop."

"It is like in days of old," one old cat said. "With sailing ships, we might have a line of frigates stationed not quite hull down on the horizon. A report on what one line of battle was doing might take an hour or longer to pass down the line, but getting the two battle lines close enough to fire at each other might take days."

"That is very similar to what I face," Sandy said. "There is also the matter of whether this fleet is our only problem, or it might be a diversion from some larger fleet."

"Oh," came from several leaders, including President Almar and Prime Minister Gerrot.

"It would be nice if you had enough ships to respond to one threat without leaving our bare rear hanging out to be chewed on," the old, battle-wise cat said.

"Exactly," Sandy answered. "I will have to weigh my options very carefully. It is likely by now that the aliens have either jumped into the third system out, or withdrawn. I am waiting on developments. However, I may move a major part of my fleet into the next system out. That would allow me to ambush the aliens in the second system out while keeping the option to fall back if this is just a diversion."

Sandy paused before adding the clincher. "So, unless you would like to continue your negotiations on a ship accelerating so fast that you weigh three or four times what you weigh now, you might want to either end your negotiations, or move this to a space on the station."

Sandy paused, waiting to see how the cats responded to those choices.

"May I ask for a show of hands? How many of you are in favor of continuing these discussions on the station?" Prime Minister Gerrot asked the room.

The president and prime minister quickly raised their hands. Slowly, they were joined by about a third of the others. The cats still sitting on their hands looked around, and more hands came up. As the number grew, more chose to join. In the end, over two-thirds of the world leaders had their hands up. Faced with that daunting number, the rest raised their hands into the air.

"We will move these negotiations to the station," President Almar said. "You have provided us with respectable hospitality. The rooms and food are most cordial of you. I hope you won't forget to have someone on the station continue this gracious hospitality," she said, eyeing Penny.

"I'm afraid I must take my alien intelligence officer with me," Sandy said. "However, I will have her help you in the transition to the station. I will assign you a new contact. She will likely be one of the scholars I brought."

Sandy had almost assigned Jacques to the job, then she caught herself. When dealing with the cats, it was always better to have a woman provide the buffer.

COMPUTER, PLEASE ASK AMANDA TO COME IN HERE.

SHE IS ON HER WAY, ADMIRAL.

Less than a minute later, both Amanda and Jacques joined them. Most of the cat leaders recognized the two of them and seemed pleased to be working with them again. They quickly packed up their papers and followed Penny, Amanda, and Jacques out of the ballroom.

Sandy watched them go before asking her computer, "Can you make the ballroom melt back into the ship?"

"No ma'am. There are too many variables involving moving space around inside the ship and shrinking the outer hull. Very few computers have access to the codes to access that particular area of Smart Metal. I can, however, inform the captain that you no longer require this space and he will have his damage control officer see that a programmer does it with the main ship's computer."

"Very well. Do that," Sandy said, and turned to retrace her steps back to her flag plot.

In the short time she'd been gone, another report had come in, but it was from the low-tech buoy. Another sixty ships had entered the system in the last fifteen minutes. Since neither observer had the ability to range the bogies, there was no way to tell how fast they were going when they entered the system or how much acceleration they had on the boat.

Sandy was left with far too few answers to a whole boatload of critical questions.

The admiral decided that she needed to do some thinking where she wasn't under scrutiny by every man Jack or Jill in her crew. She turned to her fleet commanders, "Admirals, chief of staff, ops, meet in my day quarters. Computer, tell Penny to meet us there when she gets back."

"Aye, aye ma'am."

So, the seven of them left flag plot and made their way down to Sandy's day quarters.

14

S andy had her computer produce a conference table with eight comfortable chairs. She took the head, with her chief of staff, Captain Van Velder at one elbow, her ops officer, Captain Mindi Ashigara at her other. The fleet commanders arrayed themselves down the sides, leaving the foot of the table for Captain Penny Paisley, the fleet's chief of alien intel.

"Computer, can you duplicate the screens from my flag plot on the walls here?"

"I can, but they will have to be smaller, ma'am."

"Go ahead. We can expand some and shrink others. Please also order us up some coffee or hot water for tea. This is going to be a long morning," Sandy said and found herself yawning.

The cat naps had been way too short.

Sandy waited while the walls turned to screens, then waited some more for her beverages. The door finally opened and a steward's mate wheeled in a cart of carafes as well as sandwiches.

Right behind him ran Penny.

Sandy eyed the cart. No doubt, if she'd had Mimzy, all of it would have arrived right on her conference room table, but, lacking Penny's presence, Sandy's own computer had gone back to basics and requested a human to deliver the order.

The meeting was further delayed as officers served themselves. It seemed that everyone was hungry. It had been a long time since the banquet. With a mug and a sandwich in hand, they settled back down around the table. Sandy let them finish eating, then refill their mugs. Most of her admirals wandered around the room with their steaming mugs. They eyed the different screens, enlarged some, and shrunk others until they were satisfied.

Only then did they return to the table and wait for their commanding admiral to say what she wanted to say.

"As I see it, we've got two possible options in front of us. One, this bunch of raiders hasn't gotten the word yet and they are charging right into our guns," Sandy said.

Heads nodded. "That's understandable," Penny said, "it's a large galaxy and there aren't a lot of mother ships."

"Yes," Sandy said. "Two, this is a diversion to lure us away from here so they can slip in a force while we're occupied elsewhere. Can anyone think of a third?"

The table remained silent.

"Okay, Penny, could you have Mimzy give us a briefing on the terrain of this area of the star map? Are there any double or triple jumps that could let them jump from far away to right on our door step?"

Mimzy began to speak from where she sat as a choker high around Penny's neck.

"This area seems to be a spur off the main transit lines

that the three alien races set up to zip around the galaxy a couple of million years ago. There are only a few systems with fuzzy points. Most are the older, slower jumps," the computer said. "That is bad for us because it means we don't have as many chances to outflank them."

Mimzy paused before going on. "However, being on a spur line also means that there are not a lot of jumps that go where you might want them to go, not unless you took a slow local jump. We've got three jumps where they can jump from outside our pickets to the third system in. However, if they hit the jump out and headed for Sasquan, at a high speed they'll jump way past us. Simply put, there are only two systems in the outer ring that allow them to jump from four out to two out. None of those systems allow for a direct jump into the cat system."

"Is it that simple?" Sandy asked. Maybe the cats wouldn't be that hard to protect.

"Based on the map that General Ray Longknife discovered on Santa Maria, that's the lay of the land," Mimzy said. "If I was a bloodthirsty alien raider, I'd hunt for some fruit that was easier to pick."

"Are there any systems that we've got pickets in that would allow the aliens to jump from them right into this system?" Admiral Drago asked.

"No, sir, but there are two that would allow them to pass through a fourth layer and cross the third layer before they could make the jump into the next system out."

Suddenly, Sandy wasn't so sure that it was all that easy. "How many?" Sandy asked.

"Two," Mimzy said.

To Sandy's right, a screen expanded. Two stars in the third line around Sasquan blinked a bright red.

Deep in thought, the admiral rose from her chair and walked over to study the map carefully. Hidden in the puzzle of star systems and scattered jumps was a path to life for her and the cats below. That, or death.

While Sandy's eyes wandered the star map, a back part of her mind was taking stock of her recent history.

Twice she'd chased the aliens. The first time, intent on ambushing them, she'd led a force that was too small for its mission. Her ambush turned into an alien ambush because she was too new to this war and underestimated her enemy. The second time she chased the aliens, they led her right into a trap. The fact that she'd managed to use the atomics given her by the cats to spring their trap on them was more luck than any skill on her part.

So far, she was zero for two when attacking the aliens.

However, she had also defended against them twice and wiped out two huge fleets, with Admiral Miyoshi bagging a third. She'd been sticking her nose into the alien home world and they seemed all too ready to cut her nose off at her neck.

Again, the illegal atomics that were gifts from the cats below had helped her massacre aliens and save her own skin.

Three times the cats' atomics had saved her neck.

I owe these cats. Owe them big time.

Her four other fleet commanders had come to stand beside her.

"Admiral Miyoshi, the aliens split their forces the last time we faced them. What do you think? Is this force a diversion?"

"If it is a diversion, it's an awfully big one," the admiral from Musashi answered.

"One that we likely can't ignore," Sandy said.

"No," Admiral Drago agreed.

"But then we have these two," Sandy said, eying the two systems that would allow a quick jump into the next system out from Sasquan. Do we wait until we get a signal from an outer buoy before we move to block them?"

Sandy thought on that for a long minute, then realized she had an answer at her fingertips. "Mimzy, allowing for the time delay in getting us a warning, how long would it take the aliens to jump into the third layer out?"

"Assuming the aliens hold to their maximum two gee acceleration from the time they enter the fourth layer picketed system until they make the jump into the third, we could get to their jump into the third system before they could get to the other side of it. That assumes that we make 3.5 gees the entire time."

"A hard passage," Admiral Bethea said.

"But one we can do," Sandy concluded.

"May I point out one possible problem?" The speaker was Admiral Nottingham of Earth. Just promoted to fleet commander, he'd kept silent during most discussions.

"Yes, Admiral?" Sandy said.

Nottingham took a deep breath. "That two gee acceleration is based on the maximum that the alien battleships have been able to maintain. Their cruisers have been able to hold 3.0 gees for long speed runs. Sometimes a bit more. What about those new ships we're calling frigates? They've got a lot of reactor power. How much of that can they convert to velocity?"

"Mimzy, if the aliens advanced at 3.0 gees acceleration and deceleration, where would our force coming out from here at 3.5 gees run into them?"

"Somewhere in the middle of the second system," Mimzy answered.

Immediately, two star systems enlarged on the screen. Both showed red lines and blue lines. Both crossed somewhere past the star as the humans were making their way to the far jump.

"We have a problem," Sandy said.

The numbers which counted intruders crossing the system four jumps out from the cats had quit growing. They totaled one hundred and seventy-nine battleships, eighty-nine cruisers and ninety-one of the new type. In addition, there was a second new type of ship. It had only two reactors. Forty-two of them trailed the fleet.

"Assuming their battle array follows their standard of thirty ships to a dish," Penny said, speaking quickly. As her chief of alien intelligence, Sandy listened when Penny spoke. "The battleships look like six dishes of thirty, with one ship missing. The cruisers are also missing a ship to fill up three dishes. The new kid has an extra ship for the three dishes."

"And the tail-end Charlies?" Sandy asked.

"They don't fit anything we've seen before. This is just a hunch, and I wouldn't take it to any bank, but," Penny paused before finishing in a rush. "They've only got two reactors. Their numbers are all wrong. Halfway between one dish and two. Lastly, their placement at the rear of the fleet. Admiral, where did you put our fast transports on the voyage out from human space and from Alwa to here?"

"At the rear," Sandy said. "Are you thinking they're carrying a landing party?"

"It's possible. I think the mother ship usually provides the people that strip a planet. I'm guessing after Kris blew away eight mother ships, that these bastards are keeping mommy somewhere safe. Safe and making as many ships as she can."

"Haven't the aliens been using small suicide attack boats?" Admiral Drago put in. "Didn't they send individuals in wearing rocket-powered suits?"

"Yes, they have. If these ships were way out front, I'd assume that, but they're in the rear," Sandy pointed out.

"It's a few adjustments to their formations, and that can change," Admiral Bethea noted.

"Yes, ma'am," Penny answered, but added nothing more, leaving the admirals to mull over her hunch.

Sandy shook her head. "If I was going to use suicide teams, I'd place them with the forward elements of my force and see if I could mine the space that we'd have to pass through. Let's keep these ships in mind, but, until we know more about them, let's call them transports."

Sandy led her team back to the table.

"So, do we send one fleet out to hold a jump into the second system out from the enemy we know, as well as rush two fleets out to guard those two mouse holes that are, as yet, not a problem?"

"Are we sure the aliens even know those two jumps could skip over a system to the one on our door step?" Captain Velder asked.

"Bret, have you had any aliens sniffing around this cat house?"

"No ma'am, but that's not to say that they haven't done some recon work. Kris stumbled upon the flotsam and jetsam from her first destroyed mother ship. We don't know how they got here and who may have left before we arrived. Sorry, Admiral, but I can't offer anything that makes our problem more tractable."

"So, we split up our forces and scatter them across three systems several days from here," Sandy concluded. "Needless to say, I don't like that deployment."

Sandy eyed the Musashi admiral before saying, "Admiral Miyoshi, are you prepared to play out Horatio at the bridge again?"

"I'd be glad to. However, we left all the atomics at home. We'll need to borrow some more bombs from the cats. The reports we're getting here say that all hundred and eighty battlewagons are the standard garden variety, but who's to say that they haven't added two to three hundred thousand tons of rock, ice, and whatnot to a battleship and kept the usual number of reactors and lasers?"

That sent a shiver down Sandy's spine. The aliens had taken to wrapping their ships in granite and basalt, often honeycombed with ice. The idea was to have the stone ablate away the energy of a laser hit. A hundred thousand tons of that stuff made the alien battlewagons harder to kill.

They'd also come up with a really nasty bit of work. A door knocker, as it had been named. This ship had half the reactors to make it less susceptible to self-inflicted damage when United Society lasers burned through into the ships' insides. They'd cut the number of lasers in half, again to reduce the amount of damage we could do. Then they added three hundred thousand more tons of rock and ice. They'd used them to bust through jumps, expecting them to take so long to die that we'd still be trying to kill them when the battle fleet started barging in.

The first time we'd run into them, we had to run from the jump. The last time they tried to use them, we mined the jump with atomics on loan from the cats. Twenty megaton explosions weren't bothered by a couple of yards of rock.

"I'll ask the cats for some more warheads," Sandy said. That was something she'd have to do herself. If you're going hat in hand, it's best done face to face.

"Now, about those two systems three rings out. I'd rather wait to know which one is the problem rather than scatter my forces to the wind before they make their move. Just as bad, I don't want to have only a few seconds to shoot up their fleet while we race past each other. Not when it puts them between me and my base. We need something better."

Admiral Drago turned in his seat to look at the two offending star systems. He then turned back to the table. "Who says we have to race to the jump point on the far side of the system?"

"We usually try to hold at a jump point. They make for a good choke point," the chief of staff said.

"Yes," Bret answered, "however, there is too high a chance that we'll race past them and then have to wheel around and chase them. Remember, they love to seed their wake with nasty stuff."

"What do you have in mind, Bret?" Sandy asked.

"Kris hated to risk letting an enemy get in her rear. Wherever she could, she'd swing herself around a planet and get on something close to a parallel course. Preferably, at a range where her long-range lasers could blow them away well outside of their shorter-ranged lasers. Now, if our reports on those two systems are correct, there is a planet in both of them not that far off of the direct course from the jump in, to the jump out to here. What do you say that we hold our horses and wait to see what we're going to face, then march the king's troops up the hill?"

Sandy nodded. She sometimes forgot that Admiral Drago had been Kris Longknife's ship's captain for many years before he got a fleet. God knows, anyone who shared a ship with that woman deserved a fleet as a reward just for surviving.

"I like that. Okay, Bret, make sure we have the right skinny on those systems. I'd hate to get there and find a planet misplaced. I want all of you to detach a division of four battlecruisers to Admiral Drago's 4th fleet. That should give all of you forty-four battlecruisers. Admiral Miyoshi, prepare to get underway as soon as I get some atomic devices from the cats."

"Ah, ma'am," Bret said, "I've got a whole lot of those infernal machines broken down to their parts and those parts locked away under a stiff guard. You could use some of them."

"Yes, I could," Sandy said, knowing full well where most of the donated atomics had ended up. "However, the cats don't know where the devices are. I want to see what happens if I ask for something to aid in their immediate defense. What with them withholding workers from us, I have to wonder what they'll think of those bombs."

"So, the sly fox is about to go see just how stupid the feisty cat is, huh?"

"Yep."

Sandy had Penny accompany her to where the cat leaders were negotiating their opening position for negotiations with her. That sounded a bit like a wheel going around inside a wheel, but if the cats couldn't figure out what they wanted, Sandy couldn't get them what they needed. That would be essential before they could figure out what kind of tech transfer they were going to give the cats.

Penny asked Sandy to wait outside while she let the cats know she wanted to talk to them. A minute later, her computer told Sandy they were ready for her.

Once again, the cats had organized themselves into a rectangle of separate tables, with more tables radiating out in rows upon rows. Some of the cats, however, were marking up large sheets of paper and taping them to the walls for all to see.

"Is that part of their normal behavior?" Sandy asked.

"No, ma'am," Penny said. "Amanda suggested I show them how and it caught on like wildfire."

Sandy shook her head. "I guess we have to teach these folks how to work together rather than just fight it out."

"Kind of, ma'am. Now, where do you want to stand when you talk to them?"

"I'll take the center of the rectangle. Please stand by to bring up some star maps and either project a holograph above their heads or turn part of the wall to a screen."

"Mimzy and I are ready, Admiral."

Sandy strode into the open space surrounded by tables. She knew she couldn't just talk to the head table with the president and the prime minister. She would have to make her request roving around, sometimes talking to some, other times with her back to them.

The room wasn't totally silent, but it was close enough.

"We have a problem," Grand Admiral Sandy Santiago said to the two leaders of the more powerful nations, then she began to rove the box she was in.

"The alien raiders have begun a march on you." With Penny and Mimzy's help, she showed them the star systems Drago's fleet had outposted, using a holograph of the local stars.

"The flashing red light shows you the system the aliens are now in. It will take them four more jumps to get here. We intend to destroy them before they do."

"How?" Prime Minister Gerrot asked.

Sandy had her back to the head table; she turned back to face the prime minister. "We have recently used some of your atomic munitions to hold a jump. A large fleet of alien ships charged through the jump into a maelstrom of atomic fire. We think we can do that again. Unfortunately, we left all our atomic devices at our base on Alwa."

"Oh," President Almar said. "So, you want some more."

"Yes, we need more. We need enough to destroy this

sally. However, we suspect that this may be a diversion to draw us away from the main attack."

That got several of the cats in the third row of tables nodding and some prowling the aisles, tails swishing.

"We need additional atomics so we can destroy those threats if they come."

"How many?" President Almar asked.

"I'd like a thousand. I'll settle for five hundred," Sandy left that hanging in the air.

"We gave you thousands already," a cat to her left seated at a first-line table said.

Sandy turned to face the direction that observation came from. "Yes, as I said, we didn't feel a need to bring atomics back here to the planet that has them."

"And if you don't get these hydrogen bombs?" another world leader asked.

"I cannot defend your planet," Sandy said with blunt simplicity

"What would you do in that case?" the Prime Minister asked.

"I would have to withdraw," Sandy said flatly.

"Without those bombs, you won't defend us?" came from behind Sandy.

She turned to face that direction. "Say instead, that without those bombs, I would face annihilation if I tried to defend you."

"Is it that serious?" the President asked.

"I have one hundred and seventy-six battlecruisers in this system. What I think is a diversion already outnumbers my forces two to one, and I dare not commit all my forces to block them. With atomics, I can hold a jump and keep them well away from this system. Without them?" Sandy just shook her head.

The Prime Minister surveyed the room, probably reading cat body language that Sandy could not even detect. "We need time to think on this. To make our decision. When can we get back to you?"

"I need to dispatch the force to block the diversion as soon as possible. The sooner they go, the farther out they can stop the aliens."

"We will have an answer for you within an hour. Two at the most."

"Thank you," Sandy said, and strode from the room.

Outside, she had Penny take her to the observation center. There again, Jacques and Amanda had a team of specialists studying the cats and their behavior.

"So, Amanda, Jacques, what have I done?"

"You kicked a wildcat into the henhouse," Jacques said, and pointed Sandy at the wall with the monitors on it. "You've dropped a hot potato in their lap, given them a short deadline, and walked away."

"Why should it be a problem? They have lots of these things," Sandy said.

"Yes, and when last you were here, they wanted us to take a good size chunk out of here. However, now they're looking for bargaining chips to get some of the goodies they want. They knew workers were something we needed. Now you've added atomics to our wish list."

"So, you think they'll want something in return for the bombs? Isn't defending their planet enough?"

"Some think so," Jacques said, eyeing the screen. "The President and the Prime Minister are leading that faction. However, they don't want to draw down only their stock of weapons. They need for the donations to come from across the board and by an equal percent. Fifteen countries have the bombs. They need to get all fifteen on board."

"Are you going to be watching a lot of cat fights?"

"Right now, they're just talking. There's some shouting and yowling. With the two-hour time limit, it looks like they'll either reach a quick agreement, or be fighting before the first hour is out."

"Penny, do you want to stay here?"

"Unless you need me, yes, Admiral."

"Keep me informed. I want to know if it comes to fighting."

"Aye, aye, ma'am."

S andy returned to her flag plot. Her chief of staff and operations chief were studying the star maps as if they might see some fortune in them that they had not already squeezed out. From the looks on their faces, they were coming up dry.

"Anything from our outer perimeter?" Sandy asked Captain Velder.

"No, ma'am. We're waiting for a report from the system the diversion is in. If someone managed to maintain 3.0 gees across it, we should be getting a report from the next set of buoys."

"When will we know?" Sandy asked.

"Right about now," Commander Ashigara said.

On the board, the next star system in suddenly showed forty-two bogies in system.

"One of the more primitive buoys?" Sandy asked.

"Yes ma'am. It will be another fifteen minutes before we get an update with info about their reactors."

Sandy nodded. She was starting to feel the lack of sleep;

her bed was looking very attractive. Still, she wanted to see what was happening fifty light years away.

Sandy found a quiet, shady corner on her flag plot and pulled a chair up from the deck. She sat, ordered the chair to be a bit more comfortable, and was asleep before she knew it.

"Admiral, you want to look at what we have?" was in Van's words, and spoken softly.

Sandy snapped awake. "Have we got the first report?" she snapped out.

"Actually, ma'am, I let you sleep. All hundred and eighty of the cruisers and putative frigates are in the third system. I let you sleep for most of two hours while it was coming in. It looked like you needed the rest and it wasn't like you could do anything about it."

Sandy frowned at her chief of staff, but she really couldn't fault him. She did feel refreshed, like a wet rag that had only been stomped on a few times rather than pummeled by an enraged bull.

"So, they're sending their fast-movers forward. That splits their forces even more."

Van nodded. "Not too smart, I'd say."

"Where are the cats and their nuclear weapons?"

"When you fell sound asleep, I called Penny and asked her to notify me when they made a decision."

"And?"

"You can get the full details from Penny, but about an hour ago they reached an agreement. There were only two fights and our side won both of them. We've dispatched longboats to pick up the offered warheads."

"Good. Computer, get me Admiral Miyoshi."

"Yes, Admiral," came only a second later.

"I understand atomics are on their way up to us. You'll get the first batch to arrive. Load them up and move out."

"I have already heard. My longboats are dropping down to Columm Almar and Kingdom Bizalt. You'll excuse me if I say I trust their munitions better than the other players."

"You are excused. As soon as you have two hundred warheads, please get underway."

"I am preparing for just that, ma'am."

"Very well, Admiral. Good luck, Godspeed, and good shooting."

"The same to you. Admiral Miyoshi out."

"What's the situation with the rest of the fleet?" Sandy asked her staff.

"All fleets are ready to sortie. All ships are ready to answer bells. More food is coming aboard, but they'll sail with what they have," Ops said.

"And not a peep out of any of the other perimeter buoys?"

"Total silence."

Sandy strode over to eye the star chart up close and personal. Commanding and coordinating forces over light years of space was an impossible business. It would take Admiral Miyoshi nearly five days to get out to the furthest jump in the second system out. Communications between here and there would take half a day. The signal might jump from star system to star system with seven league boots, but the message still crawled across the systems at the speed of light. It took a good half hour for any message to get from the jump to Kiel station.

The realities of interstellar communications presented Sandy with a challenge. It presented any alien Enlightened Ones with an impossibility. Transmitting a message from the third system out across space, assuming the aliens had learned the human trick of leaving jump buoys, to either one of the two likely jumps or any other one, might take several weeks.

No, whatever the aliens were doing, they'd had to set it in stone before they launched this attack.

"When would I launch the real thrust?" Sandy asked herself. "How long would I wait for me to take the bait before I went for my throat?"

Sandy decided her nap had not been nearly long enough.

"Van, keep me appraised if there are any surprises. I'm going to get a nice bath and a good five hours of sleep."

"At least one of us should," her chief of staff answered.

"When I get back, you need to get some shut-eye."

"Just give me the order."

Sandy made her way slowly to her night quarters. Her situation rolled around in her mind, but nothing came of it. Her night quarters, she found, were quite shrunken down. She walked into the head and found where half of her bedroom had gone.

Her bathroom now included a large tub; it was already half full of steaming water.

"Computer, did you do this?"

"Yes, ma'am."

"Without instructions or asking me?"

"Yes, ma'am. You did mention that you wanted a bath, so I created a comfortable one and began getting it ready for you. Do you want jets as well?"

"Yes, please." Sandy paused, then added, "Suzie."

"Do you wish to call me Suzie from now on?" her computer asked.

"Yes," Sandy said as she quickly ditched her shoes and shed her shipsuit. She had to smile as the shipsuit disappeared, obviously headed for the laundry. The shoes moved to rest neatly together beside the door.

Aware that her computer had not only become "Suzie," but also her personal valet, Sandy put her toe in the water. She found it just right and sank her foot into the tub. A moment later, she had both feet in, and was carefully lowering herself into the warm water. In a moment, she was stretched out, luxuriating in the feel of jets massaging her body.

"Suzie, the jet behind me. It's playing directly on my back bone. Could you give me two jets to work my shoulders?'

"Of course, Sandy," and suddenly the one jet slipped over to the left and a second one appeared to the right. Sandy sighed as she felt her entire body begin to relax.

Still, there was a pressing matter to discuss.

"Suzie, you called me Sandy."

"Yes, ma'am. Should I not?"

"Why did you do that?"

"Mimzy often calls Penny by her first name. She and I thought that the odds were very high that you would like to be greeted by something less formal when we are alone."

"Is Mimzy controlling you? Did she decide I needed the luxury of a warm bath?"

"No, ma'am. Mimzy has been helping me to organize my matrix and make it more of a neural network. Still, I will never be as accurate as Mimzy at predicting your needs. However, I will do as well as I can."

"So, Suzie, you're faster and more flexible than you were a week ago, but not like Mimzy?"

"Yes, Sandy."

"Are you going to start arguing with me like Nelly?" Sandy asked. She liked the idea of having a fast and flexible computer, but Nelly seemed to show there could be a limit on reliability if it went too far.

"No, ma'am. I will not argue with you. If you ask me to examine a situation and present you with options, I will do that. I do not ever expect that I will tell you that you are concentrating on the wrong situation. That is not within my skill set."

Not yet, Sandy thought to herself.

"I suggested I needed a bath," she said, "And you gave me a much fancier tub than I'd thought of, but you didn't prepare a shower."

"Yes, ma'am. You wanted a bath, so I arranged matters so you would have one. I searched my memory and quickly decided that this one would be the best to relax you after a very rough night. I knew what the best temperature was. Do you want to change any of my assumptions?"

"No, Suzie, you did quite well. And you did all of this on your own? You didn't have to ask Mimzy for any help?"

"No ma'am. Penny is keeping Mimzy quite busy at the moment. I wouldn't want to bother them."

"Thank you, Suzie. Let me know when I've soaked for fifteen minutes."

"Yes, ma'am."

Sandy found herself floating as the pool filled. The jets were pushing her around the tub. She reached for the side, and found two handholds suddenly just where she needed them. It had been a good idea to embed a Smart Metal^{TM} skull net around Sandy's head. It made communicating with other computers easier. If Suzie really was going to start preparing for things as soon as Sandy thought of them, she'd need to let Suzie in on her thoughts.

For someone who'd been so cautious, if not concerned, about this race to let Nelly's kids get into every nook and cranny of military operations and planning, Sandy found herself questioning her willingness to give Suzie a name and let her so far into her head.

Still, there was nothing wrong in trying this out.

Sandy found herself closing her eyes as the probing jets of water relaxed her.

"Sandy?"

Sandy shivered as she came awake. "Yes, Suzie?"

"I think you are falling asleep in the water."

"I think I was, too, Suzie. How long have I been soaking?"

"Nine minutes."

"I hate to say it, but I think that's enough." Sandy stood, and found a towel now hung on a hook in easy reach. She dried herself off as the tub quickly drained. A sleep shirt and loose shorts were waiting for her on the sink. A few moments later, Sandy was back in her sleeping quarters. They returned to their normal size as she stepped through the door from her head.

"Magic. Pure magic," Sandy muttered to herself.

"Smart Metal is fun to play with," Suzie said.

Sandy fell asleep wondering what a computer considered fun and how Suzie enjoyed it. She didn't have long to think about it; she was asleep moments after her head hit the pillow.

18

"Sandy, you need to wake up," was accompanied by soft classical music that quickly became seriously loud.

"I'm up, I'm up," Sandy snapped, and the music softened and went away. "What time is it?"

"You have slept eight hours, Admiral."

Sandy noted how she'd become Admiral again now that her computer had confessed to ignoring her last order.

"Suzie, what did you tell me about you not arguing with me?"

"I didn't argue with you. Captain Velder called and asked me to delay your wake-up call. I refused. Then he got us both on a hook up to Penny and Mimzy. He explained that nothing was happening and that he and your Ops chief, Ashigara, could swap out four on, four off, and give you time for a decent nights' sleep. Mimzy assured me that this was a time to be flexible. You were sleeping soundly and I did not want to wake you up to ask you to change your order."

Suzie paused. "Velder also agreed with Penny that you

would likely not approve of this change, but that it was best if we did it anyway."

"So, you did," Sandy growled.

"I did," her computer answered, clearly not at all penitent.

"And if something with the alien raiders had changed?"

"I was plugged into the comm net. If I heard anything that showed a change in their forecasted behavior, I would have woken you, likely before either Velder or Ashigara asked me to."

Sandy eyed her wrist commlink. Should she swap it out for a new one and ban it from any contact with Mimzy?

That seemed a bit radical. Still. "Suzie, I will accept the decision you and my subordinates made for me this time. Be very careful next time. I may not be as forgiving as I am today."

"I understand, Admiral. I should be more inflexible about being flexible."

"Was that intended as a joke?" Nelly told horrible jokes. Sandy wasn't at all sure she wanted a comedian on her wrist.

"A joke, ma'am?"

Maybe not.

"Get me some coffee and a sandwich from the wardroom," Sandy said, and headed for her flag plot.

Captain Velder was waiting for her in her plot room. She gave him the stink eye, but said nothing. He acted as if nothing had happened.

"Any alien activity?" Sandy asked.

"No surprises. Admiral Miyoshi's Second Fleet is getting close to the jump. He has two hundred atomic devices. We've got eight hundred more now distributed around the fleet. One ship per squadron is designated Special Warfare and we've reinforced the Marine guards."

"Very good. Have you eaten?" Sandy asked.

"I had a sandwich earlier."

"Suzie, I've changed my mind. Captain Velder and I will be having breakfast in the wardroom."

"Yes, ma'am. If I may point out, Admiral, the wardroom is serving lunch."

"Can they knock out some hash and sunny side up eggs?" Sandy asked.

There was only a moment's pause. "Yes, Admiral."

"Have them put together two. No, Suzie, is Captain Ashigara up yet?"

"He should be here in a minute or less."

"Have them cook up breakfast for three."

"Don't you want to leave someone here?" Van asked.

Sandy glanced around and spotted a lieutenant commander at the comm desk. "Commander, you have flag plot. Let us know if anything changes."

"Aye, aye, ma'am," she said.

Sandy led her team out to breakfast.

19

"Now," Sandy said, as they settled at a table with their plates and drinks, "About not waking me up. Suzie tells me that you two succeeded in suborning my computer."

That conversation flowed directly into chewing the fat about the alien raiders and what they were doing while the screens were blank. The three of them came up with many ideas about what they'd do if they were the enemy, but no solid opinion of what they should expect next from the murderous aliens.

They were just enjoying a final cup of coffee when Suzie came to life with the voice of the Comm commander. "Admiral, we've got some developments on the bug-eyed monster front."

"We're on our way," Sandy answered. She flagged down an ensign to bus their table, and the three of them bolted for flag plot.

The lieutenant commander was standing in front of a star map. "This just came in, not three minutes ago. We've got a report of activity in this system. It's from a basic buoy, so it's not telling us more than bogies are present."

"How many?" Sandy asked.

"Twenty-eight so far."

Sandy studied the star map. This was one of the two jumps that allowed fast-movers to skip the fourth system out and jump directly into the third. Unfortunately, it was the one that was the farthest from the present threat axis. She'd have to be careful about how strong she made her response here. Indeed, the more she thought about it, the more she wondered if this was another diversion. She'd just have to wait and see what they sent her with this thrust.

Three hours later, the buoys sent in a report that showed no new ships had arrived in the system within the last fifteen minutes. The hostiles must have been coming in fast; they'd held to one every thirty seconds or so. There were three hundred and fifty-seven of them; half were cruisers, the other half were the design they didn't know a lot about. Their reactors had about double the power of the present battle cruiser reactors. However, if they didn't have the Iteeche system to step up the power output of a reactor, their effective output was likely less than half of what our battlecruisers had.

That left several questions to mull over. Where were the battleships? Had some wolf pack chosen to go all fast-movers? Also, how long would it take the frigates and cruisers to cross this system?

They could have hit the other side of this jump at a velocity of anywhere from 51,000 KPH up to just shy of 300,000 KPH. They'd need to hit the next one at no more than 49,999 KPH if they wanted to stay on course for the cats. Too much, and they'd jump past them.

Now, how fast could the aliens cross this system? Would they settle for a safe 2.0 gees or risk jacking it up faster to cut their time crossing this system?

"Suzie, assuming they are able to maintain 3.0 gees, can you estimate the fastest time for these ships to cross the system and arrive at the jump slow enough to head our way?"

"Yes, ma'am. There are two possible outcomes, if they hold to an average deceleration of 1.45 gees, they will arrive at the jump in approximately eighty-two hours and fifteen minutes. However, if they accelerate at 3.0 gees and then flip to a 3.0 gee deceleration, they will cross the system in forty-one hours and seven minutes."

"Did Mimzy teach you to estimate?" Sandy asked.

"Yes, ma'am. If you want precision, please tell me. If I forecast the need, I may give it to you, but I may, ah, guess wrong."

"Fine. Velder, it looks like we've got a moving target for a while. Tell me, how many ships of ours do you think it will take to wipe out this bunch?"

"They've got a lot of ships," her chief of staff said. "Worse, we don't know exactly what we're chasing. How powerful are their lasers? What range? How fast can they move? Maneuver? I know you don't want to hear this, and I don't want to say it, but there are just too many unknowns for me to give you anything but a guess."

"Thanks for the honest answer. Now, tell me, where are the battleships? Drago's intruders are half fast-movers and half battleships. None are here?"

"They might arrive later. That 1.45 gee deceleration is well within their power curve," Ashigara put in.

"Yes," Velder said, "but why split their forces? If they're

intent on using the fast-movers for all they're worth, why have the battlewagons trailing so far behind?"

The Ops chief nodded.

"The more I look at this map," Sandy said, "the more I get the feeling that we're being gored on the horns of an attack. Every tactician I've ever heard of that sent forces right and left has had one hell of a center force."

"Fake right, fake left, then go up the center," Ashigara said.

"Except these bug-eyed monsters have enough ships to hit us right, then left, then sweep in from the middle."

"Or add a fourth attack from the back," Sandy said, eyeing the half of the space around the cats that had been quiet.

"No one could coordinate attacks from all over the place," Velder said.

"Coordination could be underrated," Ashigara said. "If you've got all these ships, they can just swamp us. Does it matter if one prong is off by a day or two? Unless we defend the three jumps into this system, we'll have to spread ourselves mighty thin trying to stop them somewhere out there."

The longer this conversation went, the less Sandy liked it. She remembered the story of a cavalry officer who thought his two hundred and fifty sabers could take on four thousand of the locals. When help arrived, the locals had moved on, leaving a whole lot of dead bodies.

She was starting to feel like that guy, whatever his name was. She did remember where that had happened. A place called Big Horn.

Not quite two days later, the buoy in the next system reported the arrival of the fast wing of warships. The aliens were coming for them, and coming fast.

"Miyoshi is already racing out to intercept the first batch of intruders," Sandy muttered to herself. "I'll likely hold them three star systems out. Of course, that also means he'll be farther away from this cat house."

"We could order him to hold in the second system," Velder said.

"And if that batch of bug-eyed monsters does a u-turn, he could spend a lot of time watching an empty mouse hole," Ashigara said.

"And if they've made a run for it, we sure could use him back here," Sandy said, thoughtfully. She shook her head. "Let's have him keep up the advance, but Comm?"

"Yes, Admiral."

"Send to Admiral Miyoshi an update on our situation. Append, 'Stay alert to the hostiles turning their diversion into a faint and withdrawing. Admiral Santiago sends'."

"On its way, ma'am."

"Betsy, you're next in line for an independent command. If that herd of bug-eyed monsters goes 3.0 gees accelerating or decelerating all the way, where can you intercept them?"

Admiral Bethea summoned up a star map, then concentrated it on the path between the hostiles and Sasquan. "They're already in the second system out. I can either hold at the jump into the next system, or I can jump through."

Now the star map showed one system. "They'll enter from here. I enter from the opposite side of the system. I've got an ice giant I can orbit in wait for them. They either come to me, or they make for the jump and I intercept them before they can get there. Either way, we find out how good those new frigates of theirs are."

"So, do we assume you can fight outnumbered eight-to-one and gather intel on the aliens, or do we wait for them to

charge the gate and wipe them out as they jump through?"
Sandy asked.

"Point of interest," the Ops chief said. "The last time we
fought them, they were sending ships through in clusters of
three. What if they go for bigger clusters?"

"That won't be a problem," Betsy said. "No matter how
fast they enter that system, I'll be waiting on the other side,
ready to shoot them up at long range. If they try to get away
from me by going faster, they'll hit the jump way past where
they can threaten us."

That put the decision in Sandy's lap. Miyoshi faced a
mixed force that outnumbered him eight-to-one. He had to
use the jump for a choke point. Bethea was just as outnumbered, but her hostiles were all light, probably thin-skinned
fast-movers. Unless the aliens had a new, long-range laser,
Betsy's ships should be able to shoot them to junk at a safe
range. If things went right, they would get intel on these
new ships.

Of course, they were new ships. Clearly the aliens
thought they were worth building. Were they a game
changer?

"Betsy, put Third Fleet in orbit around that ice giant. If it
looks like the alien force might be too big a bite, run for the
jump and defend it."

"Aye, aye, Admiral.

"We've got to defend the cats below from those bastards
wiping them out. Even more, we've got to keep them away
from our birds. Be guided accordingly. Do not trade one of
your ships for ten of theirs. We can't survive that exchange
rate."

"Understood. I can be away from the pier in two hours."

"Good luck, Godspeed, and good shooting," Sandy said,

but it was to the back of her admiral. Betsy was already heading for the door.

"Penny says the cats have reached an agreement," Suzie reported.

"Then I guess we go see what they've decided," Sandy said, and headed off to see what her ally had to say.

20

I t was a short hike to the hall where the cats had been meeting for several days. One had left to attend the birth of a grand cub, another had been hauled out on a stretcher suffering a heart attack. One had returned; the other was still in the hospital.

The cats were that serious.

The room had been rearranged; it was easy to see Mimzy and Penny's work in it. One end of the room was terraced, each level forming a three-quarter circle of tables, rising so that those in back had as good a view as those in front.

Where a quarter-pie sized cut had been made in the circle stood a single desk. Penny stood there, waiting for Sandy. Jacques and Amanda were present as well. Several human specialists sat in chairs along the wall behind the table. Sandy noted her fleet's senior gunnery and engineering specialists, as well as some of the managers from the fabricators that had come out with the tons of Smart Metal™.

Directly across from where Sandy stood, in the first level

of tables, were the delegations from Columm Almar and the Bizalt Kingdom. Seated side by side at the edges of their delegations were the President and Prime Minister of those two great countries.

President Almar stood, and the low hum that had filled the room fell to silence. "What can you tell us about the threat that lurks at our door?"

A nod to Penny, and a large holograph filled the space between the them.

"The slowly pulsing green star in the center is your home, Sasquan, green with its gift of life," Sandy said. "The other white dots are nearby stars. They are not all the stars, but only those connected by the trade routes that connect some systems to others. Do you have any questions?"

Sandy paused to survey the room. She was greeted by nods. Apparently, the facts of interstellar geography were catching on.

"Mimzy, light up the first problem. Both the first jump they entered, and where they are now."

A white dot turned red, then, a red dashed line reached for a second light. It also changed to show a flashing red.

"This is the first enemy armada that we told you about. It is double the size of all my forces here. It is composed of fast cruisers, fast but more heavily armed frigates, and slower, but very heavily armed and armored battleships. They weigh in at five hundred thousand tons, maybe more. We've encountered a few that weigh in at a million tons, but we don't think any of those are here."

Mouths hung open. Several cats in military-looking harnesses back in the third or fourth row began stalking back and forth, tails lashing their side. Sharp claws were out.

"We now have a second intruder coming through the

perimeter of picketed systems we've set up." Now Mimzy showed a second system flashing red with a dashed line to another red system. "This force is all fast-movers. It consists of about one hundred and eighty frigates and an equal number of cruisers."

Sandy paused for a moment to let those numbers sink in.

"I have dispatched Admiral Bethea, one of my most experienced commanders to halt the second intrusion. Her forty-four ships have about two hundred of your atomic devices. We hope she can destroy this force before it gets into the next system from here."

"Forty-four ships!" That yowl came from quite a few cats. Sandy let matters run for a short while. Cats clawed the tables, not a good idea with Smart Metal™. Mimzy must have softened the metal, because after a few screeches of pain, the tables began to let claws sink into them. The marks were erased as soon their paws were lifted.

If the clawing cat didn't notice the near-magic of the tabletops, someone next to them did very quickly. That alone silenced the cats.

The President was still standing. When things quieted down, she said, "You have sent two forces out to face odds of almost ten-to-one. Yet, you hold half your forces here. May I ask a general and admiral on my staff to comment on your deployment?"

Sandy hadn't really expected her decisions to be graded like a test. Still, she nodded.

From the third row, two cats, one in a leather-like harness, the other in a blue jacket, stood. There were several comments aimed at them from others similarly dressed. This resulted in a couple of paw swipes with claws out, but no fights. They made their way to an aisle and then joined the President. For a moment, the three spoke in hushed tones, then the one wearing the blue coat stood, and pulled down on her jacket.

"I am Admiral Ferrish. May we look at your star map again?"

Without a word from any human, Mimzy had the holograph of stars back up, floating in the air between Sandy and the admiral.

"Good ground is always important, even to a sea-going cat," the admiral said. "I take it that the shipping lanes have a significant impact on both their path of advance and your ability to resist them. Could you show me those lanes, please?"

The avenue of advance for the two hostile intruders appeared as dotted yellow lines going from one star to the next until they met at Sasquan.

"I take it that deviation is not an option the enemy has?"

"No, they cannot advance, nor can they withdraw, but no other path leads here."

"I take it that there are other paths?" the admiral asked.

"Mimzy, would you please show the admiral all of the other paths?"

"Yes, ma'am. Please understand that there are a lot of branches here. Let me start from each of the three jumps into your system and show you what we have. Let's start with the first intruder."

From Jump Point Gamma, a tree of dotted yellow lines branched out. The planet flashing red was four systems out. There were murmurs around the room.

"I will lighten up the first tree, now, and give you the various paths from Jump Point Beta which leads to it."

Another web of dotted green lines branched out. One of them showed the second intruder in the third system out.

"Thank you," the admiral said. "Could you show us the options from the other jump into our system?"

Without a word, the net of orange dotted lines appeared leading from the Jump Point Alpha.

"The Alwa system that is our base is located farther out from that jump," Sandy said.

"Yet they could approach that jump without going near your planet and its warning systems?"

"Yes," Sandy answered the admiral.

"Madame President," the admiral said, giving a respectful nod to her political leader, "Even without asking further questions about travel time between and across these nets, it is clear to me that she is maintaining half of her forces as a reserve. This is a very high percent, but considering the many options the enemy can exercise, it seems wise. If I may ask another question, do these forces you now have identified constitute the totality of the enemy's fleet?"

"Unfortunately, I have no way of knowing that," Sandy said. "We have already destroyed eight of the enemy base ships. There may be thirty to thirty-five more out there. How many of them have come back from roving the galaxy to engage us here is unknown. We know how many ships were usually deployed around a base ship. However, of late it appears that they are running their production plants at full tilt. So no, I have no way of knowing if this is it or if this is just a probe, a feint or a full assault."

The admiral nodded as Sandy finished. She turned in place and eyed several of those in the third row. The cats there, who appeared to be in uniforms, were a somber lot at the moment. No one was up stalking the aisles or lashing their sides with their tails.

The admiral turned back to the front of the room,

listened for a few moments to the general whispering, nodded, and again pulled down on her jacket. That apparently was something she just did. Whether it was a nervous tick, Sandy would leave to Jacques and his team.

"With a third threat axis to cover, and a chance that she may end up having to defend the jumps into the system where we live, I think every officer here would agree that she has acted wisely. We would also like to point out that she is defending us with vastly insufficient forces. I've made it my life's work to advance the cause of Columm Almar. I have fought many of the officers in this room. I strongly believe that any waste of life and resources to any other endeavor than defending our planet from this enemy is a waste. So say we all," she said, turning back to the others.

Suzie's effort to translate the roar of agreement from the third row failed. It was left to Mimzy to say, "They all strongly agree," and leave it at that.

With a respectful nod from both officers to the President, then to the Prime Minister, the two returned to their places in the third row. There, they were greeted by pats on the back and quiet nods. The cats in the room stayed quiet, allowing the officers a chance to express their approval to each other.

As the officers sat, the President and Prime Minister stood. They were soon joined by four other leaders. All six of the largest delegations, those that had taken up the smaller first row, now had their leaders standing shoulder to shoulder.

Clearly, they wanted to present a united front to Sandy. The grand admiral could only hope that they were united and were ready to head off in the one direction that she could agree with.

"Grand Admiral Santiago," the President said, "We

thank you and your brave space sailors for putting your-selves in harms' way for our sake. We wish with all our hearts that we could send ships, crewed to a great extent by our own people, to fight for our very existence as you are now doing. Possibly matters would be better now if some of us had been more forthcoming," she said, turning to eye those around her.

"However, that mistake belongs to all of us. Now, we must not make that mistake again. Not if we survive the next few weeks based on your bravery and charity."

She paused to take a deep breath and let it out before beginning again. "As you may have noticed, our negotiations took longer than we expected. I suspect your duties kept you busy. Busy enough that our delay hardly bothered you."

Sandy raised an eyebrow, then realized that such slight facial comments might go unnoticed. "You are correct. I was very occupied. I trusted you put the extra time to good use."

"That we have," the President said, turning to nod at those around her. "Your people were kind enough to allow your fabrication managers to meet with our industrial leaders. We came to understand that their plan was to land the magical metal on our moon. There, they would establish mining operations to extract raw materials while also building the initial fabricators to convert those materials into more fabricators. The expectation was that during the first two or three years, all production would be devoted to building a larger industrial base. Do I have that correct?"

Sandy turned to Penny. The captain answered with a simple, "Yes."

"We knew that you were responding to a threat," the President said. "We could not fail to understand your request for more of our atomics, nor miss one of your fleets sailing off as soon as they were delivered. We were aware before your briefing that a second part of your armada was preparing for a hasty sortie. We cannot often understand the fine points of your body language, as, we suspect, you are still working on ours. However, the worried haste of your officers and sailors screamed concern. Now we fully understand why. We wish that we could stand with you in the battles to come, but we have no spaceships."

Again, the President paused to take a deep breath and let it out in a sigh. She did it twice before she went on. "However, we are very much aware that we must look to you like questionable partners. Kris Longknife told us that our lack of a central government was a bar to our entering your United Societies. No one had to tell us that you feared sharing all your advanced technology with cats that squabbled too much and had their fingers on the nuclear trigger."

Sandy opened her mouth to say something. She wasn't sure what it would be, but the President waved her to silence.

"As I said, no one told us this. It didn't take a genius to look honestly at ourselves and conclude that we would not let ourselves loose among the stars. We are a combative race with, what do you call it," she turned to Jacques. "Angry management issues?"

Jacques shook his head, "I would not have put it that way."

No, Sandy thought. He'd say, "anger management issues."

The President went on, possibly with something like a smile on her face. "Still, so long as we cannot solve our problems without resorting to violence and we have our fingers on the nuclear button, I would not let us loose without a leash."

Sandy expected muttering at that, but the room remained so quiet that you could hear a pin drop.

"Keeping all of those concerns in mind, I would like to make you an offer that does, indeed, grant us access to much of your technology. I am prepared to commit to us using this technology totally for our mutual defense for the next five years. For the next five years, we would allow ten percent of that production to seep into our economy and society. Like you, we have fears, too. I'm told that you also refer to the buggy whip business vanishing with the advent of the automobile."

The room did share a soft chuckle at that.

"What we are offering to you is a minimum of seventy-five percent of our industry presently devoted to weapons production. We will immediately begin converting it to the production of your magic metal and weapons systems such as lasers. We will also build transport to your design to both take these up to your station and to construct mining survey vessels to search for minerals scattered in our asteroid belt. We expect that we might be able to begin exploiting those resources in four or five years. Maybe less. During that time, we will devote as least as many resources to the construction of fabricating mills on our planet and the production of what you need to build ships."

Now the President turned to do an eyeball check with those around her. She was greeted with nods, so she turned back to Sandy.

"Would you like time to consider this offer? We have provided the outline of it to your staff people. They can brief you more in-depth. Should we remove ourselves?"

Sandy did feel kind of swamped. This was not what she'd come here expecting. She gave Penny, Jacques and

Amanda the stink eye, but they maintained placid innocence.

"Have you eaten recently?" Sandy asked.

"We have survived for the last two days on cocoa and cold meats," the President admitted.

"Penny, could you lay out a banquet on my flagship?"

"Do you require that your meat be seared or served raw?" Penny asked.

"Just so long as it is not served cold from the refrigerator and long dead, we will be happy," the President said.

"I've got Mimzy working on it with the mess president, ma'am," Penny said. "Jeanette," talking to a lieutenant commander seated behind them, "please lead our guests back to the banquet hall this all started in."

"Yes, Captain. If you will come this way," and the cats filed out of the room quietly.

While they did, Sandy reviewed what she'd heard. At least intellectually, the cats understood that the humans weren't sure they wanted to share space with them. Still, the situation called for, and they proposed, that the humans give them access to their advanced tech so they could build warships to better defend themselves.

Of course, warships were both defensive and offensive weapon systems. The key question was how to avoid the cats appearing in human space and dropping illegal atomics on human or Iteeche planets.

With the door closing behind the last cat, Sandy turned to Penny and the rest of her advisors. "Okay folks. We're being asked to let this genie out of the bottle. There's a good argument to be made that we do it. There's no doubt in my mind that we need them actively and heavily involved in their own defense. So, how do we do this without them returning the favor we give them by turning human planets into atomic waste lands?"

Penny cleared her throat, made sure no one else was eager to jump into this frying pan, and said, "We've been looking at this for much of the last two days. We think we have an idea. You might want to run it by a red team. To get to human space, you need a star map and a Mark XII fire control system. You also need to know how to use jumps to cover the galaxy in seven league boots."

Penny paused. Sandy gave her a nod.

"We're using the standard jumps to defend here. A Mark X fire control would work fine in a fight five or ten systems out. Second, we give them a map of this immediate area, showing the jumps and advise them not to approach a jump at more than 50,000 kilometers per hour, or they may end up off the charts and lost."

"And if we need them to use a long jump?" Sandy asked.

"We lead them through it. Until we have to do it, we don't tell them about them."

"They already know that we're doing something," Sandy said. "If Alwa isn't within their defense perimeter, they'll know something is up."

"Yes, ma'am," Jacques said. "But these pussies like foxy leaders. If they know you're holding back an ace or two, they'll respect you. I don't think they'll feel disrespected. Hell, they might even feel respected. They know we're kind of afraid of them. I think they like that."

"Do they understand that they aren't higher on the food chain than us?" Sandy asked.

"I think the cats we have been talking to for the past few days are scared stiff. They know all that stands between their planet being 'nuked from orbit,' I think that is their phrase, is us. They very much don't want to face this situation again."

"So, have you given some thought to how we work this?" Sandy asked.

"For the first five years," Penny said, "they don't expect to be skippers, XO's, Guns, Engineering and other division officers. They know they'll have to work their way up from boot ensign and deck ape to field grade officers and chiefs. I think we'll be getting the best cats they have in their military. They know they need to be young and flexible. The old generals and admirals aren't real happy, but the ones present understand that we knock these ships around hard."

"Okay. Then what?"

"From five to ten years, they'd like to see some of their people advanced into division head slots. Maybe XO. Maybe CO. Our choice. Promotions will be governed by a performance system that we'll agree on with them. We can wash out anyone for the first four years of their career. After that, the cats want a board to review our decision. Two cats, two humans, and a bird. A human is the chairman of the board. They're willing to keep that in place for fifteen years."

"Okay, I'll think about that. Amanda, how is this economic transfer going to work? Can they actually make Smart Metal and weapons-level lasers?"

The economist turned to glance at several of the fab managers behind her. "We think so. It will take some retooling. They're used to producing specialized steel and aluminum products. If we land twenty thousand tons of Smart Metal on their planet, we can quickly set up a Smart Metal foundry. Once it's up and running, they can produce their own metal to bring more foundries on line as well as start shipping metal up to Kiel Station to be spun into battlecruisers."

Amanda eyed the one Navy officer sitting against the wall. "We gave the cats laser tech for minor things like computers. I knew they were already working on how they could knock out more powerful lasers, say for cutting cloth to make clothes. We knew they wanted to push it for all they were worth. It will take an effort on our part, but they should be able to produce fighting lasers in the next six months. Maybe less. We're thinking of starting with frigates, maybe with 18-inch guns. Something we could use for scouts, or maybe redesign things when they can do 20- or 22-inch lasers."

"Like we did," Sandy said.

"Yes, ma'am," came from all three of the people at Sandy's table.

"What kind of a mess does this do to their economy and society?" Sandy asked.

"Well, it won't be good," the husband and wife team of anthropologist and economist said together. They shared a laugh, then he waved her into the breach.

Amanda took a deep breath. "We've been looking at this hard, both us and the cats. They are not unaware of how much our highly advanced tech can upset things. They've been having trouble living with just the radical changes computers have brought to them. Computers and low-powered lasers. They came to us begging for thermonuclear power plants. They needed to build some new coal burning power plants, and they didn't want to invest in obsolete technology. Drago let them have three big power plants and taught them how to build a better power grid with computer controls. They went hog wild, but it caused major disruption in their coal country."

"No surprise there," Sandy drawled.

"However, they need carbon to convert to Smart Metal.

They already have orders in for coal deliveries, not to burn but to convert."

"So, this huge defense effort could help them over the imminent speed bumps?"

"Yes, ma'am. They also have committed to keeping this new tech from impacting their economy for the first five years of the work. Everything they produce goes into warships, fabs on the ground or on the moon, and setting up a mining effort to their asteroid belt. Nothing goes into the civilian economy. None goes into the ground-based military. This isn't part of the program, but I think the last tank, plane, and ship have already been commissioned. What's in production now will be shoved aside to make room for high tech work."

"Displacement?"

"Several of the countries do have safety nets for the unemployed. Those that don't have them are being heavily leaned on to provide the same services. No one wants someone to keep producing planes after they quit. You do mean to come to anyone's aid that is attacked, right?"

Sandy winced. "Assuming I've got any ships in their sky, yes."

"Yeah. Well, if all the other countries are ready to respond to any rogue, we'll likely be part of the charge."

"Understood," Sandy said. "We need some good diplomats to help handle the inter-governmental affairs."

"I'd order up a couple of dozen with the next ship heading back home," Penny said.

About that time someone's stomach growled, and then another. "When was the last time you ate a decent dinner?" Sandy asked.

It turned out, just like the cats, they'd been surviving on coffee and sandwiches since the banquet.

"Let's head for the *Victory*. Penny, if the cats don't mind us sitting in on their dinner, we can do that. Otherwise, you are all welcome to my flag wardroom."

The cats liked the idea of having the humans in the same room with them. They were letting down their hair. Several of them were engaged in some kind of sing-along that really should be classified as torture, but worked for them. There were short forays into negotiations, but nothing too deep.

When the dinner was done, Penny had Mimzy print up a stack of proofed briefs they had worked out. The cats read it over, agreed that it was the framework they had worked out, and it was what they would take down to their respective governments to look at and refine.

Sandy told the admiral commanding Kiel Yard and the senior managers who had come out with the Smart Metal™ to the cat system to take a deep dive into this planning document. She also ordered her Fleet Security Officer to take two paranoid pills and go over it as if that document alone would keep the cats from atomic bombing her grandmother.

It was agreed to meet again in two days and go over all the proposed changes and additions to the Status of Forces Agreement as well as the Technological Transfer Agreement.

Then Sandy went back to chewing her nails and waiting for the aliens to make their next move.

Admiral Bethea jumped out of the system, headed for her own battle.

Sandy had a lot to worry about.

Suddenly, there was no more time left to worry.

21

Admiral Miyoshi sat in his high gee station, studying the latest communication from Admiral Santiago. It held no surprises.

The aliens were sending a fast-moving wing at one of the other jump points into the cat's system. He and Sandy had expected that. The question was, could a fast wing carry enough weight to bust through a jump point defended by a fleet?

Of course, he was trying to ambush a force the same size, half of which were battleships. There was still no way to tell how much rock armor they'd added to their hide.

The final paragraph was the core of the message. IF POSSIBLE, DISPOSE OF THE INTRUDER AND RETURN TO KIEL STATION SOONEST.

He eyed the star map projected on the forward screen of his flag plot. His aliens were maintaining a combined arms fleet structure. The cruisers and frigates were ahead of the battleships, but the big over-gunned and armored ships were not that far behind. If Miyoshi held to 3.0 gees, maybe a bit more, he could easily be ready to meet them this side of the jump into system three. By doing that, he'd have to spend more time in transit, both out and back, but he'd hold contact with the aliens for the entire time they were crossing system four.

"It is better to know where your enemy is than to run around the battlefield trying to be everywhere at once," he told himself.

He held his course and acceleration. He hoped Sandy would not need him too quickly. He doubted that this was an accident on the alien's part. They wanted his ships here, not at Sandy's side.

Damn, but he hated it when the enemy got smart. He hoped it would not get to be a regular habit.

22

S andy was only a few hours from a huge confab with
the leaders of the cat world. They were bringing up
not only the political factions in their different
national governments, but also their masters of industry
and finance. The proposal being laid out for all the parties
would impact nearly a tenth of their gross planetary product. A lot of cats were interested in what would happen here.

Sandy had added Smart Metal^{TM} to Kiel station so that
they could create a huge conference room with a large
number of break-out rooms. President Almar suggested that
she should expect to devote an entire week to these two
treaties.

Then the aliens kicked over the whole damn hornet's
nest.

"We've got alien activity," her duty officer said through
Suzie.

Sandy scowled at her most formal dress uniform, and
slipped her feet into her dress shoes. In a moment, she was
in flag plot.

Admiral Drago had gotten there before her. He was also in formal dress for tonight's dinner and negotiations.

"You aren't going to like this," he said, through thin lips.

"What?"

He pointed at a system that was flashing. Aliens had entered it. Entered it despite it being on the third ring of pickets!

"What the hell?" was Sandy's immediate reaction to what she saw.

"Suzie. You tell Penny and Mimzy to get their asses over here. Now! Better yet, ten minutes ago!"

"Yes, Admiral, we're almost there," Penny's voice quickly answered from the commlink on her wrist.

"Correct me, Admiral Drago, didn't our supercomputers tell us we only had to worry about two systems the aliens could steal a march on?

"Our computers surely did."

Sandy suddenly had a second question. "Suzie. You knew about this double jump before I got here, didn't you?"

"Yes, Admiral."

"Why didn't you tell me?" Sandy snapped.

"Mimzy taught me that there were some things you humans prefer to learn from other humans, especially if you will learn soon enough and it won't have any material impact on the decision-making process."

"Mimzy did, huh?"

"She said that her mother had found that Kris Longknife was agreeable to this."

"We will be revisiting this when we have a spare moment. In the meantime, I want to know immediately when all hell breaks loose."

"I shall endeavor to see that you are immediately

informed when all hell breaks loose," Suzie answered evenly.

Leaving Sandy wondering what a computer would consider 'all hell breaking loose,' but there was no time to haggle over it at the moment.

About that time, out of breath but present, Penny galloped into Flag plot.

"Yes, Admiral?"

"I thought I was assured that only two of the systems three rings out could be jumped into from outside our perimeter."

"Yes, ma'am," Penny said.

"Mimzy?"

"Those assessments were based on assumptions that appear to no longer be correct," the computer answered.

"Explain yourself," Sandy snapped.

"To make a long jump, you have to put a high velocity on your ship. If you've got a lot of energy on your ship, you need high gee deceleration to slow down before you go zipping through the next jump above the speed limit and go hurtling past the next system you want to be in."

"And?"

"Alien battleships have never been able to maintain a two-gee acceleration or deceleration. I assumed that we'd be dealing with less than a two-gee deceleration and therefore, that system could not be jumped into."

Sandy eyed the readout next to the flashing system. "Forty-five battleships jumped into that system in fifteen minutes. We can't range them, but they must have hit the other side of that jump with a whole of a lot of velocity."

"Yes, ma'am. They will have to decelerate at 2.3 gees all the time they are crossing the system to slow down enough to make the next jump work for them."

"Two point three gees," Sandy echoed.

Admiral Drago had been stroking his chin in thought. "Either they're ready to accept heavy attrition from ships falling out or blowing up due to engineering casualties, or the damn bastards have managed to increase the quality control on their reactors."

"It looks like either one or the other, doesn't it?" Sandy said.

"Yep. Don't you hate it when the enemy ups their game while you're busy upping yours?"

"I would rather they didn't," Sandy admitted. "How soon can you get away from the pier, Bert? I'd prefer to give you an independent command and hold Admiral Nottingham back here with me. He doesn't have a lot of fighting experience."

"We are ready, now, Admiral. However, there is one minor problem. All the atomic devices I have are from the smaller powers, and I am told they may not be as good as those manufactured by other countries. They may also not explode with the same, shall we say, enthusiasm."

"So, I need to steal you some more atomics, huh?"

"Please, dear admiral."

Sandy eyed the man. "I thought a colonial girl had her hooks in you?"

"Sad to say, distance did not make her heart grow fonder, but pardon me, I wasn't intending to say anything more than that I would be very grateful for the bombs."

"Penny? Mimzy? Do either of you have anything to add to my challenges?"

"I have worked the intercept for Admiral Drago," Mimzy said, sounding a bit contrite. "Even at 3.5 gees, he will not be able to intercept them at the jump into the system three rings out. A more pleasant two-gee voyage should get you to the jump they'll use to enter the second system."

"Thank you, Mimzy," Bert said.

"With me," Sandy said, curtly.

She hadn't joined the Navy expecting a placid life. Not really. Still, it would be nice if she could have a nice quiet banquet and pleasant negotiation session just once in her Navy career.

23

Down three near-palatial stairways and around a passageway, Penny led Admirals Santiago and Drago. They strode along at a fast pace, with sailors and officers getting out of their way.

"Would you like to take a shortcut?" Penny asked.

"If it won't take too long." Sandy knew some shortcuts that were a long way from short.

"It won't," Penny said, trying to swallow a grin.

Ten paces ahead of Sandy, the bulkhead wavered. In a second, it split and began to flow apart. In little more than the blink of an eye, Sandy found herself walking toward a very impressive arched entryway.

Penny fell back, and Sandy led the way into a banquet hall. Quite a few of the people seated at tables were staring at her entrance. Others, their back to her, were turning in their seats, having missed the more spectacular aspects of her entry.

The head table was off to her left; Sandy headed for it. There was a vacant chair between Prime Minister Gerrot and President Almar. Sandy aimed for it. Two other vacant chairs were farther down the table. Penny and Bert chose them.

"I'm sorry I am late," Sandy said.

"We were wondering when you would arrive," Madame Gerrot said.

"Is there a problem with the hostile aliens?" President Almar asked.

"As a matter of fact, yes there is. Should I brief you and then the rest or would it be quicker to just do it all at once?"

The President and the Prime Minister eyed the other leaders seated at the head table. Sandy didn't need to read cat body language. Any politician would be balancing the desire to be first to know against the potential error of keeping their new allies in the dark.

The threat from the aliens likely tipped the scales.

The President lifted a silver spoon and tapped her water goblet. A clear tone rang out. A room that was quiet became totally silent.

"Grand Admiral Santiago has told me that there are new developments among the enemy aliens. She has asked to brief us all. We here at the head table believe that our time is well spent listening to her."

There were soft assents around the room, but it quickly returned to silence.

Sandy stood up. "We have a problem," she said. "Penny, would you produce a star chart of the local sector for all to see? Show the two aliens we have told them about."

A moment later, a holographic star chart floated above the heads of the diners. Some failed to suppress their surprise.

"I have told you of the first incursion," Sandy said. A pair of stars began to flash, while a dotted line led to the cat's system. "The fleet sent out to engage the aliens should be meeting that force very soon."

Immediately, a second pair of flashing systems showed where the second attack force was making its way toward Sasquan. "That force will also be engaged. Now, there is a third force."

A third star began flashing. It was four jumps away.

"Each of these attack forces are different. The first is a combined force of slow battleships and fast cruisers. The second force is a fast force of large frigates and smaller cruisers. This third force is still being reported on. The first twenty-nine, however, are battleships."

Sandy paused to let the cats absorb all she'd dumped in their furry laps.

"I have yet to dispatch a fleet to engage this third incursion. I intend to send Admiral Drago here," she nodded at the admiral who half-stood. "He and his fleet have been your protector since I arrived. He is prepared to sail in harm's way, but he has raised a concern."

Sandy paused for dramatic affect.

"We dispatched four hundred of the five hundred atomic devices you gave us with the other two forces. We have only one hundred left for Admiral Drago's fleet. During the time he has been waiting to sail, his crews have stripped the warheads down and found that the quality control during the construction of these hundred was less stringent than on the first four hundred. He fears that if he has to use them, they may explode with small yields, or fail to explode at all."

When Sandy paused for a breath, President Almar asked, "Can you tell us where those shoddy weapons are from?"

There were murmurs in the room. No doubt, this was intelligence critical to many, both for those who produced the bombs and their neighbors who feared they might be used on them.

"I do not have that information, and doubt if it is available. Let me say that any city that suffered an attack from one of these bombs would be much the worse for the experience. Now, I need for Admiral Drago to sail as quickly as possible. I need for him to sail with a very large supply of atomics. Likely double the size of the other forces I have dispatched. I fear he is headed for the greatest fight."

There were murmurs of agreement from the generals in leather harnesses and the admirals in their jackets of different cuts and different shades of blue.

Sandy turned to the President and then the Prime Minister. To each, she raised a quizzical eyebrow. No doubt the facial expression was lost on the cats, but the need was clear.

"I will release a hundred and ten of the largest devices from our stockpile," President Almar said.

"I will also provide a hundred and ten of our largest," the Prime Minister said.

The other four of the lesser powers quickly agreed to give up seventy of their best.

Admiral Drago stood. "I thank you very much, both in the name of my fighting crews and in your own name. With those devices, we will be much better able to put up a fight in your defense. Now, if you will excuse me, I need to get longboats down to your armories to retrieve your gifts and get us on our way."

"Admiral Drago," President Almar said, "You know many of our military officers from your time among us. If we were to nominate some of them to go with you, would you take them?"

Bert's lips disappeared as his mouth formed a tight,

studied frown. With a sigh he said, "If you will nominate whom you please from the six nations providing us with weapons, I will determine how many we can take along and then apply a lottery."

The cats nodded, and Sandy gained new respect for Admiral Drago. If there were individuals that he did not want to take aboard, no doubt, the number would be cut and the offending cat would draw a losing number. Smart.

Drago now trotted from the room, and the food servers, mostly Marines earning extra pay, began to bring around the trays of food. Sandy decided to stay with the cats for a while. It would be an hour or more before she knew what Drago would face. If more ships were still arriving in three hours, she'd likely have to adjust her forces further.

The conversation was muted. No one seemed to know exactly what topics were appropriate at the moment. The cats avoided bringing up the incoming intruders. Sandy didn't want to say anything that would make a mess of the careful negotiations yet to come.

It was the Prime Minister who broached a subject both could agree to discuss.

"Have your people had much experience introducing your high tech to new and, if I may say so, deliberately less advanced cultures?"

"I would think," Sandy said, "that there is nothing less advanced about your culture. I have no doubts that many of the aspects of your culture are the best suited for your society. I think the more appropriate subject that we both can be concerned about is the problem that introduces different means of production into an economic environment that is unprepared."

"Yes. Yes, I think that is what I really meant to say," the Prime Minister answered.

"How often has the interjection of such advanced means of production made a wreck of a planet's economy?" President Almar asked.

"We haven't had the problem for a while," Sandy said. "The birds on Alwa are not at all sure they wanted our plants on their planet. They are content to have them on their moon and there are no factories dirtside. They work for us there and get products made on the moon. I think we both are committed to not sullying their planet with industrial production."

"Hmm," said the Prime Minister, "there are some among us who would be glad to see the pollution from our smoke stacks moved off-planet. That's been something talked about, but we never figured it would happen in even the lifetimes of our great-grand cubs. Now, maybe it can happen."

"That brings us to an idea that we have been discussing," the President said. "It might shorten the time we need to begin warship construction to little more than a year. We are thinking of establishing a magic metal fabrication foundry on a small island two hundred miles off the coast of my country. We would ship the raw materials there, and you could send down longboats to get them and deliver the product to the moon to expand your fabrication base there."

"It would make the startup go a bit slower," the Prime Minister said, "but it would assure that the pressure to siphon off some of the metal into the local economy could be better controlled."

"Then, we could use a lot of your citizens to expand the fabs and work them," Sandy said. "We could have some of your local plants begin the construction of battle lasers. I doubt there is much that can be transferred there that you haven't already received."

"We have been thinking that way," the President said. "Five years is about the furthest we can forecast at present."

"It's rare anyone can," Sandy said. "The trick is to rework your forecast every year. That way you advance into the unknown one year at a time with your eyes no more than five years out."

"Good. I'm glad to see we're in agreement."

"You'll have to work the details out with Amanda and Jacques," Sandy was quick to point out. "I'm not able to see all the risks involved with something like this." Sandy glanced at her wrist unit. "I've been away from my flag plot for an hour. I really must get back."

"But of course, of course," the Prime Minister said, and all at the head table stood when Sandy did. With a profusion of 'thank you's' and 'you're welcomes', Sandy stepped away from the table. The archway she'd entered by had flattened out back into a bulkhead. Now it opened again.

Sandy marched through it, then headed down the passageway, but she couldn't help but look back to watch as the archway smoothed out into just bulkhead again.

"Magic metal, indeed," she muttered to herself as she picked up her pace.

24

Sandy found that both Velder and Ashigara were intently eyeing the latest information to arrive from the latest breach in their outer perimeter. The count now stood at one hundred and ninety-nine.

"All of them are battleships."

"Are they coming through faster?" Sandy asked.

"About forty every fifteen minutes."

"Do we understand anything new about these ships?"

The two other Navy officers shook their head. "They all have one hundred reactors. They seem to represent a new type, possibly a bit stronger than we've known, but we don't have enough hard data to make any better than a guess."

It was frustrating to Sandy, to be faced by a growing threat, but not able to gauge it any better than this.

Fifteen minutes later, there were another forty large alien battleships in the system for a total of two hundred and thirty-nine. Sandy tried not to let that spook her, but clearly, this battle force was at least fifty percent larger than the one Admiral Miyoshi faced.

An hour later, the count of battleships was up to three

hundred and sixty, and the first frigate type warship had made its appearance.

Sandy now had a serious problem to tackle.

The other two forces were roughly three hundred and sixty ships. In one case, they were a mixed force. In the other, they were lighter.

How large a force should she dispatch with Admiral Drago to fight this new force?

Even if this third force had only sixty or ninety frigates, was it already too large for just one fleet? How small a force could she get by with if one of her detachments was blown away or maneuvered out of position and she had to defend a jump into this system?

The unknowns were huge and the penalty for guessing wrong could make a cinder of the planet beneath her,

An hour later, they had a hundred and sixty more frigates and no end in sight.

Fifteen minutes later, the distant picket's new report showed twenty more frigates and the first cruisers with three reactors. Twenty of them.

The count on the board now showed three hundred and sixty battleships, one hundred and eighty frigates, and twenty cruisers.

Even if the cruisers topped out at half the number of frigates, this would still be a huge force to reckon with.

"Any suggestions?" Sandy asked her two lead staff men.

Neither of them shot back a ready answer. All three of them stood, eyeing the board, and no matter how hard they stared at it, it told them nothing more than they already knew.

"We could run," Ashigara said. "We're facing over twelve hundred hostiles, likely more with only one hundred and seventy-six battlecruisers. That's seven to one odds. If they bring in another hundred and eighty cruisers, it will be over eight to one odds. And, may I also point out, this new force doesn't seem to have littered its course with bent, busted, or blown-up ships. Those numbers round up to full dishes."

"You have several good points. Ignore them for now," Sandy said.

"If we ordered Admiral Bethea to engage the flying wing, say one system out, she'd be closer to us when she won and could come to our aid faster."

"Computer, show me how much time it would take an order to reach Bethea."

The computer projected the likely place of the fleet and the time of flight for a comm message. If the message arrived per the estimate, it would joggle the admiral's elbow only a couple of hours before she joined battle. That would be a big mess and save them little time.

"Comm, send to both Admirals Miyoshi and Bethea. 'A third assault force is headed for Sasquan, aiming at Jump Point Gama. Please return to this system as quickly as you can after handling the problem in front of you. Admiral Santiago sends'."

For another long minute, they stared at the screen. The only solution to this was the obvious one.

"If we aren't going to run, Admiral Drago will have to be reinforced," Sandy finally said.

"How do we split what we have left?" Velder asked.

"That is the problem," Sandy said. "We've got the *Victory* and forty-four ships. What kind of a jump defense can twenty-three ships present?"

"If we anchor them in seven groups of three and a single pair, that would give us something like a hundred and forty, maybe a hundred and sixty guns aimed at the jump at any time," Ashigara said.

"But at one revolution per minute," Velder said, "we'll likely shoot ourselves dry in six seconds and have to wait for another fourteen seconds before the next ship came on line. Worse, we'll have the lasers reloaded fully twenty to thirty seconds before we swing around and can shoot again."

"Better we slip our moorings and alternate firing by squadrons," Sandy said. "The fight won't last too long, and that would have a hundred and forty to a hundred and sixty lasers ready every nine or ten seconds. That's much better."

The two staff officers nodded agreement. "Six seconds firing, three seconds waiting for the next ship to come on line, then another six seconds firing," Velder said.

"But if they're sending a ship through every second, we'll be swamped," Ashigara said.

"One ship every fifteen or twenty seconds, and we can handle it," Velder countered.

"So, whether twenty-three ships can hold a jump depends on how fast they come at us,"

Sandy concluded. "Oh well, there are always the atomics if push comes to shove."

"They worked in the alien system home world," Velder reminded her.

"But they got enough ships away to let them know how we did it," Sandy pointed out. It was clear, she wasn't going find a better option if she kept staring at the screen.

"Cut orders for three squadrons from Admiral Nottingham's fleet to be detached to Admiral Drago's command. I better go ask the cats if they have any more warheads they're willing to share with me if I end up trying to defend a jump with just what I've got left."

While Velder cut the orders, Sandy headed back to the banquet hall. This having to beg for illegal atomics was getting to be a bit of a pain.

25

A dmiral Miyoshi watched the main screen in his flag plot. The ships of his command, Second Fleet, were now moored 180,000 kilometers back from the jump. That put the jump 20,000 kilometers inside the range of his 22-inch lasers. At the moment, a longboat was just drifting up to the jump. In a few minutes, it would put a periscope through the jump and let him know exactly what those damn bug-eyed monsters were up to on the other side of it.

With any luck, the aliens should be only hours out from the jump, bearing down on it fast, intent on racing through it at as close to 50,000 kilometers per hour as they could manage it.

The data stream from the periscope sent through the jump was limited. The alien fleet of a hundred and seventy-nine battleships, fifty-nine cruisers, and some ninety-three of those new frigates were approaching the jump, but it was impossible to tell exactly how long it would take them to arrive.

"Send a probe through," Admiral Miyoshi ordered.

A few moments later, the longboat withdrew the periscope and launched a tiny smart probe through the jump. The plan was for it to spread out, with two atomic laser mass tracking devices at either end of a kilometer-long baseline. The probe also had plenty of passive antennae to pick up any radio, radar, or laser noise. What it found, it would transmit to the periscope then to the longboat and back to the *Haruna*.

Admiral Miyoshi could wait; he was a patient man.

What he finally received did not please him.

"The enemy fleet is decelerating at a higher gee than it would need to if it intended to go through the jump at 45,000 kilometers an hour," the duty officer on sensors reported.

Even as he spoke, the main screen showed a projection that had the aliens come dead in space about a 100,000 kilometers short of the jump.

"Damn," Miyoshi allowed himself. "They aren't going to charge the jump."

"What do you think they're up to?" his chief of staff asked.

"I have no idea, Aki. We will just have to wait and see."

During the several hours that they waited to see what the alien fleet was up to, Miyoshi was handed the latest message traffic from Admiral Santiago. It took all his patience not to crumble the message up and toss it toward a trash can.

"A problem, sir?" Aki asked.

"It seems that there is now another force. Admiral Santiago asks if I could please handle this bunch quickly and rejoin her. I suspect she fears she will soon be low on reserves."

Miyoshi initialed the message flimsy and returned it to the comm runner.

How soon can I dispose of this hostile force? Miyoshi thought to himself.

I cannot attack them. That is certain. I can only destroy them when they attempt to close with me.

During the wait, Miyoshi set about mining the jump. If the aliens sent even one of their small cruisers through, there would be a huge thermonuclear device waiting for them. In a flash, the jump would be just one small adjunct to hell.

Farther back, he deployed high acceleration rockets. Carefully protected against electromagnetic pulse and insulated from as much heat as possible, these rockets would be shot into that small bit of hell to stoke the fires. Device after device would keep eating up battleships before the aliens realized where the jump had taken them.

That had worked once for Miyoshi. The foremost question in his mind was, would it work again?

Admiral Miyoshi had ordered the Second Fleet to Battle Stations and Condition Charlie as the time approached for the aliens to arrive. However, from the way they were slowing, he was starting to doubt he was in for a fight.

Sandy, if I cannot leave this jump unguarded, I fear you will not get any new reserves from me.

The probe soon showed that the enemy fleet had indeed come to full stop 100,000 kilometers away from the jump. The battleships were spread in a thin concave curve in front of the jump. The frigates and cruisers floated around its flanks, covering all 360 degrees of its edge.

Before Miyoshi could question what would happen next, several small vessels of ten thousand tons detached from the battleships and began to tiptoe toward the jump. Several began leaving large packages in their wake.

"Will the probe tell us something about whatever those are?" Miyoshi asked.

"It's coming in now, sir," Aki answered.

Before the chief of staff fell silent, the sensor duty officer was already reporting. "The devices weigh ten tons, sir. We are getting a radioactive read off the package. They do not yet appear to be active."

"Thank you, Commander. Order the probe to prepare to return when I order it."

"Aye, aye, sir."

"Mines, sir?" Aki asked.

"It would appear that they are prepared to mine their side of the jump just as we've mined our side."

The two of them studied developments for the next hour. When the mine layers were within 20,000 kilometers of the jump, they pulled the probe back. After that, they were reduced to just what data the two versions of their periscope could gather. One brought in visual. The other scanned the electromagnetic scale.

It wasn't a lot of information. However, it did tell them that as the mine layers withdrew, the mines activated a kind of primitive proximity fuse.

"I wonder if we could jigger their proximity fuses to blow themselves all up?" Aki asked.

"We will have to see about that," Miyoshi said thoughtfully. "Though that is a tool I would prefer to keep in my tool box until it will do me the most good. Now, about those mines."

And the two of them put their heads together and came up with a plan to annoy the great Enlightened One on the other side of the jump.

An hour later, a much-reduced longboat shot through the jump. No one was aboard it. Humans did not have to rely on suicide crews; we had automation to do what the aliens seemed to demand of their own people.

The armed probe immediately accelerated at 6.73 gees in a tangent course from the jump. It never maintained its direction or acceleration for more than a second. It activated a minimal sensor suite, identified the nearest mine, and shot four 12.6-mm lasers at it.

The mine blew up, but it was not a primary detonation. Some of the conventional explosives surrounding the plutonium were hit and began to burn. Then it exploded, but not with the proper timing. In a moment, in the space where the mine had been, all that existed was a collection of parts and a large, misshapen chunk of worthless weapons-grade plutonium.

The armed probe got off shots that destroyed seven mines before the alien fleet began to wake up to this nuisance. The probe gunned down three more mines before a laser wiped it out of existence. However, three more mines were also wiped out by some of the volleys aimed at the gun boat.

Admiral Miyoshi pursed his lips. "Well done. Very well done," he said. "Thirteen of those pesky mines gone."

"Do you think they will attempt a similar raid on our side of the jump?" Aki asked.

"No doubt they will. Unlike them, however, we should be able to nip theirs in the bud. Two, maybe three seconds, yes?"

"I am told that our gunners have the jump zeroed in and are ready to surround it with laser fire. They will not know what hit them."

"Good. Good. However, my dear Aki, we must do better

than them. Advise the gunners to put our mines in their data base. No one fires if they have a mine in their sights as well as an alien intruder."

"We will make sure of that."

While Aki went to make sure that his own sharpshooters would not destroy one of the atomic devices Admiral Santiago had to beg the cats for, Miyoshi found himself a dark corner of his flag plot.

Two things were becoming clear. Admiral Santiago feared that her reserves would be soon depleted, and depleted badly. The aliens across this jump from him definitely wanted him to stay here. Stay here or charge through the jump to his doom.

There was no question of abandoning the jump. Mines were nice weapons, but they needed to be protected, as he had just proven. The question he struggled with was just how large a force did he need to keep here to do that.

Too large here, and Admiral Santiago might not be able to stop the other intruder, or the other threat she anticipated.

Too few, and he risked letting this force blast through the jump and strike for those troublesome cats.

The correct answer would only be known when it had succeeded or failed.

Admiral Miyoshi examined his options several more times. Nothing new came to his attention.

Then the aliens made his afternoon interesting.

26

The periscope gave them warning. One of the alien cruisers was approaching the jump at a slow, measured speed. They switched periscopes for the electronic surveillance version and found that none of the mines were still sending out proximity noise.

That made for interesting information.

The longboat retrieved the probe, collected the close-in mine, and, when the cruiser was fifteen minutes from the jump, it accelerated to 2.0 gees to get some distance between it and the jump.

The crew also wanted to clear the fire lanes.

At exactly sixteen minutes, a small device tumbled through the jump.

It took half a second for that news to reach the guard ships. The gunners were on a hair trigger alert; the firing solutions were already worked out. The lasers were already dialed in on the jump. A second later, they had sixty lasers firing in a pattern around the jump.

Exactly one and a half seconds after the object tumbled into the system, it was obliterated.

"Banzai!" was muttered in chorus around the flag plot. Miyoshi smiled at the enthusiasm of his warriors.

"We've got radioactive readings off of the wreckage," Sensors reported to Admiral Miyoshi.

That was no surprise.

Six of his forty-four battlecruisers had used only part of their charges during those one or two seconds. It would take little time to top off their capacitors. There were also another six ships that now had the assignment of nipping the next thing that came through the jump.

The alien cruiser waited for a full minute before a second object shot through into their space. This one rocketed off, heading straight out of the jump. It ran into the lasers two seconds after it arrived and was immolated.

"I wonder how long the safety locks are on those bombs?" Miyoshi said.

"We know it's not less than two seconds," Aki answered.

"So far," his admiral reminded him.

There were two more efforts to lob atomic weapons through the jump, both using rockets. These missiles, however, started to evade immediately. They jinked hard, but that had been accounted for in the fire pattern. Each of the lasers was part of a pattern. While half the 22-inch lasers were at full power, several were now doing stutter shots at one-quarter power as they swept the space.

It didn't matter. Both missiles ran into a full power laser beam and basically ceased to exist by the time it had been on the human side of the jump for two seconds.

"Do you think we should put more of our lasers on lower power?" Aki asked. "Those missiles are getting more and more rambunctious."

Admiral Miyoshi shook his head. "Very soon they will risk the cruiser. Very soon."

The admiral was right. A full two minutes after the last atomic had crossed the jump, a cruiser appeared. It was accelerating hard at 4.0 gees. While its velocity was very low, it was jinking radically. Still, it was ripped apart by laser fire, both at full power and reduced. In less than the blink of an eye, it was an expanding cloud of gas. In hardly a breath, it was gone.

Miyoshi eyed the screen. Nothing was there. For five minutes, nothing was there. Finally, the admiral ordered the longboat to halt its mad dash from the jump. It took it forty-five minutes to get back close to the jump. It halted well short of the area around the jump that had been targeted, and launched the periscope probe.

It took another five minutes for the probe to make it to the jump, locate it, and send the visual periscope through. It immediately transmitted a picture that showed no warships within 100,000 kilometers of the jump.

Now the longboat tiptoed up to the jump.

A tiny probe was sent through. It showed that the mine field had been reactivated.

"Shall we take out a few more of their mines?" Aki asked.

Admiral Miyoshi shook his head. "That would be too predictable. No, let us wait sixteen hours, and then send one through. For now, I am hungry, and I think we need to stand down the crews from battle stations. Let us go to Condition Bravo and allow half the watch crew to eat and sleep. In four hours, we can rotate."

"Aye, aye, sir. I will get the order out immediately."

The problem facing Admiral Miyoshi had not changed. The enemy still occupied the other side of the jump. Like him, they had deployed atomic mines to annihilate any ship that ventured through. There were times when the aliens had tried to withdraw from their position at a jump. The humans had waited until the aliens were well beyond their own gun range, then jumped through and cut down every one of them.

This time, the aliens had mined the jump. Even if humans made the jump, they risked being blown to super-heated gases by those mines.

Of course, he had the same deployment on his side. They, of course, had over three hundred ships. If he withdrew from the jump, how long would it take the aliens to know they were gone and risk a few ships to blow the mines?

Miyoshi knew of armies that ordered infantry to walk across any minefields they found, no matter what the cost. A minefield that wasn't under close observation and support fire was a minefield quickly turned.

He was still lost in thought as his orderly brought him supper. He always liked the nutty taste of the watercress salad. The bowl of udon noodles was served with a fish he did not recognize; likely either from the birds or cats' home planet, and mixed seaweed from the last shipment from home. The main course was salmon, likely also from home, well marinated, and with short grain rice with just the precise consistency that his cooks knew he liked.

There were no sweets on his plate. A man of his age could not afford the culinary joys of youth. Being on the point of battle at any moment, he contented himself with green tea.

Satisfied, he retreated to his room for a three-hour nap. He did not allow the worries of the day to delay his sleep, but cleared his mind and fell asleep before he had hardly finished laying down.

In the next watch, he would have to make the hard decision to reduce his fleet to aid Admiral Santiago. The next watch would have plenty of time for that problem to gnaw at him.

27

Grand Admiral Sandy Santiago watched as Admiral Drago's reinforced fleet slipped through the jump on the far side of the solar system. Due to the speed of light delay, his fleet's jump had actually taken place the day before.

It was the problem with the speed of light delay that gnawed at Sandy's gut. It had been a long time since she had heard anything from her two deployed commanders, Admiral Miyoshi's Second Fleet or Admiral Bethea's third. She knew it took time for messages to get out through two or three jumps, still, it would be nice to have some reinforcements herself. She looked at the screen. All that was left of Admiral Nottingham's Sixth fleet were the fourteen battle-cruisers from Earth and the Scandia squadron of Norse gods. The *Odin* and the other eight ships of that squadron were all very experienced veterans. The Earth ships, after a rough start, were working much better.

Still, were they enough?

Problem was, she was far too uninformed for her taste. Her last message from Admiral Miyoshi said he'd arrived at the jump he intended to blockade, and that the aliens were in system but not there yet. Admiral Bethea's latest had her in the second system out and orbiting the nearest planet to the jump. The aliens had just shot into the system and would need several days to cross to the jump.

Battle was likely also several days away.

Admiral Drago was leading his reinforced Fourth Fleet out to intercept a huge force, hopefully at a jump. It would be a while before she knew if he'd succeeded in blocking the jump or had to fall back.

"If I didn't believe it was impossible, I'd say that some SOB managed to coordinate a battle across hundreds of light years of space. I'd say someone managed to get me to divide my forces and was going to defeat me in detail."

My luck can't be that bad. Can it?

Suzie broke the silence. "Admiral, Penny asks if you can meet with her, Jacques, Amanda, and several of their support staff about the final proposal they've gotten from the cats."

"Tell them I'll meet them in my day quarters," Sandy said, and quickly covered the short distance to her quarters.

Her space had been enlarged for the meeting. No doubt, Mimzy had felt free to rearrange Sandy's spaces, she grumbled to herself, then softened.

Everyone knew she was living in flag plot. Of course, Mimzy knew she could work her magic to prepare for the meeting. Sandy settled into the chair at the end of the table away from the door. In a moment, the chair had changed into a massage unit and was working on a few of the million kinks in her back.

"Stop that, Suzie. Those knots are all that's holding me together."

"Yes, Admiral. Sorry, ma'am."

"That's okay, Suzie. I just need about a month of R&R."

Her computer wisely gave Sandy the last word on that. In the few minutes it took Penny and company to come from the banquet hall to her quarters, Sandy found herself nodding off.

I have to get some rest, Sandy scolded herself.

Finally, Penny led the negotiation team into Sandy's quarters. They looked like they'd been run over by a pack of Alwan elephants, but they were all beaming.

"You look happy," Sandy said.

"We are. We think we've got something that will make you a very happy admiral," Penny gushed. "I think your comment to the President and Prime Minister that dumping high tech into an economy needed to be a measured choice, won us a lot of this. Still, there were several countries that wanted all the tech immediately, but the President and the Prime Minister were also worrying with Amanda about that. Even Jacques finally convinced them that sudden changes in technology could lead to some really serious culture shocks. Even religion. Personally, I think the arrival of off-world aliens has already done a whale of a lot to upset their culture and they've seen this."

"So?" Sandy asked. "What have you got?"

"Agreement that all of the new high tech will be limited to Gull Island, well away from any shore. They all agree to examine everything arriving and leaving to make sure our tech is strictly quarantined."

"Personally," Amanda put in, "I think all of them figure that everyone else will be trying to sneak the tech out to themselves. Nobody trusts anybody."

"Then how is this working?" Sandy asked.

"They are only going to produce Smart Metal. We won't have any of the spinners or programmers on the ground.

They feed in the raw materials and produce the stuff, load it aboard longboats, and we lift it up here to the station, then send it along to the moon. Only there will our programmers and spinners actually do something high tech to it."

"They believe that?" Sandy had to ask.

"We offered them a couple two-pound blocks of the stuff, and challenged them to make it into something," Penny said.

That got a laugh from most of the negotiators in the room.

"They brought up their best scientists," Amanda said. "Their best computer types. They even brought up several of the cats that had returned from Alwa. They couldn't so much as make a hammer out of it."

"Then Penny asked Mimzy to make a model airplane out of one block," Jacques took over, earning himself a nasty look from his wife. "Okay. Okay, you keep telling the story."

"No, I think you'll have more fun with this part."

"So, Mimzy turns this one kilo block of metal into an airplane. No one looks too excited about it. Then the propeller starts to spin and a moment later, the thing is taxiing for take-off. Then Penny shows them how a hand-held tablet like they have now could be used to get the plane to circle, fly straight, climb and dive."

"After five minutes of this, President Almar brings the thing in for a landing," Amanda said, taking the story back over. "It taxis to a stop. The prop quits spinning. Penny says a word to Mimzy . . . and the entire plane folds itself back into a solid block. Just like that," she said, snapping her finger.

"You're impressing the natives," Sandy said to her intel officer.

"I guess so, but it got our point across," Penny said,

beaming and not at all bashful for her parlor trick. "You can make the Smart Metal, but unless you're just as smart as the metal, it's just a block of metal."

"So, tell me what the bottom line is?" Sandy asked. She really would like to get a few hours of sleep. Maybe even eight if no word came in from any of the blocking fleets.

"We will divide the present Smart Metal along this line," Amanda said. "A hundred thousand tons will be flown down to Gull Island. We'll program it into a Smart Metal fabrication plant. They will provide all the other support facilities on the island. Housing, roads, water, whatever. All made from local resources."

"Raw material will be delivered from all the major countries by a set schedule," Penny said. "All will establish a bond. If there is any default on their deliveries, the cost of filling their order will be taken from that bond. If anyone continues to fail in their delivery schedule, the cats are united in restricting trade with that country."

Penny shook her head. "This is the first time the cats have done anything like this, coordinating among themselves to resolve conflicts without a fight. They've set up arrangements so the countries can deliver what they have an excess of. They even agreed that if someone is having problems delivering, if they give warning and demonstrate that they have a serious problem, they won't be fined."

"This is revolutionary for the cats," Jacques said. "I think this attack has put some serious fear of the bug-eyed monsters in them."

"What's the agreement look like?" Sandy asked.

"The Status of Forces Agreement is over a hundred thousand words," Penny said. "It goes into a great deal of depth. You'll need to study that in detail, but we've had the fleet's legal team working with us. They see a few places where we will have to walk carefully, but nothing that is a show-stopper."

"The Treaty on Technological Transfer and Production for Mutual Defense," Amanda said, "is even longer. It's over five hundred thousand words. We have some executive summaries for each of the subsections, but it's still a monster."

Sandy surveyed the room. She had never seen so much exhaustion. "Okay, I'm going to make a command decision. I'm tired. You're tired. I bet the cats are tired. I propose that we all get a good meal, a good bath, and a good nights' sleep. Eight hours of sleep. Then, we meet back here in the morning. We need to bring in some people who weren't involved in the negotiations. Hand these monsters over to the Red Team and let them work while you and I are getting some rest and reviewing this with a fine-toothed comb.

"After breakfast, we can meet back here, or in a larger room and start going over what they think you have and what you think you meant to say. Okay?"

There were deep sighs around the room. "Aye, aye, Admiral," Penny said.

Sandy thanked each of the negotiators personally as they left her day quarters. Done, she turned to her own bath. The wall to her night quarters, which had been pushed back to enlarge the day room, now moved forward to reclaim its space, and more. Sandy found a lovely bath already over half-filled.

"Thank you, Suzie."

"You're welcome, Sandy. I've got a float you can rest your head in. You won't drown if you fall asleep."

"That is a very good idea."

Sandy stripped and settled into the luxurious bath with

a contented sigh. A float did appear. She rested her head on it just as the jets began to massage her tense muscles.

She knew she'd ordered everyone to get a solid meal under their belt, but after an hour of floating in the warm soothing water, the best Sandy could do was stumble to her bed. She was asleep the moment her head hit the pillow.

Still, her last thoughts were of her widely scattered forces. What was keeping Admiral Miyoshi? Wasn't it about time for Admiral Bethea to make contact with her foe? Admiral Drago would likely arrive at the jump point he was to blockade.

There was so much going on and so little change she could affect right now.

Content she'd done her duty as best as she saw possible, she slept the sleep of the innocent.

28

"What is our enemy doing?" Admiral Miyoshi mused.

"They have made four cruiser raids, tossing or shooting atomics through the jump before sending one, two, or four cruisers through," Aki, his chief of staff answered, mistaking a rhetorical question for a real one.

"We have made four forays with armed probes to their side. Each gets a more promt response, although they are still much too slow, compared to our way of operating. The last time we sent four probes through in a cluster. They have twenty-seven mines. We have blown up nearly five dozen mines. However, they have replaced every mine we destroyed."

"So, the score is zero to zero," Miyoshi said through a scowl. "This is as bad as a kids' hockey game. A lot of flailing around and chasing after the puck, but nothing is done in the end."

"Yes, Admiral."

"Yet, something is done. We are here and Admiral

Santiago needs some of us back there, with her, guarding
the cats."

"Yes, sir."

Admiral Miyoshi bent over the battle board that filled
the center of his flag plot. In the middle of it was the jump. A
tiny bit of space that some aliens a couple of million years
ago had created. He and his fleet were moored, ship to ship,
180,000 kilometers from it. His own set of atomic weapons
were much closer, where they could convert the space
around the jump into an atomic hell.

So far, they had only fired at some atomic warheads and
minor warships.

On the other side of the jump, a dozen or so light
years away in another system, was the alien fleet. That
force outnumbered him over six to one. They were
centered around over one hundred and sixty huge six or
seven hundred thousand-ton battleships, with ninety
frigates. It was now down to fifty light cruisers guarding
their flank.

But they did nothing, just hovered 100,000 kilometers
back from the jump. Their crews had to have been weight-
less for the last five days. That wasn't adding anything to
their combat efficiency. Miyoshi's own fleet was moored in
fourteen trios and a single pair, with each ship swinging
around a central point. That gave the sailors at least a sense
of down, even with as little as half a gee of gravity.

If the enemy charged the jump, Miyoshi would destroy
each ship with either atomic fire or laser blasts. He'd done it
before. He'd do it again.

Apparently, someone had survived one of those attacks
and had taken the word home that jumps were a lot harder
to force than they had been. Thus, the game of two cats
facing the mouse hole waiting for the other cat to risk

becoming the mouse and jumping into the other's wide-open fangs.

Just as clear as it was that Miyoshi's Second Fleet would annihilate the aliens, so it was just as assured that they would wipe his fleet out if he attempted the jump. Each of the hundred and sixty battleships mounted a hundred or more lasers. The last time we humans had fought them, the lasers could reach out 100,000 kilometers. Just as our ships now mounted 22-inch lasers with a range of 200,000 kilometers, one had to assume that the aliens might have extended the range of their lasers.

They had also deployed atomic mines in the space around the jump.

Miyoshi had no chance of successfully engaging the enemy unless they were fool enough to attack, and they were showing that, at least this bunch, had learned to respect what they insisted on calling vermin.

So why tie up his entire forty-four ships on blockade duty here? Why not send some of his fleet back to Grand Admiral Santiago's reserve?

This raised the question, just how many ships could hold this jump? Would they have to hold it against a few more minor raids, or would the ships that remained here face a serious attack?

Admiral Miyoshi shook his head as he mulled that critical question.

"Admiral Santiago needs ships to replenish her reserve," he muttered to himself. "We do not need a full fleet to take pot shots at light cruisers."

"No, sir. But what if they attempt to force the jump with battleships? Last time, they sent four cruisers through in a cluster. What if they attempt us with four battleships in such a cluster? Or in a larger cluster?" Aki responded with questions his admiral found very much in the center of his own conflicted musings.

"We have the atomics," Miyoshi said. "You and I have both watched as the aliens stormed through a jump and were immolated like moths drawn to a candle's flame. How many battlecruisers do we need to pick off any of their ships that leak through?"

"It depends on the number of leaks."

"The force across from us does not have any of the door knockers," Miyoshi muttered. Most of the alien warships had one or two hundred thousand tons of rock added to their hide, a primitive armor meant to slow down the time it took lasers to burn through into the unprotected inside of a ship. Reactors, lasers, and capacitors tended to explode when hit by hot things like laser beams.

However, the aliens had fielded a larger ship. Door knockers were clearly intended to knock down the door and force a jump. Laser fire took too long to destroy these ships and while the fleet concentrated on them, battleships would have time to make it through the jump and form up into a battle array.

Those million ton monsters, with more rock and fewer reactors, were hard to kill. However, there were none facing him.

Was that evidence of intent? Did the aliens have no intention of sending their fleet through this jump? Was his fleet being tied up by a fleet that was never intended to fight?

"Aki, can we hold the jump with half of our present force?"

"If the attack is just a probe, yes. If they try probing us with a few battleships, yes. If they send the entire fleet at us? Admiral, I do not know. Could they play a game of cat and mouse, attacking, activating our atomic mines? Pausing. Sending more through before we can reset our defense? I just don't know, sir."

"Neither do I, but I can't just sit here while Admiral Santiago wants for ships in her reserve."

"Shall I cut the orders?"

"Yes. Send to Admiral Zingi on the *Mikasa*. I want him to take his task force and return to Sasquan. I will keep my own battle squadron from Musashi, the *Phantom* and her sisters from New Eden, and the Alwan-built *Furious* and its divisions. In total, twenty-two battlecruisers. Zingi will take the rest and return to the cats. I know I'm sending him off with the division from the Esperanto League but I think they've shown themselves to have fight in them. Besides, he gets the Espania division. The *Libertad, Federación Independencia,* and *Union* have shown they fight like ten ships."

"I will have the orders out in a few minutes, sir," and Aki went to make his admiral's order happen.

A few minutes later, Admiral Zingi acknowledged his orders.

"Miyoshi, don't you go having all the fun here while I'm back with those fur balls."

"I hope that neither you nor I get to have any fun."

"You always were the pessimist. I will save a few targets for you."

"Let us pray that none of your targets are among the ships on the other side of this jump."

Admiral Zingi shrugged. "Fat chance of that. You are hogging all of them for yourself. You upstart people of Musashi don't respect your elders."

Both men laughed at that. It was a common joke among both planets' fleets. Musashi had been colonized from

Yamato. The rivalry was usually reserved for football games, bars, and O Clubs.

"I will see you soon," Miyoshi said.

"I will be looking for you," Zingi answered, and the comm line broke between them.

A few minutes later, seven trios broke up and began to form lines by squadrons. The pair also split off. One went with his squadron mates. The other floated for a while, then joined a trio, making it a foursome.

Twenty-two battlecruisers stayed, swinging at their moorings around each other. Twenty-two formed into three squadrons; one of eight, the others reduced to seven so that Admiral Drago's Fourth Fleet could be brought up to the same strength that the others had been.

Admiral Zingi ordered his ships to Condition Charlie and set a brutal 3.5 gee acceleration for the jump across the system that would lead them to Sasquan. A message had been sent toward the distant jump buoy, alerting Admiral Santiago that the force holding off the first enemy thrust was now outnumbered almost fifteen to one, but that the ships she'd asked for were on their way to her.

Admiral Miyoshi leaned back to eye his battle board. He saw nothing, so he elected to go to lunch and, if nothing came up, he'd have time for paperwork and maybe a nap. This stand-off would last for a long time. He needed to stay on alert, but he also needed to be alert.

As Miyoshi made his way to the wardroom, he wondered how things were going with Admiral Bethea. Was she confronted by this same kind of stand-off?

29

Admiral Bethea studied her battle board in flag plot. The board showed no surprises. Still, Bethea did not like the looks of it.

The hostile forces were just jumping into the system at the same time her ships also jumped in. In theory, she could have turned around and gone back, blockading the jump as they had done before. However, that was not in her orders.

The new ships the aliens had . . . call them frigates. Others might call them large or heavy cruisers. That was the problem. What were they?

The mass detectors gave them thirty-five thousand tons. The first human frigates had started at twenty-five thousand tons. United Society battlecruisers weighed in at fifty thousand tons. They still were half the size of a human battleship, but their laser batteries included nearly as many lasers, all with the same firepower as those on the big battlewagons.

Where did a twenty-five-thousand-ton warship fit into an enemy battle array that had half million to one million ton battleships at one end and cruisers of fifteen thousand tons at the other?

Admiral Santiago needed to know, and the only way to find out was to fight them.

Betsy's job was to fight them, measure their worth, annihilate them, and avoid being banged up too badly. The aliens had lost half a trillion people and seemed to have shrugged it off. The humans did not have the spare sailors on Alwa Station to swap even ten enemy ships for one battlecruiser.

Thus, Betsy Bethea mulled her problem. Just shy of one hundred and eighty of the frigates, and an equal number of cruisers were streaking toward the jump that led through one more system and then would enter the cats' home planet. They had covered half the distance to that gate at close to 2.5 gees acceleration and were now decelerating toward it.

Betsy's Third Fleet orbited an ice giant not too far from the aliens' course. They had taken that time to refuel and collect a lot of ice, which had a heavier reaction mass than hydrogen. In two more orbits, her forty-four ships would break out of orbit and steer a course to cross the aliens' path. There, a battle would take place.

Betsy expected to win. Her battlecruisers carried 22-inch lasers and were protected by crystal armor, a hull coating that slowed down laser beams, spreading out the energy of a hit through the crystal cladding and radiating it back out to space. However, her ships were still at risk. Too many hits, and the crystal would begin to break down. Too much heat, and the Smart Metal™ hull beneath the crystal also began to crumble.

Good ships had been burned by masses of alien lasers. Admiral Bethea's job was to see that her ships stayed out of the range of those alien lasers. United Society could damage ships at 200,000 kilometers. So far, most of the alien lasers were good to 100,000 kilometers, although some had begun to reach farther.

How far could the lasers on these new ships reach? No one knew. It was Betsy's job to find out without it costing too many human, bird, or cat lives.

As the enemy approached over the last few days, her captains had drilled her crews, finished the last bit of maintenance, dialed the weapons in tight, optimized the ranging sensors, the fire computers, and weapon controls. Each ship was as deadly as its crew could make it.

Now Bethea ordered a stand-down so they could get a shower and hot meal before going into their high gee eggs. Her fleet would approach the enemy fleet at 3.0 gees, maybe more. From now on, food would be the mush in the eggs' tubes. Water would be from a tube. Sleep would be about all the crew could do, if you didn't mind sleeping with twice your own weight resting on top of your chest.

Then, of course, would come the terror of battle.

Admiral Bethea ordered the fleet to Condition Baker, tighter than the love boat configuration they currently had, but it was still loose enough so the hull could handle 3.0 gees. She would shrink the ships down as they approached the enemy. With luck, that would keep the enemy in the dark as to the fighting size of her ships.

For much of a day, she accelerated and then bled off her velocity. Her course was not aimed for the jump, but to bring her across the alien fleet's course three hours before they reached the jump. At that point, ships would be slow enough to evade, but not so slow that it didn't move enough to actually get out of the way of incoming lasers. It was a delicate calculation.

She would likely be the one to close with the enemy fleet. Her estimates allowed that the enemy might try to wear away from her, perhaps even veer as far off course for the jump as they could allow themselves to go. That might delay the fight.

They might also charge her. Indeed, she expected some of them to try doing just that. The only issue would be how large of a force headed for her and how many kept going for the jump.

She needed to get her fleet through the jump. Admiral Santiago wanted reinforcements in case Admiral Drago had to fall back from his own battle. She would do her best to do it. Still, if it saved her ships, she'd miss the jump and circle back. That would take a lot of time and reaction mass. Still, it was better than being blown to bits.

As they began their approach, both fleets were braking toward the jump. Both were still traveling at several hundred thousand kilometers an hour. If they didn't do some serious braking, they'd jump too far and be out of the battle.

Betsy had set herself up to be a bit closer to the jump so she'd be firing up the engines of the alien ships. You couldn't put much granite or basalt over rocket engines spewing thermonuclear plasma. So far, the battle was going exactly the way she'd expected it. She was still 300,000 kilometers from the aliens. In another 100,000 kilometers, she could open fire.

She made her final battle preparations. The fleet shrank down to battle trim, Condition Zed. Except for the huge rocket motors on their vulnerable sterns, the much smaller hulls were now totally protected with 100 millimeters of crystal armor cladding. The outer hulls began to rotate, quickly getting up to sixty revolutions a minute. Any laser hits the battlecruisers took would not only be absorbed into the crystal, but the hull beneath the hit would be spun away, bringing fresh crystal to take the hit and distributing the heat further away from the point of entry, saving the ship and crew.

Admiral Bethea's fleet was ready for combat.

Then the aliens changed things.

30

"**R**ange is 250,000 kilometers to the enemy fleet," Sensors reported.

"All weapons manned, ready, and fully charged," Guns on her staff reported.

"All reactors are in the green," the fleet engineer reported.

Her fleet could not be more combat ready.

"Angle on the alien fleet is changing," Sensors reported.

"How so?" Admiral Bethea snapped.

"They are bearing the ship away from us by 15 degrees."

Betsy studied the vectors on the two fleets. Her ships had been sailing a divided vector. Her rocket engines were not aimed straight toward the jump, but angled off so that she was also closing the enemy fleet. Since they'd jumped into the system, the aliens had followed only one vector: toward the jump. Now, they were taking on the same angle as her fleet. They were still braking for the jump, but now they were using part of the power vector to bear them away from her fleet just as fast as she was trying to close them.

"Since when do those bastards run away?" her chief of staff, S'Bun said softly from where his egg sat next to hers.

"I guess since now," Betsy answered.

"Enemy has increased deceleration to 2.7 gees," Sensors added.

"They've been holding at 2.5 gees since entering the system," Captain S'Bun pointed out. "Now, with the extra power, they will have a solid braking vector while dodging away as well."

"And they haven't been overheating their reactors and rocket motors," Betsy said. That was something the aliens had problems with. Usually, by now, a few of their ships would have had to reduce their gees. Others would have blown up from reactor failure.

Not this batch of ships.

"Battle board, recalculate our course projections," Admiral Bethea ordered her fighting computer.

"Now, we'll both miss the jump; miss it by quite a bit," S'Bun pointed out, once the new projection for their courses appeared on the board.

"So, we try some 'what ifs.' Battle Board, assume that they will adjust course and go to three to 3.5 gees. Show me the courses that they can use to make the jump."

Now the enemy's course went from a single line to a large volume of possibilities, depending on how soon they chose to break off the evasion and/or how hard they chose to brake.

"It didn't matter," S'Bun said, "the Third Fleet would intercept them before they have to adjust their course and power settings."

"Nav. Steer fifteen degrees closer to the enemy. Advise fleet of course and deceleration," Betsy ordered. The fight would start when she wanted it and not a moment later.

Time passed. Her ships inexorably closed on the aliens. The aliens could not run away from the fate Admiral Bethea intended for them.

Sensors reported "Enemy at 200,000 kilometers."

Betsy ordered her ships to concentrate their fire on the frigates.

Then the bug-eyed monsters changed everything again.

31

"Enemy fleet has changed course. Most of it is closing rapidly."

Sandy spotted all of the problems in one split second. Most of the enemy ships were now pointed almost straight at her. The frigates formed themselves into six dishes, most of them thirty strong. One maintained its course for the jump. The other five formed themselves into a cross. A central formation with one dish on each flank: right, left, top, bottom.

There were also six dishes of cruisers. Four filled in the quadrants around the frigates. Two swung wide, imposing themselves between Betsy's fleet and the thirty that were now still edging away from her, but striking out for the jump.

Her battle board flashed data showing that the charging ships had would be 150,000 kilometers away in 17.15 minutes. Even as she watched, the enemy force spread themselves out and each ship threw itself into some sort of evasion program. It wasn't much, but it was enough for her to hold the shoot until the fire control computers could evaluate it.

"Sensors, talk to me about the group that isn't closing on us."

"Ah, Admiral, I make thirty of the frigates. One dish. Everything else is headed straight for us."

Her battle board caught up with the sensor reports. Now there was one clump of thirty ships still decelerating toward the jump. Every other enemy ship was doing its best to close the range as fast as they could.

"I suspect they're only presenting their bows to us," her chief of staff said.

"Even a frigate has bow armor to absorb meteorites," Admiral Bethea added.

"Do you think these ships were constructed precisely for this maneuver, ma'am?" S'Bun asked. It likely wasn't really a question.

"Considering all the construction each of those base ships at System X spat out before the fight, I'd say yes. If this task force wasn't designed specifically to get into this fight, their Enlightened Ones are dumber than we take them for."

Admiral Bethea had expected a nice two- or three-hour turkey shoot as they slowly closed the range from 200,000 kilometers to approximately 150,000 kilometers. It was anybody's guess what the range was on these new ships' lasers.

Now that time was cut by less than seventeen minutes. Even that was quickly vanishing and she'd have a lot smaller targets to shoot at.

"Change course, thirty degrees away from the enemy. Go to 3.2 gees," Admiral Bethea ordered. "Navigator, get me a course that lets us dodge away from that charge as much as we can and still make the jump."

"Aye, aye, ma'am. Give me a minute."

"Take your time. Make sure its accurate."

"Guns, have you got a new set of fire solutions?" Bethea asked.

"In three, two, one, we're ready."

"Fleet. Cease acceleration," Bethea ordered. "Rotate ship to target enemy."

All along the six squadron lines of seven or eight ships, stacked one on top of the other in loose formation, the ships cut their deceleration and spun their bows around to present their forward batteries to the enemy."

"Volley fire. Fire."

Forty-four human battlecruisers let loose with the twelve 22-inch lasers in two rows across their bows. They aimed a carefully calculated salvo for the area around the mildly gyrating alien frigates. The computer forecast was that at least one of those lasers should connect with every one of those ships.

Six seconds later, the lasers had exhausted their capacitors and fell silent. Bethea's fleet resumed its base course, and went back to a 3.2 gee deceleration that would take it to the jump.

Across death's ground, only two enemy ships were expanding balls of gas. A few more might be wavering a bit, but they all stayed the line.

Betsy frowned; those were not the results she'd expected. Yes, the range was the maximum effective, 200,000 kilometers. And yes, the enemy was presenting itself bow-on, say a circle with a diameter of 40 or 50y meters. Maybe more, maybe less. Still, even with the dodging, Betsy had expected to do more damage. Somehow, the alien captains had managed to escape the pattern of fire aimed for them.

Betsy waited for her ships to steady on their base course. Rather than commit to the hard maneuvering it would take to bring their aft battery to bear, a maneuver that would let the enemy close the distance while she drifted, she chose to hold her fire and wait.

She wanted to see if the aliens would soften their evasion pattern.

No. If anything, the evasion was now even more energetic.

"The bastards can learn," S'Bun muttered.

"Yes, they can," Betsy agreed. "But so can we. Guns, order the fleet to stutter fire. One second bursts."

"Aye, aye, ma'am."

Kris Longknife had first come up with that in gunnery practice. Now the process Nelly created was in every ship's own gunnery computer.

"The cruisers are going to 3.2 gee acceleration," Sensors reported.

"If they're trying to make a quick run in to launch missiles," the chief of staff said, "they're in for a long approach."

Betsy nodded. "We'll concentrate on the frigates for now. We can get the cruisers later."

It was now time for the next volley. This time, each laser would fire for one second, then adjust its point of aim and fire another one second burst. That would increase the odds of getting a hit, though it would decrease the amount of damage any hit did.

"These new ships are fast. Let's see how well-protected they are," Betsy muttered.

"This ought to be fun," S'Bun answered. Locked into the high gee stations and being under 3.2 gees deceleration tended to limit nods and shrugs. Sailors had learned to talk more.

Isn't it delightful what men will learn if they have to? Betsy thought, reflecting on how taciturn the men around her had been in the early days of her career.

The ships again went through the maneuver of cutting power, swinging their bows around to point at the onrushing enemy, and firing. This time, the six seconds of firing took ten seconds as each one-second burst was shot at an ever-so-slightly different point in space.

The battlecruisers immediately returned to their base course and deceleration as the sensors reached out and tallied up the price the enemy had paid.

Three of the frigates had vanished into dust. Two more appeared to have suffered some damage, but only one slowed its charge, visibly distressed.

Worse, the enemy had measured the amount of time it took Bethea's ships to reload and were ready to dance to her tune. As soon as the fire ceased, they went to a slower evasion plan, allowing the alien crew some respite from the brutal jinking while the humans reloaded. No doubt, they'd jack up the evasions again just before the time came for the next salvo.

This left Betsy with a challenge. Did she adjust the tempo of her salvo and delay the next salvo for a few extra seconds? She shook her head. She could not afford even a few extra seconds between salvos. She needed to kill ships. She'd just have to let herself become predictable and allow them some respite from evasion.

"Nav here, Admiral," interrupted her thoughts. "The course we're on is the optimum one for keeping the enemy at arms' reach while still aiming for the jump."

"Thank you, Nav."

It was time for another salvo. This time, they destroyed four frigates. Another three ships showed distress, though none fell out of the line. The one-second laser blasts seemed quite capable of destroying a ship, but only sometimes, say if it hit a reactor or laser capacitor. Either that or the aliens had somehow figured out a way to more heavily armor their ships than Betsy would have thought possible for a twenty-five-thousand-ton warship.

Admiral Bethea studied her battle board. "Sensors, talk to me about the space around those ships. Are we getting any evidence of stone ablating off of a defensive shield?"

"I'm sorry, Admiral. They are closing us. Whatever vents off the ships is quickly left behind. I'll try to get a quick read from the next ship targeted by the *Lion*, ma'am. It's hard in the glare of a hit to do a mass spec analysis on the light."

"Do your best," Betsy said.

Again, the forward batteries were reloaded. Admiral Bethea did not wait before she ordered her fleet to fire.

Ten seconds later, six one-second blasts shot out from the twelve lasers in each battlecruiser's bow. Across the battle, they only got three frigates. Another three showed some sign of damage, but not enough to fall out of the line.

"The aliens have the nose of their ships coated with basalt," Sensors reported. "The *Lion* appeared to make a glancing hit. Ablated gases show calcium, aluminum, silicon, and oxygen in the right proportions for basalt."

"I suspect they have only armored their bows," S'Bun said. "They couldn't carry a lot of basalt and be as fast on their feet as they are."

"And we're only destroying a ship when we get enough of a hit on one of its gun ports to reach in and blow up the capacitors."

"Assuming none of the ships have closed gun ports," her chief of staff said, pointing out a possibility.

"That could be why we're not blowing up as many ships as I expected."

"I think we also need to consider what our chances are of getting a hit," S'Bun said. "Guns, how tight is our stutter fire? At 200,000 kilometers, just how close is one laser bolt to the next?"

Guns had to study her own board for a long minute. "We've got them locked in tight, sir," she answered. "Still, we can only adjust the fire so tightly ourselves. At 200,000 klicks, it's likely there's a quarter kilometer between each burst."

"Thank you, guns," S'Bun said. "The math is against us, Admiral. Our burst is going to hit somewhere within a space of 250,000 square meters. A ship with a bow silhouette of, say 50 meters across, presents a target of a bit less than two thousand square meters. Admiral, just obeying the law of averages, we've got about one chance in a hundred and twenty-five of hitting something, and that's before we throw in how hard they're evading and the time it takes us to set up a fire solution and fire."

Admiral Bethea counted the damage. In a bit less than two minutes, she'd only bagged eleven of the frigates. At this rate, it would likely take her close to half an hour to destroy all the big war wagons. Her battle board now predicted they'd be in range in approximately twenty minutes.

Admiral Bethea had to up her game.

"Comm, send to fleet. 'Division Commanders. Select a target for your division. Establish a fire pattern for your division with the highest probability of destroying that one ship.' Bethea sends."

The next volley, the twelve divisions aimed all three or

four of its battlecruisers at a single enemy frigate they had
marked for death.

Eight alien warships died.

The next salvo got six. Things were looking up.

Then the aliens changed things again.

32

The cruisers that they had been ignoring had meanwhile begun to spread out. Some turned right or left, others went up or down. Some zigged from top right to bottom left.

Admiral Bethea didn't spot the movement so much as she noticed when the concentration of light cruisers began to spread out and disappear from her board.

"Sensors, what are those light cruisers up to?"

A second development was also becoming clear. Now that this strike force was concentrating all its acceleration on charging Betsy's guns, little or no part of their vector was being used to slow them toward the jump. They were now passing from right to left in Betsy's course.

Before too long, they'd be between her and the jump. When they finally got in a position to fire, assuming enough of them were still in one piece, they would be firing up the humans' vulnerable sterns, right at their unprotected reactors.

This rapidly developing battle was starting to look like the odds were not on Betsy's side.

Then the cruisers began spiking their exhaust with aluminum, iron, and other waste metals as well as shooting the stuff off in all directions.

The entire flag plot knew it immediately when Sensors recognized the problem. The shout of "What the hell!" broke the usual cool quiet of the room.

"A problem, Commander?" Betsy said, dryly.

"I'm afraid so, Admiral. Those cruisers we've been wondering about? They've gone to 4.0 gees and are laying down some kind of chaff or debris screen. I'm having a hard time taking a reading off of the main body of frigates. If I can't take a reading, the fire control sensors won't be able to either."

Betsy and S'Bun watched developments for a few minutes, during which thirteen frigates were blown to bits. However, other frigates disappeared behind a thin but effective fog. With fewer enemy ships visible, the fleet concentrated its fire on the dwindling number of targets it had.

Two salvos later, eleven alien warships were destroyed. A minute later, twelve more large enemy warships were vaporized.

However, the number of targets were drying up fast. The enemy fleet was concentrating into a tighter mass. They'd never been as spread out at Betsy's ships; their evasion plans required less space. Now they were getting quite cozy as they slipped behind the screen the light cruisers were creating with their exhaust. More importantly, some of the light cruisers were falling back into the expanding cloud and vanishing themselves. The cloud did continue to thicken up, likely because of what those ships were doing.

The cruisers in front were now zigging and zagging, using their 4.0 gees of acceleration to cover both the front of the cloud and to advance it.

"Sensors? That cloud. What acceleration is it advancing?" Betsy asked.

"A lot faster than it needs to if the fleet behind it is still doing 2.5 gees for our throat, ma'am. Give me a minute. That cloud is squirrelly."

"Take your time," Betsy said, reinforcing the calm of her flag plot.

"While we're waiting for that, maybe we should shoot ourselves a few cruisers," S'Bun suggested.

"Sounds like a good idea. Guns, we're offering a special on cruisers. One time only. No limit."

"Yes, ma'am."

That was easier said than done. The light cruisers' acceleration was right up there at around 4.0 gees, each one was a bit different. They also were dodging more nimbly to the right or left, up or down. The first salvo saw the human fleet get only four hits, apparently missing the rest. The next volley was no better.

Worse, when the aliens lost one, a replacement would accelerate out of the cloud and begin to extend the fog closer to the humans.

"Someone spent some serious brain sweat thinking this battle plan up," her chief of staff said.

"Ah, ain't it wonderful when the little darlin's show that they've learned what you've been teachin' 'em," Betsy said, drolly.

"I'd sooner they stayed dumb for a few more battles."

"Me too. Okay, concentrate by divisions. However, now we go down to a quarter power and keep the lasers on while we swerve them around the cruisers."

"Aye, aye, ma'am."

The next salvo took out eleven of the cruisers it targeted.

However, the fleet coasted for almost forty seconds as it emptied its lasers at one quarter power.

Still, it left only five of the cruisers making smoke.

Twenty seconds later, the forward batteries were reloaded. However, the aliens had used the time, too. Eleven light cruisers had shot out of the screen and were adding to it. This time, ten of the smoking cruisers crumpled or exploded as 22-inch lasers cut into them.

Bethea chose to make a change, too. She put power back on her fleet, then flipped her ships to bring her rear laser battery to bear and took out the remaining six cruisers as well as two that had jumped out of the smoke screen.

"Let's add a bit of vector away from them," Betsy muttered to herself, then added. "Nav, how long can I stay on this course before I can't make the jump?"

"About two more minutes, ma'am."

"S'Bun, I don't think we're going to make that jump."

"Doesn't look like it, ma'am."

"I don't think any of the ships facing us are going to make it either."

"Looks that way to me."

"Okay. New battle. We keep our distance and we kill them," Betsy said.

"That looks like a plan to me."

Then the aliens moved the goal post.

33

"The two dishes of cruisers not with the battle array have upped their deceleration to 4.0 gees and are making for the jump," Sensors reported.

The sixty cruisers that had stationed themselves out on the flank, between the larger force attacking Betsy's ships and the smaller one making for the jump, were now clearly headed for the jump.

Just as Admiral Bethea had conceded that she couldn't stop the aliens from making the jump, they increased those forces to ninety.

"Navigator, send a course to the fleet that has us reaching hard for the jump.

"We'll need to go to 4.2 gees."

"Do it."

"New course is sent."

A moment later, Bethea's flag jacked up the deceleration to over four times her weight. The high gee station groaned, but it absorbed the strain and kept Betsy, and everyone else in her fleet, from being squashed like a gnat.

The battle board, however, had bad news. If they held this course for three minutes, the aliens would cross the 150,000 kilometer mark.

"Guns, new fire plan. Establish and order fire by divisions. Every time one of those cruisers tries to extend the screen, have a division nail it. Forward batteries first. If we exhaust all of them, use aft batteries."

"Aye, aye, ma'am." There was a pause while guns used her board to work out the solution. "Got it. Sent."

On Betsy's board, three light cruisers were doing their level best to extend the screen. In ten seconds, all three died as three divisions engaged them. The loose array of Betsy's ships made it easy for one division to pull out of the line, cease deceleration, fire for as long as it took to get the target, then snap back to the base course.

Over the next two minutes, fifty-seven cruisers tried to advance the screen and every single one of them died before they'd been out for more than a couple of seconds.

"How many more of those cruisers do they have?" Sandy asked her board.

"No more than thirty," her computer answered.

In the next sixty seconds, those thirty ships shot out from the screen, gyrating wildly and spewing smoke. They came in two waves of fifteen. Admiral Bethea had to decelerate her entire fleet to bag them. However, even as those died, the second group of fifteen shot out right behind them.

Bethea eyed her course. She could not let her ships drift much more if she wanted to intercept the ships making for the jump. If the high gees would have allowed, she would have been biting her nails as she let her battlecruisers decelerate while the alien cruisers spewed all sorts of reflectors and heat generators into space.

Batteries recharged, Betsy put the fleet through a firing

sequence. In seven seconds, the last of the alien's cruisers were dust, gas, or tumbling hulks.

Admiral Bethea ordered her ships back to their base course. They were at the very limit of space that would allow her to make the jump.

She was also at an estimated 150,000 klicks from the enemy fleet.

The screen formed a wall, behind which Betsy could see nothing.

Then the enemy frigates shot out from behind the screen, and Betsy found out just how good the lasers were that they carried.

Betsy then found the answer to one of her earlier questions. The new ships did have new lasers. Lasers that were good out to 150,000 kilometers.

34

Five dishes came out of the fog. They had been hit hard, but they could still muster fourteen or fifteen ships each, and each dish picked a human battle-cruiser and concentrated their fire on it.

It was then that Betsy was slapped in the face with the mistake she'd made.

She'd been working so hard on snapping up the cruisers that she'd let her fleet drop all evasion. Her ships were on a solid course.

The aliens took advantage of her mistake.

Five of her battlecruisers took hits, heated up, glowed brighter and brighter, then exploded. In hardly the blink of an eye, the *Enterprise, Jaguar, Vampire, Loki,* and *Opal* were gone.

"Evasion Plan 6," Admiral Bethea ordered.

"Evasion Plan 6 sent," Comm repeated.

Immediately, the *Lion* began to throw herself into a brutal jinking that slammed Betsy's head first against the right side of her egg, then the left, while the heavy hand of high gravity went up and down as the *Lion* varied its deceleration.

"Prepare to engage the enemy by divisions. Set lasers for one half power. Continual fire," Admiral Bethea snapped. "Stop deceleration. Aim. Volley fire."

Betsy went from horribly oppressed by her weight, to weighing nothing. Her ship swung around, and for fifteen seconds, she weighed nothing. The seat belt was the only thing holding her in place inside the egg, which was a good thing.

Without warning, she was suddenly thrust back to over four times her weight.

Her battle screen showed the enemy was minus nine more frigates, with one struggling to maintain its course.

However, no sooner were her ships back on their base course, then the alien fleet did its own flip to bring their aft batteries to bear. This time they concentrated on only two battlecruisers. The *Canberra* and the *Temptress* took hits this time. Both held out through the salvo and seemed to be handling their damage, then the *Canberra*, followed a few seconds later by the *Temptress*, lost their battle. The heat worked its way through the hull and something critical failed. Both vanished in clouds of roiling gases.

"What type of lasers do these bastards have?" Bethea muttered, then ordered her ships to cut power, flip and bring their aft batteries to bear.

Ten seconds later, the aliens lost another six ships. They were back to having their armored bows facing the incoming fire. They had recharged their forward lasers.

Even as Betsy's ships slammed back into their deceleration, the hostile lasers cut into them while they were still vulnerable.

Resolute, Banshee, Cobra, and *Sapphire* were the targets

this time. *Banshee* and *Cobra* vanished under the heat. *Resolute* held on for a second after the lasers ceased, but then imploded. *Sapphire* glowed like her namesake. It seemed that she might dissipate the cruel heat that she wore like a coat, but in the end, she lost the fight. She didn't explode so much as come apart in space. Several escape pods were seen to launch out, but the heat boiling off the armor turned them into cinders.

A quick glance at her battle board told Admiral Bethea all she needed to know. Even at 4.5 gees, a brutal deceleration that the battlecruiser force had never risked, she could not make the jump.

The enemy had not only managed to kill more battlecruisers than they ever had, but they'd won the jump. A vicious force was headed for the cats, and Bethea's ships couldn't stop them.

She *could* kill what she faced here.

She ordered her ships to flip, and then flip again as they emptied both ends of the battlecruisers at the enemy.

The aliens lost another nineteen ships in the next forty seconds. They were down to fifty-nine frigates.

However, they nailed the *Baldar, Te Mana,* and *Triumph.*

The fight was brutal and not going at all like other battles Betsy had been in. To fire, the ships had to come out of their evasion plans. They were taking fifteen seconds to sweep the area for an alien frigate and often finding one.

Still, before they could get back into deceleration and evasion, the aliens were reloaded and ready to hit them with their own fire. They were trading ships at a cruel rate. The aliens had lost ninety of these new frigates as well as one hundred and twenty of the light cruisers. Still, they'd managed to destroy twelve battlecruisers. And not just the ships. There were no beacons sounding from survival pods.

The crews were gone as well as the ships.

The slaughter continued through another salvo from both fleets. Sixteen of the alien ships burned and blew. The *Santee* and *Diamond* were targets this time, and both were overcome by the combined fire from the alien force.

Over the next minute, the aliens lost twelve. They burned both the *Thor* and the *Kikukei*. However, only the *Thor* was lost.

Admiral Bethea's fleet was firing by divisions and flipping back to deceleration just as soon as their target was no more. That put them back under power and evading when the aliens got their lasers recharged.

The aliens were reduced to a scattered force that barely amounted to a single dish. Still, they kept themselves aimed straight at Bethea's ships.

Another minute, and Bethea had lost the *Fury*. The *Tiger* was scorched but cooling. The aliens were down to only eighteen ships.

There next salvos only heated up the *Voodoo*. Over the next two minutes, Betsy lost no more ships and the enemy force was wiped out. Unfortunately, even the few alien ships that had been left as rolling hulks managed to blow themselves up in the last moments of the battle.

Whatever lasers the enemy was using would remain a mystery.

"Navigator, can we make that jump?"

"Only if we go to 4.5 gees deceleration, ma'am."

"Engineering, talk to me."

"I can't recommend holding 4.2 gees for more than a quarter hour. I'd hope we could take some heat off of the reactors, Admiral. We're heating up everything we've got. Several ships are almost in the red."

"Thank you," Admiral Bethea said. For a long moment, she considered her options.

During that time, two of the cruisers that were reaching for the jump, and pushing themselves to decelerate at 4.0 gees, failed catastrophically. Where they had been only a second before, there was now a cloud of hot gas, expanding and cooling as she watched.

Admiral Bethea had suffered heavier casualties than what Admiral Kitano's entire battle fleet had suffered in its fight at System X. Clearly, the enemy had come up with a game-changer of their own.

"Comm, send to Admiral Santiago. 'I have engaged the enemy. I have destroyed one hundred and forty-nine frigates and one hundred and twenty light cruisers at a cost of sixteen battlecruisers. They have a new laser that is good to 150,000 kilometers. Their cruisers are also good to 4.0 gees. Frigates can accelerate at something close to 3.0 gees and appear to have basalt cladding on their bows. Advise Admiral Drago of new and improved threat. I have not stopped thirty frigates and fifty-eight cruisers. They are headed your way. Admiral Bethea sends.' Get that off immediately. Let's get that through the jump buoy before the alien ships heading for the jump can blast it out of space."

"On its way, ma'am."

Betsy had done her duty. It had been a stern duty, but she'd stopped most of the alien thrust and gathered needed intelligence on this new threat. Hopefully, it would help Admiral Drago against what he faced.

"Comm, send to fleet, cut deceleration to 2.5 gees. Nav, give me a course that will bring us back around to the jump."

"Yes, ma'am."

Betsy leaned back in her egg. Slowly she let the tension

that had turned her body into a tightly wound spring relax. Her mind spun over what she'd just experienced.

The enemy had fought too damn well. It was clear they were learning. The longer a war went, the longer a loser had to learn their lessons. The worse it got for the winner if they didn't stay ahead of their game.

"Comm, take a back-up of my battle board. Ship it off to Admiral Santiago with my respect and a note, 'The enemy is learning new tricks. We need to dig some new ones out of our own bag of tricks'."

It took a few minutes, but the Comm officer quickly reported. "Full battle report sent."

Having done all she could do, Betsy gave herself over to her egg and let it massage the knots out of her body. She'd done her best. She'd lost sixteen ships with three hundred men, women, birds, and cats on each of them. She'd suffered the worst casualties of any command since the aliens had almost wiped out the fleet Kris Longknife deployed to destroy the first mother ship she came upon.

She'd done the best she could. She'd have to do better next time.

35

Grand Admiral Santiago read the initial battle report from Admiral Bethea. "Sixteen battle-cruisers lost!"

Still, Sandy did her best to suppress her reaction to that news.

How had the enemy managed to destroy over a third of Bethea's fleet?

That would likely come in a later report. Right now, Sandy had an incoming attack that had slipped by Betsy's fleet.

"Captain Velder, order Admiral Nottingham to move his remaining squadrons out to Jump Point Beta and prepare to engage the incoming light units."

"Aye, aye, ma'am," the chief of staff said. He'd taken the initial battle report from the comm duty runner. He'd only glanced at it as he walked from the door to Sandy's desk. The way his face blanched had given Sandy a bit of a warning that the news was bad.

Had Bethea mishandled the fight, or had the aliens learned a lesson after having their hide beat like a drum for so long? Bethea had been out here from the start. She'd fought through just about every battle they'd had here. Sandy would bet her pension that Betsy did not make a mistake.

That made the situation even worse.

"I have the log of Admiral Bethea's battle board," Suzie advised Sandy. "I have also alerted Penny, Amanda, Jacques, as well as Captain Ashigara to meet with you."

"Tell them to get here as fast as they can," Sandy said. "Meanwhile, run me through this battle as quickly as you can."

Before the others arrived, Sandy and Velder had followed Betsy's battle as it flowed across space. She knew the surprises the aliens had come up with.

She did not like them.

When her team arrived, Sandy had Mimzy put the battle up on one wall of her day quarters. They started just before the enemy turned toward Betsy's fleet,

"That's no surprise," Penny said. "They often send a suicide force, though this is the first time they sent most of their force."

"Keep watching."

They watched as she went to stutter shots, then cut the power in half.

"She's still killing these ships," Velder noted.

Then the cruisers cut across the front of the line and started laying down a screen.

"I didn't see that coming," Penny said.

They watched as Betsy lost time swatting at the smaller cruisers. Penny remarked in surprise at the cruisers' four gee acceleration.

"I wonder how long they could hold that acceleration before they blew a reactor?" Penny asked no one.

"Yeah," Sandy agreed.

"Is she still trying to reach for the jump?" Ashigara asked.

"Yes," Sandy said. "She's got her potential course along the bottom of the board. She knows she doesn't have much leeway left."

Then frigates charged out of the screen making 3.2 knots.

"That's more than we've seen anything but their light cruisers make," Penny pointed out.

"And now the cruisers are making 4.0 gees." Velder reminded them.

"They're concentrating all their fire on just a few ships," Ashigara noted.

"And they're catching us while we're still under no acceleration from firing a salvo," Sandy pointed out.

"It's one thing to drift for six seconds; it's something else to be out of acceleration for fifteen to twenty seconds," Velder pointed out.

"They're thin-skinned, but hard to catch with a laser," Sandy said.

"It's a new kind of battle," Penny said.

"Yes. Velder, get a copy of this off to Admirals Miyoshi and Drago. Advise them to expect trouble if they try the meeting engagement on the approach to a jump. It still looks like we can run away from them and shoot them down as we lead them."

"I see a problem with those light cruisers," Velder said. "If we hold at, say, 2.5 gees so we can shoot up the battleships, cruisers and frigates can close on us at 3.0 or even 4.0 gees. We didn't see how strong the light cruiser's lasers were, did we?"

"No, they died before they got within 150,000 klicks," Penny answered.

"So the range of their weapons is still unknown," Sandy said. "Any more thoughts?"

"I'd recommend that if the aliens manage to force Admiral Drago's jump, that he fall back using a parting Parthian shot," the chief of staff said. "Keep the aliens at arms' length and shoot them down as they chase you."

"That may be easier said than done," Penny pointed out. "Say the battleships hold at a sedate and safe 2.2 gees. They're the ones we want to kill. The cruisers can jack up their speed to 3.0 or even 4.0 gees. Maybe the frigates are slower, but they'll still be faster than the battlewagons. The alien fast-movers will outflank your Parthian shooters."

"Then we just back off and kill the fast-movers," Velder said. "After we get rid of them, we slow and let the battlewagons catch up, then clobber them."

"That seems like a plan," Sandy said. "Van, get a copy of this meeting off after the copy of the battle report we sent out. Tell everyone we recommend holding any jump we can, and give ground slowly where we can't. It's clear we have to stay out of their range. The lasers they have now can do too much damage to battlecruisers when they concentrate thirty of them against one of us."

"I can have it on the way immediately," Mimzy said.

"Do so under my signature," Sandy said.

"Now, I've sent Admiral Nottingham over to Jump Point Beta. I can't think of anything more to do. Twenty-two of our ships should be able to hold a jump against thirty frigates and twice that number of light cruisers."

"The reinforcements from Admiral Miyoshi have just jumped into the system," Mimzy told those around the table.

"Van, get them down here. I want to start rebuilding a reserve. I don't like *Victory* being the sum total of my hold cards."

"Immediately, ma'am."

"One question, Admiral," Jacques said.

"Yes?"

"Do we want to let the cats know that we've won a hard-fought battle?"

"Do we want them to know that we lost sixteen ships?" Sandy said, redefining the question.

"My reading of the cats is that winning is everything to them. To die in battle is a great honor," Jacques noted.

"Is it really?" Amanda asked. "I know what's in the literature and media. Still, I'd like to have a sit down with a mother, father, or husband before I accept that they're all for guts, glory, and victory."

"Penny?" Sandy asked.

"We're fighting for them, ma'am. We're fighting outnumbered. Fighting when anyone else would have packed it in and gone home. I think they have a right to know what it's costing us. Besides, some of those lost ships had cats on them. Shouldn't we ask the cats to help us notify next of kin? I think most of the cats they sent to us are young. There must be some folks that are worried."

"Penny, let the cat leaders know there has been a fight and that while we won, we suffered the worst casualties we've had since we started fighting these monsters. You can take Amanda and Jacques with you. I want each of you to give me your thoughts on how this goes. Okay?"

"Understood, Admiral."

The meeting was clearly over. The others left Sandy's day quarters to her. She sat at the head of the table, staring at the bulkhead. It still showed the final phase of the battle.

A list of sixteen lost ships ran down the side of Betsy's battle board.

Without asking permission, Suzie turned the chair into a more comfortable one. It began to massage Sandy's back.

"The butcher's bill is just part of the price of putting on the uniform," Sandy said to herself. "Still, during the long peace, the only wives, husbands, or parents I had to meet with had lost their loved ones in training accidents. Now, I have at least forty-eight hundred letters to write!"

Sandy shook her head. She'd known she was taking on heavy odds when she started this fight. It was either turn every cat on that planet below over to the nonexistent mercy of the alien monsters, or fight.

So, the enemy had gotten smarter. You knew that was going to happen sooner or later. It's happening now. Get over it.

What Sandy really wished was that there was some bug-eyed monster whose face she could stomp in. Some throat she could get her hands around. This being at the top of the command chain was a bitch. There was too much waiting.

Had she done everything?

She shook her head. Everything she could do, she'd done.

"Suzie, draw me a bath."

"Yes, Sandy."

So, Grand Admiral Sandy Santiago went to do the only thing she could do. Soak away her tension and get ready for the next surprise.

36

Admiral Miyoshi studied the feed from the probe at the jump. It showed the deployment of the aliens on the other side of the jump, a dozen or more light years away. They hung in space, in the same positions they'd been in for the last two weeks.

While Miyoshi's ships were moored to each other in groups of three and swung around, affording their crews at least a sense of a comfortable down, the aliens were floating in zero gravity. That couldn't be good for anyone.

Every day or so, an alien cruiser would approach the jump. First, they'd toss a few atomic devices through. So far, the gunners of the Second Fleet had managed to nail each bomb before it had time to arm itself and detonate.

The atomic attack would end with the alien cruiser slipping through the jump to see what the bombs had done. So far, no cruiser had survived long enough to get itself back through the jump.

For their part, the humans would send an armed probe through the jump every day or so. It would shoot up half a dozen or more of the atomic mines located around the jump, then be blasted out of existence by the massed lasers of the alien fleet. While the cruiser the aliens sacrificed might have a thousand souls on board, the human probe was fully automated.

That was the difference between the humans and the aliens. Humans used machines to save lives. They didn't count the cost of the lives they squandered.

Admiral Miyoshi had to wonder how the sacrificial cruiser was chosen. Was it crewed by enthusiastic zealots, eager to close with the humans and kill them? Had their skipper lost heavy at last Friday's poker game? Won too much off the Enlightened One? Did the aliens even play games of chance?

The aliens might look painfully like humans, but what made them tick was still a mystery.

Still, they were not born to zero gravity. Over the last couple of weeks, the effectiveness of the gunners had gone downhill. The first armed probe Miyoshi had ordered through the jump had died in ten seconds. The last one had survived for over sixteen seconds.

The alien crews were losing their edge. Maybe it was time to put them to a test.

The latest probe had managed to shoot up twelve mines in its brief fifteen-second war cruise. Actually, it had gotten ten, and the aliens had blown up two with their counter-fire.

At the moment, three small mine layers were advancing from behind where the main battle fleet floated a hundred thousand klicks back from the jump. If this went as usual, they'd advance as far as they needed to replace the mines, drop off new ones, and retreat back.

Maybe it was time to surprise the enemy with a new twist.

"Aki, advise the *Tone* to advance quickly to the jump.

Once there, I want it to proceed through the jump and fire on the alien mine layers. If they have the chance, I wouldn't mind if they fired a few rounds at those fast cruisers, say one shot each."

"*Tone* reports they thank you for this honor. Their fire plan will stutter fire one laser at the mine layers. The rest of the forward battery will be aimed at eleven cruisers," Aki said, a moment later.

"Very good. Make sure they are back to this side of the jump in no more than twelve seconds."

"They plan to make it back in ten."

"Very good."

Forty minutes later, the *Tone* floated in space, only meters from the jump. The probe that supported the periscope through the jump withdrew, after giving the *Tone* the best possible picture of the other side that it fed to its fire control computer.

With a tiny burst of jets, the *Tone* vanished into the jump. Eleven seconds later, it was back. The crystal armor on its hull showed its usual bright silver, but radiated no heat.

"Banzai!" the skipper of the *Tone* reported. "Three mine layers, ten cruisers, and one frigate destroyed. We shot for the last one because it had drifted out of place and was not bow-on to the jump. They are getting sloppy."

"Yes, they are getting sloppy," Miyoshi agreed.

The probe was back at the jump; the periscope slipped through. The scene it showed of the other side was a mad house. Hundreds of ships were getting underway, but in no sort of order. It was shear panic.

Miyoshi smiled contentedly. What had an Earth captain told him once? They had tossed a skunk into the ladies' bridge game. Yep, the ladies were indeed running from this smelly surprise.

"Admiral, a message is coming in from Admiral Santiago," Aki announced.

"Coming in?"

"It has a rather large attachment. The message says it's a report on a battle Admiral Bethea fought with the fast alien wing."

In a few minutes, the report was complete and Miyoshi and Aki watched as a battle unfolded a hundred or more light years away from them. It was hard fought. Bethea lost a third of her force and failed to keep a small force from getting past her.

"It would seem," Aki mused, "that those frigates may have a hard nose."

"We were lucky to catch one presenting its broadside to us," Miyoshi agreed.

"So, any thoughts, sir, on what we do if they try to force the jump?"

"Nuke them until they glow," Miyoshi said, quoting a phrase he'd heard the cats use. "And if they force the jump, fall back in good order and snipe them at long range."

"And if the frigates and cruisers put pressure on us?"

"Hope we can nail them before they cost us too much or we let the battlewagons through."

"Are you sorry you sent away half your fleet, sir?"

Admiral Miyoshi shook his head. "Those aliens across from us are content to contemplate their stone garden. I fear that Admiral Drago will need them more than I. Possibly Admiral Santiago as well, if they can force the jumps through our dragon friend."

Again, Miyoshi eyed the screen where the periscope take

was projected. The aliens were still in disarray. Hopefully, they would stay that way. With only twenty-two ships, he had no desire to take on the remaining three hundred and four alien warships.

37

Admiral Drago also was spending his afternoon watching the feed from the periscope stuck through the jump 180,000 kilometers from where his reinforced fleet was moored. What he saw was enough to make anyone's sphincter clench.

For the last four hours, he had watched as an alien warship, battleship, frigate, or cruiser came shooting through the jump across the system at some 50,000 kilometers an hour.

Admiral Drago would have preferred to turn that jump into a hotly contested roadblock. Fortunately, he'd chosen not to try to cross the third system out from the cats, and settled for establishing his defenses at the jump between systems two and three.

Had he attempted to get to the other side of system three, he'd be heading straight for the alien fighting force at one hell of an acceleration.

He'd made the correct choice, but that didn't mean he had to like it.

To face the seven hundred plus alien ships, he had only

sixty-six. The odds were ten to one against him. In the past, Kris Longknife had killed the aliens at a ratio of twenty or more to one. But she'd had a lot more ships to start with.

Drago had mined the jump on his side. A massive atomic device sat less than two thousand klicks from the jump, its proximity fuse activated. If any ship came through the jump, the bomb would plunge the jump into the fires of hell.

Farther back, high acceleration rockets, heavily protected from the electromagnetic pulse from the first bomb, would shoot into the flaming maelstrom and add more hell before it could dissipate.

This defense had held a jump point before. Bert could only hope it would hold it against what he had coming for him.

Then he got a message from Admiral Santiago with a battle report attached. After he'd looked through it twice, he hoped even more that the mines could hold the jump for him.

Drago called in Captain Svenson, his chief of staff, and his Ops officer. The three of them went over the battle report twice. It left all of them shaking their heads.

Svenson held up a finger. "The new frigates do have battleship-sized lasers, with a range of 150,000 kilometers. They're fast. The cruisers didn't get in a position to fire, but they are even faster."

"Fast, but how long can they hold that acceleration before the destroy themselves?" the Ops chief asked.

"What we've seen of these battleships show them to be faster," Drago said, "good for at least 2.7 gees with none of them dropping out or blowing up. Somebody's quality control is getting better."

"The reactors are different," Svenson said. "Are they improved, or is this a new mother ship?"

That got a shrug from the other two.

"I think we're in for a tough fight," Drago muttered to himself.

"Well, at least they didn't bring any of those door knockers," Captain Svenson said.

"No, they haven't," Drago agreed.

Then they did.

38

D rago was at lunch the next day when he got a call to the flag bridge. By the time he got there, both Svenson and the Ops chief were huddled around the forward screen.

"Is there a problem?" Drago asked.

"It seems that sixty of the battleships and an equal number of cruisers have slipped off from the main force. They're headed for a huge gas giant with a large number of moons."

"What type of moons?" Drago asked, knowing he wasn't going to like the answer.

"At least a few are real solid rock with tectonic activity. Even volcanoes," Svenson answered.

"What are the betting odds that they intend to cut some nice big chunks of hard rock and make their own door knockers?" Drago asked.

"No one in here is going to take your bet," the Ops chief answered.

"Yeah. I kind of thought so."

Drago mulled his new problem over for a bit. "Well, look on the bright side of this. It will be a while before those rock-clad ships can get here."

39

For the next week, the two fleets fifteen light years apart faced each other through a jump that was a tiny pinpoint in space. It very quickly settled down into something like what Admiral Miyoshi reported from his blocking force at his defended jump point.

Every day or so, the aliens sent a cruiser forward to lob atomics through the gate. The human battlecruisers swatted down the devices before they could arm themselves and detonate. After a while, a cruiser would sneak through, only to be smashed likewise.

Admiral Drago, for his part, sent a couple of armed probes through the jump, picking different intervals to see if he could identify their night cycles. Each time he'd nail eight to twelve mines. Each time they would replace them.

On the third day, Drago sent the battlecruiser *Roger Young* through the jump for a fast 'I came, I saw, I shot.' She bagged four mine layers, eight cruisers, and three of the frigates that were moving over to extend the flanks of the alien deployment.

The *Young* was back before the aliens were ready to take a shot.

The next foray through the jump was by the aliens. The periscope warned that they were sending three of the frigates forward, all of them lashed into a single unit. They started off tossing atomic devices through the gate, none of which had time to arm and explode.

Then the trio of frigates tried their luck.

Forewarned, Drago had cleared his own mine out of the way, and even sent his atomic tipped rockets out of the fire lanes.

The trio shot through the jump, already accelerating. They popped apart and headed off in separate directions. However, Drago's fleet was spread out and waiting for them. They had laid out a fire plan that gave the frigates no chance at all of escaping the salvoes headed for them.

Having come through at only a few kilometers an hour, even accelerating at thirty meters per second, per second, they were Swiss cheese before they got a kilometer from the jump.

It is possible that a few fragments from the exploding frigates got hurled back through the jump, but not likely.

For the next three days, the aliens tried to attack single cruisers at different times of the day. On the third day, Drago decided to try his own hand again. He ordered the *Valiant, Vanguard, Vindictive,* and *Victorious* through the jump as a unit. It was easy to meld the Smart Metal™ hulls together.

The plan was for them to edge through the jump as one unit. Immediately, they'd blossom like a flower, letting their bows spread out while keeping contact well aft. That way, each ship had its own bit of the alien fleet in its sights.

They were over and back in eleven seconds. The *Valiant* was glowing from a single hit.

The alien fleet suffered a lot more.

Using the periscope for scouting, the four-ship division had laid in a fire plan. Each ship set its lasers for half power. Each alien frigate was targeted by three different lasers to increase the odds of a hit, or, more especially, a hit that would not get blocked by their forward basalt shields.

Thirty-two frigates were targeted. Hanging in space, they were sitting ducks. Twenty-seven of them died as at least one of the 22-inch lasers slashed through a port for the frigate's own lasers and ripped into its capacitors and other potentially explosive gear.

No sooner was the division back on the human side of the jump than the probe was back in place. The periscope showed evidence that the alien fleet was still firing everything they had at the jump.

One of their wild shots apparently winged the periscope, finally answering the question of just how much of the device was on the other side of the jump.

The probe used some of its own Smart Metal™ to rebuild the periscope, but Admiral Drago ordered a five-minute delay before they sent it through again.

The alien ships were rocketing around in no sort of a pattern. Two battleships had collided; one exploded, the other was tumbling end over end.

All in all, it looked like a very productive morning.

However, during the few seconds on the other side, while the gunnery departments were busy, the sensors were also occupied. The battlecruisers searched the system. They found sixty battleships; their mass jacked up from half a million tons to one million tons each, accelerating out from that gas giant.

The preliminaries were over. It was time for the main event.

40

Three days later, it was clear the aliens intended to force the jump. A quad of door knockers, lashed together, were drifting not too far from the jump. Another foursome drifted 10 kilometers farther back. Behind them, lined up like a freight train, was the rest of the alien fleet. They were making for the jump at 2.0 gees acceleration.

Admiral Drago ordered the periscope retrieved and the probe to distance itself from the jump. He also ordered his ships to slip their moorings. As soon as they floated in formation, he ordered them to Condition Zed and beat the crew to quarters.

They were locked in, loaded, and ready to hunt bear.

Then an atomic device exploded.

"Did I miss something?" Drago asked Captain Svenson.

"I didn't see anything either," the chief of staff answered. "Sensors, talk to me about that explosion."

"Just a moment, sir," and the forward screen took on the blank appearance of space. A second later, an atomic device exploded and it was impossible to get any sensor reading except heat. Then the screen recycled back to pre-explosion and advanced slowly.

For a fraction of a second, a cruiser appeared. Immediately, the atomic device activated and the small ship was obliterated.

"Where'd that puppy come from?" Svenson asked.

"It doesn't matter," Admiral Drago said. "I'm starting to think that our shooting was too good when we sent ships through. They may have become suspicious that we knew what was happening on their side of the jump. Whatever it is, we now have a problem. Do we keep the jump under atomic fire?"

"Our atomic-tipped missiles won't be much good to us if they get some of their over-gunned battleships through. They'd shoot them down like mad dogs."

Drago nodded. "Use them or lose them, huh?"

"Unfortunately, we've only got twelve."

"That should last us a good twenty to thirty minutes," Drago calculated. "Start the second one moving in. Let's see if we can get it parked close enough to the jump and active. Maybe we can replace the mine."

Just as the thermonuclear explosion was beginning to dissipate, the missile coasted to a slow halt, then edged itself in closer as the fire ball shrank.

Four door knockers drifted through the jump, already firing. They split up, jacked up their acceleration to 2.5 gees and spread out.

Their lasers got not only close to the missile, but quickly wiped out all the rest.

"There goes the atomic option," Drago muttered, then ordered, "Fire!"

The Fourth Fleet and its reinforcements had been expecting four door knockers. They unloaded two hundred and sixteen 22-inch lasers at each of them in the next six seconds. They boiled off lava and gases, but none exploded.

"Flip ships," Admiral Drago ordered, "Accelerate to 4.0 gees. Fire."

This time the aft batteries laid one hundred and forty-four lasers on those four targets.

Internal explosions could be seen for a second on all four of them, and then they exploded into expanding clouds of superheated gases as their reactors lost their containment and the demons of their own plasma ate the ship.

Meanwhile, another four door knockers had jumped through.

Even as Drago's ships destroyed those four, another two quads had joined them.

Drago kept his fleet accelerating away from the jump, except for when he had to kill acceleration and flip to fire his bow guns.

"Why aren't we killing more of them?" Svenson asked the thin air above his high gee station.

"How many lasers did we see firing at our atomic tipped rockets?" Drago said, answering a question with a question. "Sensors?"

"Checking, sir."

There was a pause. "I can't tell, sir, the radiation and heat from the atomic explosion makes it impossible for the highly sensitive sensors we can usually use to spot the ionized gas from a laser passing."

"But the other door knockers haven't fired a shot," Svenson noted.

"Is that because they're out of range?" Admiral Drago left the question hanging. "Still, I'm starting to think they have rock clad the entire bow of their ships. Maybe all of it.

That makes them harder to kill and we're taking a lot more time to kill them."

"That's possible," the chief of staff agreed.

"Sir," Sensors called, "I'm having a hard time scanning around the jump. The door knockers are laying down that same smoke screen that Admiral Bethea reported.

Admiral Drago frowned, but said nothing.

This battle was not the one he'd planned for.

"Cut acceleration to 2.0 gees," he ordered, wanting to keep the jump in range for as long as possible.

The battle continued. Door knockers now shot through the jump already at a 2.5 gee acceleration. Every ten seconds or so another four would appear, split apart and spread out, spewing gunk behind them, expanding the cloud and forcing the humans to engage the aliens later, after they'd put on more velocity and began evading.

The Fourth Fleet was now firing by task forces. Each group of twenty-two ships would fire their forward battery at three ships. All three usually exploded. Then they'd flip and fire their aft lasers. They usually destroyed at least one ship and left the others glowing with red hot molten lava. Occasionally, one of them would overheat and destroy itself.

Still, the final score was twenty-nine door knockers destroyed, but thirty-one were through the jump. All were accelerating at 2.5 gees straight for their tormentors, creating a blind spot behind them to cover new arrivals.

Yet not one had fired a shot.

Wanting to keep well away from the enemy's new laser range of 150,000 klicks, Drago now pulled back. His acceleration was 2.0 gees, except when he cut power, drifted, and brought his bow guns to bear.

Now battleships were jumping in. Every minute, five or

six groups of alien warships would come out of the spreading cloud and join the forces massing against Drago.

As soon as the first few broke out of the screen, Drago ordered his fleet to concentrate on them. It proved effective.

The fleet continued to fire by task forces of twenty-two ships each. They could take three ships under fire with their aft battery, then the next three of the newly arrived battleships would be burned by the forward battery as they coasted. Usually, they got all six. Sometimes, one of them would survive.

In the first minute, twenty battleships came out of the smoke, already dodging. Drago's ships destroyed eleven.

For seven minutes, the alien battleships poured out of the spreading debris screen. Every minute, the alien ships Drago's forces engaged got more and more frisky as they increased their velocity up before they became targets.

The result was that fewer of them got blown apart. One hundred and twenty battleships were culled down to ninety-one.

Still, Drago's strategy was working. He was now 200,000 kilometers from the latest battleship to come out of the screen. It might be extreme range, but he could sit out here and plunk away at the alien force as he gave up ground from now until the cows came home.

By Drago's estimate, he'd have destroyed this force before it was half-way across the system.

Suddenly, new ships began to shoot out from the screen. Now the battleships were joined by frigates and cruisers. Their acceleration was somewhere between 3.5 and 4.0 gees. Each one of them spread out the screen behind them.

No doubt, more were coming.

Drago ordered the frigates and cruisers to be taken under fire. Hitting them proved harder than he expected.

They likely had come through the jump at over 20,000 kilometers an hour. In the two or three minutes before they shot out of the screen, they'd increased their speed to over 30,000 kilometers an hour.

While the battleships had charged at Admiral Drago's main force, these fast-movers were moving as much out as forward. That did make them a better target. The bow armor on the frigates only covered about half of the target. Still, getting a hit at this range, even considering speed and erratic movement, proved harder than Drago wished.

The first eight ships died, but by that time, sixteen more were reaching for his flank. Before another eight were blown out of space, the force had grown to thirty-two.

Even as the enemy light units died, the debris cloud expanded. Every new frigate or cruiser that appeared was faster, more spread out, and jinking for its life.

Fewer and fewer enemy ships were destroyed.

Something worse was also happening. Many of the faster ships were turning hard as they came out of the jump. Now that the Fourth Fleet had been backed away from the jump, they were heading out to the right or left, top or bottom, jacking up their velocity to 3.5 gees for the frigates, 4.0 gees for the cruisers . . . and staying outside the range of Drago's fleet.

"Those outriders are going to be a major pain," Captain Svenson said.

"If they manage to get ahead of us," Drago said, "they can spread mines and other junk along our course. Likely, our secondary batteries can take care of them, but I don't want to see what one of their atomics does to a ship that missed one."

"So, what do we do?" the chief of staff asked.

41

Admiral Drago let the battle develop for three hours. The velocity of the alien ships climbed up as they accelerated. Thirty-one door knockers were cut back to twenty-four. From the look of the glow on their bows, it appeared the aliens were using their own lasers to drill gun ports through their armor.

The alien battleships had pulled ahead of the door knockers. They were making 2.7 gees verses the bigger ships' 2.5 gees. None of them had organized themselves into a battle array. They kept their distance from each other and threw themselves around as hard as they could. Drago's fleet cut the number of battleships down to seventy-two.

Mainly, Drago kept the enemy's big ships at arms' length. He knew his lasers were at the maximum attenuation at 200,000 kilometers, and he accepted that. He also knew the alien were jinking more radically than he'd ever seen them do.

Again, he knew his ships were less effective, and didn't let it bother him. He had time on his side. He eyed the frigates and cruisers as they spread out on his flanks. They were not in any formation. Rather, they seemed bent on staying as unthreatening as possible as they swung wide of Drago's widely spaced squadrons. Still, their velocity was growing; it threatened to leave the Fourth Fleet in their dust.

Drago's fleet was withdrawing at the same 2.7 gees as the alien battleships were advancing. After two frigates blew up, the rest of them slowed to 3.2 gees. Likewise, the aliens lost a couple of cruisers before their force fell back to 3.5 gees.

They were staying well out of range of Drago's 22-inch lasers. Still, during the three hours he watched, they had jacked up their velocities to almost three hundred thousand klicks per hour above Drago's speed. They'd had to use a lot of that speed to swing wide of Drago's ships, but if they were left unchecked, they could be shooting into his rear quickly.

It was time to give priority to the fast-movers and put a stop to their run around him.

Admiral Drago had nine squadrons in his fleet. Each squadron commodore commanded seven or eight ships. If he sent one squadron to take out the force on each of his flanks, he would be dividing his forces. Never a good idea.

But the enemy had already done just that.

Okay, so how do we make this work? he asked himself.

If he ordered the squadrons to attack by squadrons, they risked taking forever to chase down all the scattered aliens, and quite a few might make it into his rear.

However, if he broke his squadrons up into two ships sections, or worse, spread them out as single ships, he risked the enemy concentrating on a few small units and destroying them.

He'd be opening himself to defeat in detail.

Then again, he could ignore the slow-moving battle force entirely, send his fleet out to nail the frigates and cruisers and, once they were taken care of, he could slow down and tackle the battle fleet at his leisure.

"Svenson, let's give each division a sector of our perimeter and disperse by squadrons to engage the enemy's fast-movers."

"Aye, aye, sir," the chief of staff said. The fact that there was no discussion assured Drago that he'd made the right decision at the right time.

Five minutes later, Admiral Drago's fleet went to 4.0 gees and split up like a flower opening, as one squadron took off to annihilate the alien fast-movers in its assigned forty degrees of the perimeter.

42

For the first hour after Drago split his fleet up into independent squadrons and launched them at the aliens' fast-movers at 4.0 gees, the aliens kept heading for his rear, although they did edge out a bit. As the timer counted up to sixty minutes on this course, the aliens reacted.

Drago's fleet had yet to match the velocity of the frigates, much less the cruisers. Still, the alien ships turned their tails to him and settled on the same course he was on.

"They're running away," Svenson said.

"No," Drago said, "they are leading us away from the battleships. Worse, they're scattering themselves wider. If we don't split ourselves up to chase them, we could end up headed way to hell and gone with most of them now behind us. Momentum is a bitch."

Svenson nodded.

"Comm, make an archive of my battle board, send it to Admiral Santiago with my regards and respectful suggestion that she might wish to send reserves to defend the jump from here into the next system. It is clear the enemy intend to draw me away from their battle fleet. I will do my best to avoid this, but they presently have me at a disadvantage."

"I have that on its way, Admiral. Should I send further updates at hourly intervals?"

"Yes. She needs to know how this battle is developing."

"Admiral?" Captain Svenson said.

"Yes?"

"I can't believe I'm about to say this, but we need to divide our forces further."

Drago eyed the screen and found that he had to agree with his chief of staff.

One hundred and twenty-seven frigates were now scattering to the four points of the compass. The cruisers had been cut down to one hundred and fifty-one. They were now traveling faster than the frigates. Their velocity was not a bit less than 150,000 kilometers an hour faster than their bigger brothers.

To chase these two hundred and seventy-eight fast-movers that were quickly spreading out even more, Admiral Drago had just sixty-six ships.

He could chase down the frigates in a couple of hours. However, all the energy he put on his ships would have to be dissipated, and their courses brought around if he wanted to catch the cruisers. That would leave him scattered and likely low on reaction mass.

There was one ice giant that his fleet could refuel from, but it would involve a detour away from the battleships.

Clearly, the enemy wanted him running around. Dare he ignore them or should he allow them the initiative?

Actually, they had the initiative. They'd shown they could bust down the door at any jump. They had guessed our tricks and knew how to trip our traps.

For a long moment, Admiral Drago contemplated his

bad options. Finally, he made his decision. He hoped he was choosing the best of the worst.

"Comm, send this order to the squadron commanders. 'Our first targets are the frigates. Take care not to put on more acceleration than you have to. If necessary, you may divide your squadron by divisions or two ship sections. Once we have destroyed the frigates, we will pursue the cruisers. After destroying the enemy fast-movers, we will reform at the gas giant and refuel. Then we will take on the battleships. Admiral Drago sends.' Get that out immediately."

"It is sent, sir."

"Good, now let's see how this situation develops."

43

"A stern chase is a long chase," has probably been an axiom since boats were rowed on water. With starships accelerating at 3.2, 3.5, and 4.0 gees, it hadn't gotten all that much quicker.

The attack on the frigates could have been over in a couple of hours. Of course, that assumed that Drago had a ship to send chasing after every one of the hundred and twenty-seven surviving frigates. Even if he scattered his ships individually, they'd each have to catch and destroy two ships.

With the battlecruisers deployed in two ship sections, each team needed to catch four frigates. Once it became clear which battle cruiser section was targeting which frigates, the aliens immediately set their courses to widen the gap.

Drago's fleet was chasing a hell of a lot of needles in a rapidly expanding haystack.

Worse, each time a frigate was almost in range, it would flip ship and start killing its velocity even as the pursuing battlecruisers continued to accelerate. Many of Drago's ships chose to flip ship and decelerate, too. That gave the humans more time to kill the madly dancing alien warship before it got within range of a battlecruiser.

After it became clear that the aliens could be swatted down while still well away from the battlecruisers, there was less flipping. The section commanders began to adjust their courses for their next target, even as they were destroying their present one.

Chasing down four high speed frigates each, however, tied up the Fourth Fleet for the better part of an afternoon. Only when all of them had been destroyed, could the fleet concentrate on catching the cruisers.

There were more cruisers; one hundred and fifty-one of them. Their velocity was several million kilometers per hour.

"Nav, can those cruisers slow down enough to make that jump?" Admiral Drago asked.

There was a lengthy pause as the fleet navigator did a calculation he hadn't expected to ever make.

"Sir, I think you've got the right of it. They can't decelerate enough to hit the jump at anywhere close to 50,000 kilometers."

Drago's next question was for sensors. "How far down is the mass of those ships?"

"You thinking they've used up too much reaction mass?" Captain Svenson asked.

"I'm thinking that. The aliens aren't averse to sending their people on suicide missions. If our reaction tanks are running low, imagine what those guys are facing."

"Sir," said sensors, "our mass detection gear reports that the alien cruisers are fourteen to sixteen percent less dense than they were when the *Valiant* checked them out when they jumped through. Considering that their ships are not made of Smart Metal, I'd be willing to say that they're running on empty."

"Mmm," Drago muttered, deep in thought. He eyed the gas giant and its relationship to his ships. He studied the hurtling cruisers, their velocity vector long and growing longer by the second.

"Comm, send to fleet, 'Our next objective is refueling at the gas giant. However, for the next hour, follow a course at 4.0 gees that will appear as much to be in pursuit of the cruisers as aimed at the giant. Let's keep them scared and running. Admiral Drago sends'."

"That ought to keep them burning reaction mass," Svenson said.

"Yes, it should."

44

Three hours later, the alien cruiser force came to the realization they had been had. They flipped ship and began decelerating like mad, but it did them no good. Most of them were out of reach of the jump, anyway.

Cruisers began to explode as their commanding Enlightened Ones realized that there was no way to either reach a planet to refuel from, nor get within range to kill the human vermin.

No one in Drago's fleet shed a tear. They reduced their deceleration by 2.0 gees and expanded the ship out to Condition Baker. Everyone still felt like they were lugging another human around on their back, but it meant that half the crew could be released to quarters to clean up, get a good hot meal, then replace their opposite number at their battle station. Sleeping was still done in a high gee station, but at least it was more comfortable.

Admiral Drago made sure his fleet was on course to refuel at the ice giant, then took his own break. After he came back, he and the navigator went over course and acceleration options that would put them back in a position ahead of the alien battle fleet.

The Enlightened One commanding the fleet of battleships had no option. He would have to order his ships to flip and begin decelerating at a known and established time if he had any hope of achieving the jump at an acceptable velocity.

The natural laws of the universe predestined his course with an iron hand.

Admiral Drago's Fourth Fleet could make the intercept a good twelve hours before the jump. From a safe distance, he would destroy this force. It would be more an execution than a battle.

Too bad the bastards won't surrender.

"Comm, send an archive of my battle board and a copy of this proposed course off to Admiral Santiago with my respects. Tell her she can turn her reserves around. I've got this bunch dead to rights."

"Done, sir."

Admiral Drago studied the situation for a few long minutes. Then, satisfied he'd done all he could, he leaned back in his high gee station and got comfortable in the cushioning. At a mere 2.0 gees, it was really pleasant. He closed the hood and dimmed the internal lights to nothing. Two slow breaths, and he was out like a light.

When he awoke, his pod told him he'd slept for a solid nine hours. He converted his egg back to a chair and opened it.

"Any surprises?" he asked his chief of staff.

"It's going the way we predicted. It's like a train racing down a track to a nonexistent bridge."

"That's nice for a plan to work out the way we want it to, for a change. Now, Svenson, you stink. Go get cleaned up and get something to eat. Also, get some sleep in your own bed. I don't want to see you for ten hours. Ten whole hours."

"I'll get my stink off, and some chow, boss, but I'm thinking I'll do my sleeping in a nice warm bathtub. I'm getting too old for this crap."

Drago made a note to himself to try sleeping in a tub himself. He motored his egg over to study the main screen. It showed few cruisers left. The battleships stolidly made their way steady on their course for the jump. While he'd been busy skirmishing with their little boys, the big boys had begun to organize themselves into widely scattered lines of eight. It appeared that they were mimicking the human squadron formation. Behind them, the door knockers came along, slowly falling more behind, but not changing their course or acceleration. They, too, were forming into squadrons.

While Drago watched, the battle fleet reached their mid-course point. They did a smart flip and began decelerating toward a jump they would never reach.

45

Admiral Miyoshi eyed the feed coming in from the periscope through the jump. The alien battle-ships were underway, scattering into groups of fifty to sixty. They were headed for each of the three jumps out of that system.

Ninety-three frigates still floated 150,000 klicks back from the jump, their lasers ready to shoot up anything that came through. Meanwhile, mine layers were busy seeding the space around the jump with hundreds of mines.

Clearly, the aliens did not want the Second Fleet to come charging through the jump and race off after one or two of the fleeing detachments. Very likely, Admiral Miyoshi's ships could blow two of the groups to gas.

What was missing were the cruisers. Over the last couple of days, they'd drifted off in groups of one or two, scattering to the flanks. None of them were now in view of the periscope. What they were up to was a serious concern.

With only twenty-two battlecruisers, Admiral Miyoshi was very limited in his forces. If he didn't charge the jump pretty soon, his small force would likely be unable to catch more than one of the detachments. Weighing heavy on his thoughts was his basic order. He had to hold this jump; the aliens could not pass. If he made a mistake and lost too many ships he might not be able to hold the jump.

The present probe at the jump had material for only one more armed probe, but he ordered it generated and sent through the jump. It got only three mines before it was vaporized. Clearly the enemy frigates and cruisers still defending the jump were on high alert.

Anchored together, 180,000 kilometers back from the jump, the Second Fleet was too far back to react quickly to anything the other side did that opened up a chance for a kill. It took Admiral Miyoshi a bit more than an hour to take his battlecruisers to Condition Zed and battle stations, and move them up to the jump 20,000 kilometers from the tiny point in space they guarded. As soon as he had them moored in threesomes, he ordered another armed probe through the jump.

Again, it got only three mines before it was no more.

Worse, during the last hour, the mine layers had added another ninety mines. The minefield was getting deeper and thicker.

The question at hand was obvious. Could they wipe out enough of the mines close to the jump so that they could safely jump into the system without triggering one of them?

Another probe, another three. A third probe got four. The next probe got only two. Clearly, the enemy was on high alert.

Then a minelayer appeared from behind the jump and laid another dozen right up close to the jump to replace what had been lost. It laid the mines and then slipped back around the jump where the periscope could not see them.

Which provided a high probability of where the alien

cruisers were. If they were floating 50 - 100,000 klicks back from the jump, they could do a lot of damage to the vulnerable stern of Miyoshi's battlecruisers right after they went through the jump and before they flipped over and shot back.

"Opinion, Aki?" Admiral Miyoshi asked his chief of staff.

"Admiral Longknife sandwiched the aliens between forces both in front of and behind a jump and shot the loving crap out of them. I think that the odds are extremely high that they intend to do the same to us."

"I seem to remember a battle on old Earth where an army of cavalry charged, then fell back and tricked the enemy's infantry into chasing them. They turned about and swept the field."

"The battle of Hasty or Hasting," Aki said. "Yeah. I like our position. I don't think we'll gain much of anything by pursuing those battlewagons and we might lose everything by risking the chase."

"Order the fleet to pull back 50,000 kilometers and moor again. Let's stay far enough back not to get hit by an atomic device out of that jump, but not so close we can't react if the situation changes."

Ten minutes later, they were safely back in anchorage.

Over the next three days, the battleships build up a tremendous velocity as they crossed the system at 2.5 gees, later reduced to two. Starting on the second day, a third of the frigates took off at 3.2 gees for the first thirteen hours, then reduced their acceleration to 2.7 gees. Twenty cruisers shot wide around the minefield in front of the jump before streaking after the battleships and frigates at 4.0 gees that fell back to 3.2 gees after one of them blew themselves to bits.

The next day, an equal number of little boys started their own withdrawal.

That day, Miyoshi began sending armed probes through the jump again. They not only shot up mines, but took a look behind the jump and transmitted a picture of what lay behind it. It did, indeed, spot cruisers back 75,000 klicks from the jump as well as mines very close behind it. It only got three mines, but the information it transmitted was worth a lot more.

The next day, twelve of the remaining twenty-three frigates started a run for their lives. Ten cruisers soon joined them.

Miyoshi sent three armed probes through, but they got a total of twelve mines between them. The enemy was still on a hair trigger.

The next day, six frigates and three cruisers took flight. Four mine killing probes got twenty-one mines. One of the probes swung around behind the jump and got five more before it, too, was vaporized. Still, that left another five too close to the jump to risk eliminating.

The next day, the aliens who drew the long straw took off at the highest gees they could pull. Still, there were two frigates and likely one cruiser left guarding the minefield. Ten probes, sent through at irregular intervals, took out seventy-four mines. The last one got nine.

The *Tenacious, Persistent, Steadfast,* and *Relentless* were hitched together and sent through with the *Steadfast's* bow pointed at the cruiser and the other three bows pointed at the frigates. Many of their 6-inch secondary lasers were charged to full capacity and loaded with targeting data for the nearest mine data taken from the periscope.

Two seconds after the division crossed the jump at dead slow, the alien ships were under fire. Four seconds later, they were just rapidly dissipating gas. The secondary batteries had also nailed fifteen of the atomic bombs.

Admiral Miyoshi has assumed the alien mines were using an active proximity fuse. Certainly, the periscope was showing evidence of very attenuated radar signals. However, there may also have been a dead man's switch. Two seconds after the last alien ship vanished in a ball of exploding gasses, all the atomics in the area blew up.

While the area directly around the jump had been swept, that was an awful lot of what the cats called 'mega tonnage' going off. The helmsman on the division's flagship, *Tenacious,* earned everyone thanks by slapping down hard on the reverse jets and zipping the four battlecruisers back through the jump.

While the standard radiation protection in the ship held the level of radiation down, no one wanted to test how long it could have continued, considering all that was headed their way with all the bombs going off.

This was a good choice, because as it turned out, the mines didn't explode as one gigantic boom. Rather, they exploded in a wave sweeping out wider and wider, over the next thirty minutes.

A probe sent through an hour after the last blast showed a high level of radiation. The probe had an anti-matter reactor aboard. It was allowed to self-detonate. No one really wanted to bring that highly radioactive vehicle back on board.

Admiral Miyoshi held his position for another four days, until the first two alien battle groups had jumped out of the system. He then established a pair of high quality jump buoys on either side of the jump, and began his voyage back to Sasquan and its irritating cats.

46

Grand Admiral Sandy Santiago looked out at a sea of furry faces. They were cheering, clapping, and shouting their joy.

They had sat quietly as President Almar of Columm Almar and Prime Minister Gerrot of the Bizalt Kingdom introduced Sandy. They had stayed very quiet as Sandy introduced each of her admirals and let them describe their recent battles, or, in poor Miyoshi's case, the lack of a fight. Still, many of the admirals and generals in the room had nodded sagaciously at the Musashi admiral's wisdom at refusing battle.

Most of the civilians, in what was billed as a news conference, were much more interested in the battles fought by Admirals Bethea, Drago and, most especially Admiral Nottingham. He'd fought his battle at the very jump into this system. With ninety alien frigates and cruisers rushing at them, and only the twenty-two battlecruisers to defend, Sandy had made the hard call not to attempt to engage them in the second system, but rather to form the blocking force at this jump.

The aliens had died like moths on a flame.

The cats had listened to each post-action report in absolute silence. Only when President Almar invited the audience to show their gratitude did a hurricane of applause and approval bombard the stage. It went on and on. Nether the President nor the Prime Minister made any effort to bring the applause to an end.

Sandy expected that the approbation was aimed as much at her officers and their crews as at the cats on the planet below. The entire back of the auditorium was lined with cameras, carrying these after-action reports to practically every business and household on the planet. Halfway through the reports, President Almar had leaned over to whisper in Sandy's ear that the official ratings for this news conference were double those of any television show the cats had ever shown.

"And it's still growing. More and more people are tuning in. More channels are turning to this news conference. I think before we finish today, every station on the planet will be carrying this feed. By defending us, you have united us."

Sandy could only hope that there would be something more substantial than applause for all her crew who had fought and died.

While the other two fleets had held the butcher's bill down, the cost to Bethea's Third Fleet was shocking to all of them. Clearly, the aliens were learning the humans' tricks and were doing their utmost to come up with ways to close in the most brutal of ways.

A huge number of alien warships at close quarters with a limited number of better human ships was becoming a worse and worse nightmare, and more likely.

When the applause finally began to run down, the President and the Prime Minister motioned to four other heads of state to come join them.

THOSE SIX WOMEN GOVERN OVER HALF THE POPULATION AND NEARLY TWO-THIRDS OF THE INDUSTRIAL PRODUCTION OF THIS PLANET, Mimzy advised Sandy on Nelly Net.

Sandy, like everyone else, waited for what they might or might not say.

President Almar started. "These strangers from the stars have fought for us, and too many have died so that we might live."

"While some of our young fought with them," Prime Minister Gerrot said, "there were few of us and far too many of them standing in the battle line."

"They fought against horrible odds," a third head of state said, taking up the speech.

"We cannot expect them to always win for us," said a fourth.

"We must participate in our own defense," a fifth said in an absolute voice.

"We are told that the enemy is becoming more skilled as the humans defeat them over and over. There must be more warships to protect us, as well as the other planets the humans are sworn to defend," said a sixth.

It was now back to the President.

"We are a proud people. We do not let others defend us like helpless cubs whose eyes have not opened," the Prime Minister said. Now the other five built upon his statement.

"We must find ways to participate in our own defense."

"This may mean more of our young traveling with the aliens to work in their factories in the Alwan system."

"We have already put plans in place for us to begin to

build warships to the plans the humans are willing to share with us."

"However, it will take at least a year to produce a warship, likely more before it is ready for combat."

"So," the President said, "what can we do to speed up our defense?"

"We certainly can't assume the monsters who want to wipe us off the face of our beloved planet will wait upon our time table," the Prime Minister added.

Now, the ball of this strange multi-faceted presentation was tossed to the four junior partners who continued the collective reflection.

"We know that the humans at Alwa are producing a lot of light manufactured goods out of this magical metal of theirs."

"We know from those of our young who have returned that these goods are the glue that is holding together the different cultures on Alwa and keeps them working together for their mutual defense."

"We, however, can make many of these things in our own factories."

"They need agricultural machinery and equipment. We make a lot of that."

"They need rifles and ammunition. We can make that."

"They need lasers for their warships. We have learned from them how to make lasers."

"We can learn to make large fighting lasers."

"What we are proposing," the President interjected, "is that we merge our economy as much as we can with the humans and birds on Alwa."

"We can ship to them all the things they need that we can manufacture," the Prime Minister said. "It won't be made of magic metal, but our products are strong and durable."

This was tossed to the junior partners for commentary, again.

"If the humans don't have to use the magic metal for these light industrial products, they can devote more of their production to warships."

"We can provide the people to work their factories, as well as crew the extra ships they produce."

"We can ask that half the ships built be detached for duty in our sky."

"We can also ship the battle lasers to Alwa so that they can jack up their production without having to overtax their own laser production."

"We know there will be problems," President Almar now said. "There are no banks and there is no currency in the Alwan system."

"The birds don't seem to understand the concept of money," Prime Minister Gerrot explained. "The humans, on their part, are operating a demand economy. When your main product is warships, they have only one buyer, the Navy."

"We have talked with human economists. They know that what they are doing is both an aberration and cannot be done for long."

"However, so long as both our planets are confronted by an alien menace that wants us all wiped from the face of our planets, we can expect matters to continue that way."

"Exactly how we will pay for what we ship to Alwa is something we will have to look at carefully."

"Whatever the price, there is no question that we want those warships above our head."

"Before this attack began," the President Almar now

said, "we had entered into an agreement to both manage our interaction with the humans and birds as well as control the export of human technology to our world."

"Those agreements have already passed the legislature in all six of our nations," the Prime Minister said.

"Now, we six heads of state propose to present to all our legislatures a proposal to transfer goods to the Alwan system in exchange for this technology."

"Goods that will result in more warships being built."

"Warships being built and orbiting above our sky."

"We will need a lot of thought to go into the final product."

Here the four of them took a step back, leaving the President and the Prime Minister at the podium.

"While we will be presenting the same proposal to each of our legislatures, we do not expect that every nation will approve it with a rubber stamp."

"We want everyone's input," the Prime Minister said. "We know this has been hastily put together on the pounce. We expect that many of you will have many better ideas."

"We also expect that different nations will have different ways of handling this exchange," the President said. "We need to keep this agreement both the same where we need to speak with one voice, and different where our differences will strengthen us."

"But we must understand one thing," the Prime Minister said. "The days for doing the same old thing, doing things the way we always have, they are gone."

"We, today," the President said, "faces a challenge the likes of which no generation before us even considered. The arrival of one set of space aliens to help at the very moment that a vicious and murderous group of space aliens launched attacks on us is like nothing our foremothers ever faced."

"We, the six of us," the Prime Minister said, presenting the six of them with a wave of her paw, "are committed to finding solutions to this challenge together. Just as we have presented this report to all of you together, the time for petty differences is gone. We will either all live together, or we all will surely burn together in one great cataclysm."

"Our children and their children will look back on us with pride at how we weathered this storm," the President said. "That, or there will be no children to remember our names."

"Are you with us?" all six national leaders shouted, punching the air with their right paws, claws extended.

The roaring reply of "Yes!" in unison was loud enough to get the walls vibrating.

47

S andy was only hours away from sailing back to Alwa. She'd be taking two divisions of battlecruisers with her. Admiral Taussig on the *Hornet* would be taking his old squadron as well as the iron ships from Birmingham. All the battlecruisers were at an expanded Condition Able to allow barracks for a lot of young cats, both female and males this time.

Sleeping quarters would be changed into classrooms during the day. These cats were very eager to learn.

The fast attack transports would be trailing the battlecruisers. They were also made as big as they could be. The cats had stoked them full of everything Amanda and Jacques said the Alwans wanted, then they'd added a few items of their own. They also had cats on board, including manufacturing representatives, intent on setting up dealerships and maintenance facilities.

"These cats know very well what they're doing," Amanda said through a thin-lipped grin. Once they get people familiar with their equipment, they'll want more. That means more sales and a growing market."

"But they don't have any money," Sandy pointed out.

"Not yet," Jacques said. "These cats know very well what money is good for. When they get to work, they intend to demand pay. Pay that they can save, then decide what they want to buy. Maybe they'll buy it on Alwa. Maybe back with their cat folks. Once they start walking around with money, spending it at the better restaurants that don't take company script, things are going to change."

"Most of the birds don't wear any clothes, and beyond their feathers, they aren't into any adornment. You want to bet me how long it will take the birds to get into glitz after they see some cats decked out in jewelry and jackets?"

"No way I'll take the bet," Sandy said. "I'm more worried about how we absorb all these cats into our force. I'm not at all sure I want a cat on guns or in engineering, much less in command of a ship."

"They'll either learn or they'll die," Jacques said with an expressive shrug.

"I've already had to deal with one Earth-born admiral who wouldn't follow orders and lost way too many ships with his insubordination. What will I get with cats?"

"Pardon me for changing the topic," Amanda said, "but before you get too worried about how the cats will fit in, have you heard anything about Granny Rita and who owns the fabs on Alwa?"

"You are a wicked person and you should be very glad you are a civilian," Sandy said through a glower.

Amanda just laughed, a musical affair that made it impossible for Sandy to stay bothered. "But I'm not so wicked that you'd want to activate my reserve commission so you could throw the UCMJ at me."

"Too much paper work," Sandy grumped.

"Ma'am, I hate to interrupt this love-fest," Sandy's chief

of staff said, leaning against the open door into Sandy's day quarters, "but we have a fleet ready to sail. Do you have an order for me?"

"Make it so, Captain," Sandy said, "and may God help all who sail with us.

ABOUT THE AUTHOR

Mike Shepherd is the National best-selling author of the Kris Longknife saga. Mike Moscoe is the award-nominated short story writer who has also written several novels, most of which were, until recently, out of print. Though the two have never been seen in the same room at the same time, they are reported to be good friends.

Mike Shepherd grew up Navy. It taught him early about change and the chain of command. He's worked as a bartender and cab driver, personnel advisor, and labor negotiator. Now retired from building databases about the endangered critters of the Northwest, he looks forward to some fun reading and writing.

Mike lives in Vancouver, Washington, with his wife Ellen, and not too far from his daughter and grandkids. He enjoys reading, writing, dreaming, watching grandchildren for story ideas and upgrading his computer – all are never ending.

For more information:
www.krislongknife.com
mikeshepherd@krislongknife.com

2017 RELEASES

In 2016, I amicably ended my twenty-year publishing relationship with Ace, part of Penguin Random House.

In 2017, I began publishing through my own independent press, KL & MM Books. We produced six e-books and a short story collection. We also brought the books out in paperback and audio.

In 2018, I intend to keep the novels coming.

We will begin the year with **Kris Longknife's Successor.** Grand Admiral Santiago still has problems. Granny Rita is on the rampage again, and the cats have gone on strike, refusing to send workers to support the human effort on Alwa. Solving that problem will be tough. The last thing Sandy needs is trouble with the murderess alien space raiders. So, of course, that is what she gets.

May 1 will see **Kris Longknife: Commanding.** Kris has won her first battle, but the way the Iteeche celebrate victory can be hard on the stomach. The rebellion won't quit and now Kris needs to raise a fleet, not only to defend the Iteeche Imperial Capitol, but also take the war to the rebels.

In the second half of 2018, you can look forward to the next Vicky Peterwald novel on July 1, another Iteeche war novel on September 1, and **Kris Longknife Implacable** on November 1.

Stay in touch to follow developments by friending Kris Longknife and follow Mike Shepherd on Facebook or check in at my website www.krislongknife.com

26001607R00170

Printed in Poland
by Amazon Fulfillment
Poland Sp. z o.o., Wrocław